"Have you ever thought of having kids of your own?"

Grace was pressing her luck with the question, but Tuck didn't seem upset.

"Sure, when I was younger. And if I'm honest I'd have to admit that when I look at Jesse, I wonder how it would feel to look into the face of my own child."

"Do you know that you're a wonderful man?"

"Care to back up those words, ma'am?"

Grace lifted an eyebrow. "How?"

"Dancing." Tuck grabbed her hand and pulled her into the den. He poked a button on the stereo system and the sounds of a beautiful slow waltz wafted through the room. He moved back the area rug and flipped off the lights. They were enclosed in a world all their own.

"You're trembling," he whispered against her hair.

"I think I'm a little afraid of what's happening between us." She hadn't realized what she was feeling until she heard herself say the words.

"What's happening?"

"I don't know. Maybe that's what I'm afraid of."

Dear Reader,

It's always sad when something comes to an end. But I'm not sad I had the opportunity to share the McCain family with you. If I've taken away anything from these five stories, it's that I'm very grateful to you, the loyal reader.

When I wrote *A Baby by Christmas*, I hadn't planned novels for each McCain brother. But after the book came out I got letters asking if I was going to write about Jake's half-brother. Eli's story, *Forgotten Son*, came out in 2005.

I received more letters asking about Belle Doe, a character with amnesia, so I wrote *Son of Texas*. Beau's story, *The Bad Son*, followed in September 2006. I probably received the most mail about Jeremiah (Tuck) Tucker, foster brother of Eli and friend of the McCains. You didn't want me to leave him without his own happy ending, so I'm very glad to tell you this is his story. And I'll tell you a secret—it proved to be the hardest to write.

Tuck is an easygoing, down-to-earth Texas Ranger who devotes his life to helping abused and neglected children. In the previous books, high-maintenance career woman Grace Whitten and Tuck were always at odds. They're two people with nothing in common, but something draws them together. It's taken four rewrites and to prove Tuck and Grace belong together. And I'm really hoping you'll agree.

Thank you from the bottom of my heart for your interest in the McCains and Tuck.

Until the next book,

Linda Warren

P.S. It always brightens my day to hear from readers. You can e-mail me at Lw1508@aol.com or write me at P.O. Box 5182, Bryan, TX 77805 or visit my Web site at www.lindawarren.net or superauthors.com.

ADOPTED SON
Linda Warren

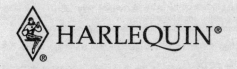

TORONTO • NEW YORK • LONDON
AMSTERDAM • PARIS • SYDNEY • HAMBURG
STOCKHOLM • ATHENS • TOKYO • MILAN • MADRID
PRAGUE • WARSAW • BUDAPEST • AUCKLAND

ISBN-13: 978-0-373-71440-7
ISBN-10:   0-373-71440-8

ADOPTED SON

ABOUT THE AUTHOR

If you could own any horse it would be...A quarter horse that can turn on a dime. **Favorite Western?** *Lonesome Dove*. **Favorite Western state?** Texas. I'm biased; I live here. **Best cowboy name ever?** Rowdy Yates. I always remember that name or maybe I remember Clint Eastwood. **Cowboys are your weakness because...**they are what you see: real men—hardworking, hard living, just needing the right woman to love 'em. **Favorite hurtin' song?** *My Heroes Have Always Been Cowboys*. **What makes the cowboy?** The hat—it's part of him and he has a certain way of wearing it that lets you know he's the real thing.

Books by Linda Warren

HARLEQUIN SUPERROMANCE

I dedicate this book to the readers who've e-mailed and written to me asking about the McCains and encouraging me to write another book about the family. And especially to those readers who come to the signings and stand in line waiting for a book. You keep me writing. You keep me going. Thank you.

ACKNOWLEDGMENT

A special thanks to Dottie Kissman and her daughter Phyllis Fletcher for sharing their Austin with me. And to all the nurses who answered so many of my questions.

Also Sergeant Frank Malinak, Texas Ranger, for so graciously answering my pesky questions.

Any errors are strictly mine and all characters are fictional.

CHAPTER ONE

"OFFICER DOWN! Officer down! We need help."

Gunshots punctuated the frantic call that came through on Jeremiah Tucker's police radio. He listened closely to the dispatcher's response.

"There's a pile-up on I-35. Hold on. Help is on the way. We're routing someone there now."

Tuck's hands gripped the steering wheel. He'd known of the wreck, and had taken a detour on 12th Street through an Austin residential area. He was near the address, and unable to ignore a fellow officer in trouble. He swerved onto Springdale Road then sped down another street and whipped into a trailer park.

As a Texas Ranger, he didn't usually answer calls. His job was investigating crimes, but this was different. Every second counted and it sounded as if the officer was short on seconds.

He pulled up behind a police vehicle, both doors of which were flung wide. An officer knelt on the graveled road, half lying against the seat of his squad car, shouting into his radio.

The trailer faced the road. Two old rusty vans were parked to the right, and a dog pen was to the left, shaded by a large oak tree. An officer lay facedown in the middle of the overgrown yard.

Tuck jumped out and ran to the officer by the car. "What's the situation?"

The officer gasped for breath, one hand clutching the radio, the other clutching his upper arm as blood spurted through his fingers. Blood pooled on the gravel and his blood-covered gun lay on the seat. "We answered…a domestic call. As we walked up to the trailer some-one…someone opened fire. I crawled back here, but Brian is hit bad. I can't get to him. The idiot keeps…firing." He gasped another breath. "Where in the hell is everybody? Brian needs help."

"They're on the way." Sirens blared faintly in the distance. "Take a deep breath and try to relax."

"I can't, man. Brian is…"

"Let me take a look at your arm. Relax."

"Help Brian, please," the officer wheezed and slumped onto the seat.

Tuck checked his pulse and then the wound. A bullet had ripped straight through his upper arm, tearing open flesh, muscles and veins. Tuck's main concern was the bleeding. He reached for his handkerchief and tied it tight above the wound. Soon the bleeding stopped. He felt the officer would be okay. He'd just passed out from loss of blood.

The sirens were drawing closer, but weren't close enough. Tuck surveyed the scene and glimpsed a rifle poking out of one of the windows. The dog pen was made out of chicken wire and two pit bulls thrashed at the fence, testing the strength of the flimsy wire and barking aggressively at the downed officer in the yard. Any minute the structure was going to collapse like a cheap umbrella.

Tuck didn't have any time to waste. Bending low, he darted to his vehicle, all the while keeping an eye on the rifle and the dogs. The officer on the ground moaned and Tuck knew he was still alive, but he needed medical attention immediately.

Several shots exploded, kicking up dirt around Brian. One nipped Brian's shoulder. His body jerked. Tuck had to do something fast or the officer didn't stand a chance.

Without another thought, he zigzagged toward the house. A shot blasted near his head, knocking off his hat. The sound burned his ears, but Tuck didn't pause. He rolled and landed up against the cool aluminum siding on the front of the trailer—the rifle above his head.

Adrenaline chugged through his body like hillbilly moonshine. He sucked in a controlling breath, knowing the guy couldn't get off a shot at that angle. Staring at Brian, Tuck debated how to get to him. Suddenly he heard loud voices, a woman's and a man's. He couldn't make out the words, but they were angry. The curse words he heard clearly.

Standing slowly, Tuck considered the situation. The rifle was to his right. He could jerk it out of the man's hands but before he could act, the gun was pulled inside. The voices grew louder, as did the cursing. The trailer shook from the impact of something thrown against a wall. Tingly sounds of glass breaking mingled with loud thuds.

Curtains covered the windows so Tuck couldn't see what was going on inside. The only uncovered opening was the small pane on the front door. Taking a deep breath, he eased up the concrete steps. The voices weren't close now—they'd moved farther down the trailer. He took a quick peep through the pane and saw complete chaos—broken furniture, dishes, junk, clothes and clutter everywhere.

But no people.

Drawing back, an image registered in his mind. It couldn't be. He glanced again to make sure he wasn't seeing things. He wasn't. Among the clutter was a small boy, probably not even two years old, sitting in a corner chewing on a bag of dog food.

OhmyGod!

His heart sank, but he couldn't let himself think about the boy now. He had to get to the officer while he could. Leaping from the steps, he sprinted to Brian, grabbed him beneath his armpits and pulled him toward the trailer out of harm's way.

Agitated, the dogs threw themselves at the fence, barking, growling, wanting a piece of the officer. And a piece of Tuck. He kept one eye on them, praying the wire would continue to hold.

The sirens rolled closer. An ambulance and police cars roared up the street and came to a screeching halt, spewing gravel onto the trailer. Quickly, Tuck searched for the officer's pulse. It was faint, but it was there. He was still alive. Thank God. Tuck sagged against the trailer.

Two officers ran to his aid, guns drawn. Three more officers followed, crouching beside Tuck.

"What's happening?" an officer asked.

"Not sure. There's a man in the trailer with a rifle."

Tuck gulped a breath. "I heard two voices, a woman's and a man's. And there's a kid, too."

"Damn."

"This officer needs medical attention," Tuck told him. "Another officer by the squad car has been hit."

"Damn. We have to get him out of here. Has the shooter fired lately?"

"No. I think he's at the end of the trailer by the dog pen. This is your best chance to move Brian."

The officer motioned to the ambulance and it slowly backed in. "Hold on," he said to Brian. "We got you covered." He then shouted orders to the others.

Two other officers grabbed a gurney and had Brian loaded in seconds. The ambulance pulled away, stopping by the squad car to pick up the other wounded officer. Sirens blared full strength as the ambulance tore away.

Shots rumbled through the trailer then there was total silence. Even the dogs quieted down.

Officers wearing protective vests and carrying high-powered automatic weapons swarmed the trailer. One kicked in the door and they charged inside. Tuck followed. He had one goal—to get the kid out.

In the narrow hallway a man and a woman lay in a pool of blood; blood also coated the walls. They appeared to be dead. Drug paraphernalia was scattered on the kitchen table. Tuck turned away and walked directly to the child.

The boy was dirty, his hair matted, his clothes stained and ripped. A telling smell emanated from him and Tuck knew he probably hadn't had his diaper changed in a while. The kid seemed oblivious to what was going

on around him. He continued to chew on the small bag
of dog food.

Tuck squatted down. "Hey, buddy, that's not for
you." He reached to take it away and the boy grunted
and bit his hand.

"That's not nice," Tuck said, and tried to take it again.
The boy shook his head and held on with both arms.
Tuck recognized the kid was hungry.

"Oh my God!" one of the officers said, staring at the
kid.

"Keep an eye on him." Tuck stood and searched the
cluttered cabinets for food. He found nothing but
dishes, pots and pans, junk, beer, cigarettes and liquor.
"I'll be right back," he told the officer. "Don't take your
eyes off him."

Tuck hurried to his car. He always kept peanut butter
crackers in the glove compartment in case he didn't have
time to eat. Going up the steps, he held open the door
for the justice of the peace, who had just arrived on the
scene. He would have to declare the people dead before
they could be moved to the morgue. Another ambulance
rolled up, waiting among the swarm of police cars.
Neighbors gathered outside in the cool March breeze.

Tuck went back to the little boy, who was still clutching the bag, his slobber all over it. He squatted again,
showed him the crackers and handed him one.

"I'll trade you, buddy. You…"

His words trailed off as the boy grabbed the cracker
and stuffed it into his mouth. Before Tuck could react,
the kid snatched the other crackers out of his hand,
poking them into his mouth as fast as he could.

"He's starving," the officer remarked.

Tuck stood. "Yeah. And he's filthy. He's probably been neglected for a long time."

"Sergeant Dale Scofield," the officer said and stuck out his hand.

"Jeremiah Tucker, Texas Ranger." They shook. "I was passing through the area and heard the call."

"Thanks for the help."

The crime scene people had arrived and Tuck and the sergeant stepped over trash to get out of the way.

"What do you think happened here?" Tuck asked, although he already had a good idea.

"This is a rental property and my guess is the woman was turning tricks and the man was a dealer or a pimp. There's a naked man dead in the bedroom. Something went wrong that ticked off the shooter. Maybe he came home and found her with a guy she wasn't supposed to be with. Who knows? An investigation might turn up something, but we'll probably never know what really went down." The sergeant glanced at the boy. "What kind of mother brings a kid into this type of situation?"

"A very bad one," Tuck replied, watching the boy as he continued to wolf down the crackers. "Has Child Protective Services been called?"

"Yeah, someone is on the way. And the animal shelter's picking up the dogs."

Two paramedics pushed gurneys inside, waiting for the word to remove the bodies. Tuck reached down and picked up the boy. He figured the kid didn't need to see anything else. The boy swung at him with his fists, making angry sounds, but Tuck gathered him up to get

him out of here. The kid was like a wild animal and Tuck
had a hard time controlling him.

An officer ran to him with a box of doughnuts and a
plastic cup of cola with a straw in it. "Sarge said to find
all the food we could," he said. "This is it."

"Thanks," Tuck replied, trying to hold down the kid's
hands. "Just put it on the hood of my car."

"Sure."

Tuck sat the boy on the hood, again noting his
powerful odor. "Hey," he called to the officer. "See if there
are some diapers in the trailer. He needs to be changed."

"Will do. And the name's Mike."

"Thanks, Mike."

The kid snatched the drink and sucked greedily on
the straw. Evidently he'd had sugary drinks before.

"Hey, buddy. Slow down." Tuck opened the half-
empty box and wondered if the boy could eat a
doughnut or if too much food all at once was good for
him. He closed the box, deciding to just let him drink
the cola. They'd have him in the E.R. soon enough.

The little boy's face was dirty and his matted hair
greasy and long. Wary brown eyes glanced at him from
time to time much as a starved animal would—on guard
in case Tuck tried to take the drink away.

Anger churned inside Tuck at what had been done to
this little life. Out of the corner of his eye he saw the
bodies being loaded out. How could a mother do this to
her own child?

Mike came running back. "I couldn't find any
diapers, but here are a couple of towels."

"Thanks." Tuck placed them on the hood.

"I have diapers." A lady in her fifties walked up with a diaper bag slung over one shoulder. "I'm Opal Johnson, caseworker." She glanced at the kid. "So this is the little boy I was called about?"

"Yes, ma'am," Tuck replied, and introduced himself.

Opal wrinkled her nose. "I assume that odor is coming from the baby." Without waiting for a reply, she plopped the bag on the hood and pulled out a diaper and baby wipes. "Let's see if we can't make him smell better."

Tuck spread out the towels and laid the boy down. He didn't object; he was too busy sucking on the straw. Tuck held the cup to one side so it wouldn't spill all over the kid.

Opal pulled the boy's pants down and undid his diaper. "Oh, no!"

"What?" Tuck glanced down and his stomach burned with fury. Urine and feces clung to the baby's butt in infected sores. It looked as if the baby's diaper hadn't been changed in days. He had to be in tremendous pain.

"Watch him for a moment, please," Opal said.

"What are you going to do?"

"Call for another ambulance." She reached for her cell in her pocket. "This baby needs medical attention immediately."

Tuck looked down at the boy, chewing on the straw. "It's going to be all right, buddy. I promise." He patted his chest and the boy slapped his hand away. "That's okay. You hit all you want. You deserve to hit someone."

"An ambulance is on the way," Opal said. "It was headed for the wreck on I-35, but all casualties have been picked up so it's coming here."

"Good."

Tuck helped Opal bundle up the baby in the towels as an ambulance whizzed into the drive. Opal carried the boy to the paramedics, talking to them for a minute before running for her car.

The ambulance screeched away and Tuck hurried to Opal. "May I have your phone number? I'd like to follow up with the boy. See how he's doing."

She gave him a strange look but rattled off her number. Tuck reached for the pad in his pocket but realized he'd lost his pen, probably somewhere in the yard.

"Don't worry, Ranger Tucker," Opal said, starting her car. "I'll call you."

Tuck heaved a sigh as the vehicles disappeared out of sight. He was left standing alone while the crime unit members worked inside the trailer. Neighbors stood in their yards, talking and watching. Tuck's hat lay on the lawn and he walked over and picked it up.

The March wind ruffled his hair and he swiped a hand through it, staring at the bullet hole in the top of his hat. Damn. He'd bought the Stetson about two months ago and had just broken it in. Oh well, better a hat than his life.

He crawled into his car with a weariness he hadn't felt in a long time, the weariness of life and its cruelties. In his line of work he saw a lot of cruelty, but this particular incident hit close to his heart.

Tuck himself had been abandoned as an infant, left in a cardboard box at the Tuckers' mailbox. The Tuckers, who took in foster children, had adopted him. He'd often wondered about the woman who had left him there. When he was younger he'd carried a lot of resentment about being thrown away, but as he grew older he realized the enormous gift he'd been given—the gift of a life. His mother had to have known the type of people the Tuckers were, and must have known they would give her son the best.

And they had.

How Tuck wished that little boy's mother had been as selfless.

LATER TUCK SAT in his mother's old rocker on his porch, soaking up that feeling of home. He still lived in the Tucker house, outside of Austin, and he probably always would. His mixed-breed terrier, Samson, better known as Sam, and his Siamese cat, Delilah, called Dee, lay at his feet. The cedar from the porch columns wafted to his nostrils, calming him. Laden rosebushes, his mother's pride and joy, covered the back fence. Soon they'd be in full bloom. His horses galloped in the pasture, enjoying the brisk wind blowing through the Texas Hill Country.

This was home.

After a harrowing day, it was always great to come back here, the only home he'd ever known. His parents were gone now, but his foster brother, Eli, lived about half a mile down the road on the same property. He and Eli were the two kids who stayed forever with Jess and Amalie Tucker. Eli's mom was Jess's niece and she'd brought Eli to live with her uncle when Eli was thirteen. At that age Eli had been wild and uncontrollable, rebelling against a father who'd never claimed him.

But Ma and Pa worked their magic and Elijah

Coltrane turned into a fine young man, becoming a Texas Ranger just like Jess Tucker. That's all Tuck and Eli ever wanted to be.

They'd inherited equal parts of land, but Tuck had inherited the house. Even though he had family close, some days he felt so alone.

All his friends were married and had families. He was the lone bachelor, but marriage wasn't for him. He wasn't sure when he'd first decided that. Eli said it was because he didn't know who his parents were, but Tuck thought there was so much more to it.

It probably had all started when he'd turned sixteen, got his first vehicle and started dating. He had a crush on one of the popular girls in school and he'd asked her out, but she didn't want him to pick her up at her house. He'd always met her at the mall or the movies. Thinking that was strange, he'd told her that he would pick her up at her home. He had a truck and he wanted to show it off.

She'd told him he couldn't because her parents didn't approve of him. That shook him. He was a good kid; he was Jess Tucker's son. She said it wasn't anything against him personally; it was those other kids his parents took in. Their parents were druggies, drunks, felons, and her parents didn't want her anywhere near those types of people.

Tuck reminded her he was one of those people. She said he was different, but he wasn't. For the first time he realized there was a stigma attached to foster kids and abandoned kids. He never dated the girl again, nor did he want to. He was proud of his parents and he hated that the seed of doubt had been planted in his mind.

In college he fell in love for the first time. Rachel said she loved him, too. They started to make plans and they talked about children. He'd told her that he didn't want to have children of his own. He tried to explain that he felt it was selfish of him to bring his own children into the world while there were so many others who needed a good home. She informed him quickly that she wasn't raising someone else's troubled kids.

He saw her in a different light then, but realized that he was asking a lot of her and broke it off. He was glad he found out her opinions before instead of after the marriage, though. A love he thought was forever died suddenly. That was an awakening in itself. The most powerful love he'd ever known was the love his parents had given to foster kids. It was selfless. Empowering. He saw it every day of his life as he was growing up.

So many abused and abandoned kids had come through their home. Under Ma's and Pa's love and care he watched battered kids grow strong, confident. All it took was one caring person to change a life.

He wanted to do that—to give back what he'd been given as a child. Ever the optimist, he had given love another try. Bethany worked at the courthouse and he saw her often. They talked about the future and she told him he was a wonderful man for wanting to help others, especially children. He relaxed, feeling secure in their love. Soon he asked her to marry him and he was happy in the knowledge that he'd found someone who understood him.

Her girlfriends had thrown them a big engagement party. There were a lot of people there whom Tuck didn't know and he was eager for the evening to end.

Toward midnight, he went in search of Bethany. She and a couple of her friends had disappeared about thirty minutes before.

He went upstairs to the bedrooms. A door was slightly ajar and he heard her voice. He thought they were talking girl talk and he didn't want to intrude, but then he heard his name and something kept him rooted to the spot.

Even today he could remember the conversation almost word for word. Hannah, Bethany's friend, said how brave Bethany was for agreeing to Tuck's plans of taking in foster kids and not having any of their own.

"Oh, please," Bethany had said. "Tuck doesn't mean any of that stuff."

"He seems pretty serious to me."

"After we're married, I can change his mind, and if I accidentally get pregnant, well, oops."

Tuck pushed opened the door then and as they'd stared at each other, they'd known it was over. That pain cut deep and his trust in women took a tumble. He didn't want a woman to change him or pay lip service to his wishes and plans. He wanted a woman to love him for who he was and he'd finally accepted that wasn't going to happen. So he decided he could achieve his dream alone.

He took a swallow of beer, putting the past out of his mind. His thoughts strayed to the little boy. Tuck had called the hospital and they said he'd been treated, sedated and was resting comfortably. He'd go to the hospital first thing in the morning.

He heard a car drive up, but he didn't move. It was

probably Eli. Living so close together, they had keys to each other's houses. Eli would check the house first then the back porch.

"Hey, Tuck. We thought we'd come for a visit." The French door behind Tuck opened and Eli stepped out onto the porch with his six-month-old son, Jesse, in his arms. He had a diaper bag slung over one shoulder.

"Hi." Tuck smiled at his nephew, a replica of Eli except for the blond hair, which was like his mother's. Tuck held out his hands and Jesse wiggled to get to him. Eli plopped Jesse onto his lap.

Tuck raised him into the air and the baby gurgled loudly. "I see him almost every day and each time he seems to get bigger." In that respect Jesse took after Eli, who was over six feet, well built and muscled.

"I know. It's hard for Caroline to cart him around in the carrier." Eli tousled his son's hair. "So how was your day?"

Tuck told him about the little boy.

"Ah, man. That's bad."

"I'll check on him again tomorrow. I hope they find him a good home."

"They will." Eli shook his head at the whole ugly mess. "I need a beer." He turned back into the house. "Want one?"

"I got one," Tuck replied, pointing to his beer on the table.

Jesse was fascinated with Tuck's shirt pocket, sticking his fingers in and out, chewing on his fingers and then doing it again.

"You're one lucky little boy," Tuck told him. "You have parents who will never let you down."

Jesse bumped up and down on Tuck's knees and made cooing sounds. Unable to resist the baby, Sam reared up on Tuck's thigh, wagging his tail. Jesse wriggled trying to get to the dog. Smiling, Tuck let him touch Sam and Jesse's excitement grew.

Eli came back, a Bud Light in his hand. "Do they even know who the little boy is?"

"They're investigating now."

Jesse gurgled again, drawing their attention.

Eli sat on the edge of the other rocker, watching his son. "I'm thinking about calling him Jess. I know Jesse was on Pa's birth certificate and Caroline liked it at the time, but now that he's older I like Jess. It's what everyone called Pa, anyway."

Tuck rolled his eyes. "Could you be more transparent?" Eli and Caroline had decided to name their son after Eli and Tuck's foster father.

"What?"

"Jesse sound too feminine for you?"

Eli took a swallow of beer. "Maybe."

Tuck bounced the boy on his knee. "What does Caroline think of the idea?"

"She rolled her eyes just like you did."

Tuck laughed, and it felt good to talk nonsense with his brother. "Pa said as he grew older everyone started calling him Jess. It will probably be the same with Jesse."

"Yeah. And Caroline won't think I'm a macho pig."

"Caroline doesn't ever think that about you."

"Hmm. She understands me better than anyone."

Tuck raised an eyebrow. "And believe me that's not easy."

"Come on, I'm a big old teddy bear these days."

Tuck just grinned. Caroline had changed his brother for the better. He was softer, more approachable. He and Caroline were good for each other. Tuck envied that. He wasn't jealous because he was happy for them. They'd found something rare—true love.

He wasn't so jaded by past experiences that he didn't believe in love anymore. He did. But for him life was different. His goals were different from most men's. He knew a lot of his attitudes had to do with the circumstances of his birth, but so far he hadn't found a woman to change his way of thinking.

At his age, he didn't think that was ever going to happen. That was fine, too. He was content with the choices he'd made.

"Is Caroline working tonight?" Caroline was a professional photographer and often worked late.

"No. She had a magazine shoot this morning that ran into the late afternoon. Mr. Fussy Pants here is teething and wouldn't sleep when he was supposed to. Caroline is soaking in a hot tub and I'm giving her some quiet time."

Jesse tried to jam both fists into his mouth, chewing away as slobber ran down his chin.

"He's trying to eat his hands," Tuck remarked.

Eli dug in the diaper bag and handed Tuck a cloth. He waved a teething ring in front of Jesse. "Chomp on this for a while, son." Jesse clamped onto the ring.

Tuck wiped Jesse's chin. "Does he keep y'all up at night?"

"Sometimes."

"Why don't you go home and unwind with Caroline," Tuck suggested. "I'll watch Jesse."

Eli jumped to his feet. "You got a deal." He kissed the top of Jesse's head. "Daddy will be back later." Eli paused in the doorway. "This is where he's supposed to cry because I'm leaving him."

"He's not going to cry." Tuck bounced Jesse up and down. "He's happy with Uncle Tuck."

"Yeah. I'll pick him up later."

"Take your time. I don't have plans."

After Eli left, Tuck grabbed the diaper bag and went inside. Sam followed. Dee decided she'd rather stay outdoors. He gathered toys out of the bag and eased down on the area rug. Jesse crawled all over him instead of playing with the toys, the teething ring firmly gripped in one hand.

Jesse poked his fingers in Tuck's eyes, ears, nose and mouth. Tuck wiped away slobber and just enjoyed the wonder of this curious child. He thought about kids and how some were born into privilege and others into horrible circumstances. Trying to understand why would be impossible. And he probably wasn't supposed to. That's why there were people like Jess and Amalie Tucker—to even the odds.

At that moment he felt incredibly lucky.

Maybe that's why he felt so strongly about his plans to one day refurbish the farmhouse and take in foster children. Every child needed a chance like the one he'd been given.

A knock at his back door interrupted his reverie. He swung Jesse into his arms and got to his feet.

"We got company, Jesse." He wiped away more slobber. "Wonder who it is?"

He stopped at the door. Grace Whitten, Caroline's sister, stood on the other side of the screen. He pushed it open, his heart knocking against his ribs the way it always did when Grace was near. He never quite understood that because the woman could annoy the hell out of him with very little effort.

"I'm sorry to bother you, Jeremiah."

He tensed and felt that seething annoyance creep up his spine. No one called him Jeremiah but Grace.

"But I was over at Caroline and Eli's and no one answered the door. I…" Her words halted as she held out her hands to Jesse. "Come to Auntie Grace. I should have known they were here. Both their vehicles are at their house."

Jesse practically leaped into her arms.

Traitor.

"Hi, precious," Grace cooed as she walked in without an invitation.

"Don't call him precious," Tuck said, closing the door.

Grace turned to face him. "Why not?"

The objection had come out of nowhere and he couldn't explain it. Maybe it had something to do with the talk he and Eli had had earlier about the macho stuff. He could blame Eli, but obviously he had issues about boys being boys and girls being girls. Or whatever. Grace had a way of making him nuts. He'd blame her. That was easier.

He waved his hand. "Never mind."

Grace glanced around his kitchen and den for Caroline and Eli. He watched the patrician features of her face. She had to be the most reserved, uptight woman he'd ever met. Her exterior was cool, composed. Always. He'd never seen her any other way and he'd known her for four years.

Grace was a dedicated career woman. Dressed in a navy suit, white silky blouse and high heels, she wore her blond hair pulled back in a neat knot at her nape. Not one hair was out of place. Ever. Perfect came to mind when he looked at Grace.

Perfect and beautiful.

Untouchable beauty.

Like a mannequin on display.

He wondered what would happen if he reached up and took the pins out of her hair. Would she be transformed into a woman with emotions and needs? He shook his head to rid himself of that insane thought. Grace was the head of the Whitten Law Firm, following in Congressman Stephen Whitten's footsteps. Everything in her life she did to please her father.

He often thought that Grace was programmed not to show emotion. But the moment she held Jesse he knew he was wrong. Her features softened and her green eyes sparkled. He had a hard time looking away, which surprised him.

"They're not here."

It took a moment for him to realize what she was talking about. "No. Eli and Caroline are not here."

"Where are they?"

"At home."

She nuzzled Jesse's face. "I was just there. They didn't answer the door."

"They're busy."

"What are they doing that they can't answer the door?"

He hitched an eyebrow. "A husband and wife are home alone. I have the baby. Use your imagination."

"Oh." A slight flush stained her cheeks, but her composure quickly returned. "I'll call Caroline later."

Sam reared up on her skirt. "Down, Sam," he said.

"Oh, my." She brushed at the skirt with her hand as if to rid it of germs while juggling Jesse in her arms.. "Do you think it's wise to have a dog in the house with the baby?"

He clenched his jaw. "Caroline doesn't have a problem with it."

They stared at each other and as always the battlefield lines were drawn. His way. Her way. No in-between.

"I'd better go," she said stiffly.

"That's a good idea."

He reached for the baby, but Jesse had Grace's blouse clutched in his fist. As he took Jesse, the baby didn't let go. A button came undone, then another, revealing a lacy bra and a rounded breast.

Grace grabbed her blouse and Tuck tried to pry open Jesse's little fingers. In his efforts, Tuck's hand brushed against Grace's soft, pliable skin. Her delicate perfume filled his senses and a jolt of awareness shot through him. He stared into Grace's eyes and what he saw there shocked him.

Was she attracted to him?

Or was he attracted to her?

CHAPTER TWO

STARING INTO Jeremiah's sensuous dark eyes, Grace felt as if she were teetering on the edge of something momentous. Her heart did a fancy two-step in her chest. All she had to do was reach out and touch him to feel the fire and warmth she saw in his eyes. That action would take her to places unknown and awaken…

As if sensing her need, his strong body tensed and she collected herself. She quickly kissed Jesse's cheek and walked out, clutching her blouse together in her hand. A musky whiff of aftershave seemed to follow her.

Why did every encounter with Jeremiah turn out like this—bad? They just never made the connection that could make them friends. Or much of anything else. A family acquaintance—that was the sum total of their relationship.

Driving home, she tried to put the incident out of her mind.

At her apartment, Grace slipped out of her clothes, folded them neatly and laid them on a stack to take to the cleaners. Running a hand across her collarbone to her chest, she could still feel Jeremiah's fingers against her skin. Her response to his touch had been a delicious sensation that melted her bones.

Had her eyes given her away? For four years now

she'd wondered what it would feel like if he touched her intimately. Wonderful. Heavenly. And she tried very hard to hide it. She was good at hiding her emotions.

She wasn't sure when she'd acquired that ability—probably when she was young and her parents would leave her and Caroline with the nanny while her father was campaigning or furthering his career. Caroline always spoke her mind, but Grace kept her feelings inside, wanting to be perfect for her father. Back then that had been important to her. Now being her father's puppet was wearing a little thin.

Her work had always completed her, but lately she was feeling a restlessness she couldn't explain. Or maybe she could. Her life that once filled her every need now instilled in her a sense of dissatisfaction. After much introspection, she recognized the cause. Somewhere along the way she'd lost sight of who she was. Her career was rock solid, but the woman in her was fighting for survival.

She knew that. And still she struggled.

She wasn't a big success in the romance department. Men who found her attractive always wanted something from her—a job, a step up the ladder or an introduction to her father. Well, that wasn't quite true. There had been men who had liked her for herself, but nothing serious had ever developed. She'd had a couple of flings in college, which left her wondering what the fuss was all about.

From an early age she knew she would follow in her father's footsteps and become a lawyer. That's what was expected of her and she never saw her life any other way. Her focus was on her career. After becoming a lawyer and with several years of experience under her belt, she took over the Whitten Law Firm, which had been held in trust for Stephen Whitten's daughter. She started at the top of the ladder, but she had to fight every day to stay there.

Romance had taken a backseat in her life until she was introduced to Jeremiah Tucker. When she'd looked at his tall lean frame, chiseled features and dark penetrating eyes, her mouth and brain fell out of sync, which was very rare for her. As a lawyer, she was always in control. But the first time they met she'd insulted him. She hadn't meant to. He just had a strange effect on her. She hadn't realized until later that it was sexual attraction. Sadly, the feeling wasn't something too familiar to her.

After Eli had introduced them, she questioned why anyone would call him Tuck when Jeremiah was such a pretty name. The way he'd looked at her spoke volumes, but being a Ranger he was very polite and never mentioned her rude behavior. After that, Grace had a hard time getting her foot out of her mouth in his presence. Something about Jeremiah always short-circuited her mouth and her brain.

How she wished he had the same attraction for her. But he thought she was bossy, uppity, neurotic and about as appealing as global warming. He tried to avoid her at all costs, which was no secret to her. With their connection to Eli and Caroline that wasn't always possible, though. He tolerated her because of them.

Her fingers splayed across her chest. How could one touch make her feel so—she thought for a minute—so alive? Her skin felt warm and her senses danced like pixies drunk on cheap red wine.

She must be coming down with something, she thought as she slipped into lounging pajamas. *Pixies drunk on cheap red wine.* Ridiculous. One touch shouldn't make her think such silly things. She wasn't sixteen years old. She reached for her briefcase and headed to her study to work.

With her mind deep in legal issues, her hand rested on the spot he'd touched.

Damn you, Jeremiah.

TUCK LAY AWAKE wondering about the incident with Grace. They'd been thrown together at weddings, parties and family gatherings but tonight was different. She seemed different. He was different, too. He had to admit that. The shock of touching her soft skin had knocked him for a loop.

What had he expected her skin to feel like?

Annoyed with the stupid question, he flipped over. He made a point of keeping Grace at arm's length. Now he wondered why he'd felt that need. The answer was easy. Grace was way out of his league and a neat freak, almost to the point of being obsessive. She drove him crazy.

Staring into the darkness he realized she was driving him crazy now. She'd left so quickly that he hadn't had a chance to gather his thoughts or apologize. Just as well. He didn't feel inclined to change the status quo of their relationship. Grace wasn't a one-night stand or a woman he could walk away from without a guilty conscience. And he would eventually walk away. He somehow always did.

As he drifted into sleep, soft green eyes stared back at him.

Grace's eyes.

THE NEXT MORNING Tuck went to his office early, checked his messages, made a couple of phone calls and then headed for the hospital. He met Sergeant Dale Scofield in the lobby. They shook hands.

"How are your officers?" Tuck asked.

"Great. Both are going to be fine. Darren's wife is waiting to take him home this morning. Brian was hit in several places, but not in any vital organs. Thank God. The surgeon said he should recover completely." The sergeant looked at Tuck. "I'm so glad you came on the scene when you did. Your quick action probably saved their lives. Thank you."

"No problem," Tuck said, feeling uncomfortable. He was a lawman. His actions came naturally and praise wasn't required or easy to accept. "I'm glad I could help."

"How's the baby?" Dale asked, and Tuck was glad to change the subject.

"I'm on my way to check on him. Did you find out any info on the mother?"

"Yep. Nicole Harper is a fine piece of work. Her mother had the little boy until about three months ago. His name is Brady, by the way. She assured her mother she was clean and getting her life straight."

"Is the grandmother going to take Brady?"

Dale shook his head. "No. She's in the last stages of lung cancer. That's why she let Nicole take the boy."

"Are there any other relatives?"

Dale rubbed his jaw. "I haven't had time to check. Our workload is bursting at the seams. CPS will handle it."

"Do you mind if I lend a hand? I want to make sure Brady finds a good home."

"Heck, no. That little boy needs all the help he can get."

Tuck thought the same thing. "Do you have any info on Nicole or the men in the trailer?"

"We've received calls there before. The guy, Cliff Davis, is a small-time drug dealer with a temper. The calls were about drug deals and twice about him beating Nicole, but she refused to press charges. My officers interviewed a few neighbors and they said there was a steady stream of guys going into the trailer. They knew something wasn't right, but didn't want to get on Davis's bad side."

"Did no one think about Brady, an innocent kid in the middle of that environment?"

"Evidently not. Sad, isn't it?" The sergeant checked his watch. "I've got to get to the station. Thanks again for your help yesterday."

They shook hands again. "No problem."

Tuck took the elevator to the pediatric ward. Opal was at the nurses' station so he walked over to her.

"Ranger Tucker." She pushed her glasses up the bridge of her nose and handed a file to a nurse. "I was just fixing to call you." Opal's dark hair was threaded with gray and the lines on her face denoted a life of toil and anguish—all given selflessly.

"How's Brady?" he asked.

"Know his name, do you?"

"I met Sergeant Scofield in the lobby."

She sighed. "This one slipped through the cracks."

"What do you mean?"

"Nicole Harper has been in the system for a while and we slipped up. After the last visit, the caseworker filed for a random drug check. She suspected something wasn't right, but she became ill about three weeks ago. No one was reassigned to Nicole's case and the test wasn't done. This is unacceptable."

Tuck liked this woman. Fighting for children was her top priority. "What's the story on Nicole Harper?"

"She was raised by a single mom and had a pretty normal childhood until she got into high school. Then she started doing drugs and finally dropped out. She went to work at a fast-food place and got involved with the manager. When she became pregnant, she tried to stay clean, but right before Brady was born the boy-friend, Braden Hollis, died in an auto accident. Nicole spiraled out of control then. Wilma, her mother, couldn't handle her. Nicole delivered Brady and quickly got back with her old friends and the drug scene. CPS took Brady away from her when a motel clerk called and reported her for prostitution and doing drugs with the baby in the room. Wilma was granted temporary custody."

"Didn't CPS try to get her some help?"

Opal touched his face. "You sweet man, I bet you believe in fairy tales, too."

"What's wrong in believing there's a better life? Sometimes it just takes one person to accomplish that."

"Nicole Harper got hooked on drugs fast and furious

and that's all she thought about—how to get more drugs."

"Still…"

"She was offered help many times. She always refused. Six months in jail changed her some. When she got out, all she wanted was her kid. Wilma was battling lung cancer and thought Nicole had changed. But it wasn't long before she was back with the old crowd. It's hard to break that cycle once it starts."

"Why wasn't Brady taken into custody then?"

"Did I mention that Nicole is a very good liar and knew how to put on a show? I love my kid. My kid is the most important part of my life. Yada. Yada. Yada. Once the caseworker leaves, she's hitting the bars looking for guys and drugs. And the kid is usually left home by himself, or worse, taken along. We just never could catch her at it—until it was too late. We have so many cases it's difficult to keep a constant vigil on these girls."

Tuck knew that. It was just a sad scenario that the kids were the ones who paid. "How's Brady this morning?"

"He was so violent in the E.R. that they had to sedate him. He was just scared. They checked his vitals, started an IV and did blood work. Nobody knows how long he's been neglected and we have no idea what he's been eating. He could have even been drinking from the toilet."

Tuck winced.

"I've seen it before. He may only be fourteen months old but even at that age a kid fights for survival. He could have digested nonfood items, even toxic items. They're testing for drug exposure, anemia and lead poisoning. The main concern was dehydration, so that's the reason for the IV. They want to keep his electrolytes under control. Since his sores are infected, they've started a round of antibiotics through the IV."

"What's going to happen to him?"

"I'm on my way to talk to Wilma. I know she won't be able to take him, but there might be a relative who wants to raise him." Opal threw the strap of her big purse over her shoulder. "How would you like to come with me, Ranger Tucker? Get an up close and personal view of life's real fairy tales."

"I'd love to, but first I'd like to take a look at Brady, if that's okay."

"Sure. Follow me."

They walked across the hall to a room full of baby beds. A large glass window gave the nurses a clear view of each crib from the nurses' station. Two nurses were attending to the needs of children with various ailments. Opal stopped at a bed against the wall.

Tuck removed his hat and stared down at Brady. He lay on his stomach, completely naked except for a small blanket covering his upper body. His bottom was bloodred and had ointment spread over it.

"They'll put a diaper on him as soon as he wakes up," Opal said. "They've debrided his wounds and applied a barrier cream."

Brady's hair had been shaved off and Tuck saw the infected sores on his scalp, too. He fought the anger churning in his stomach.

Opal glanced at him. "They had to shave his head to clean the sores and remove dead tissue. There are sores between his toes, too. It had been a while since he'd had a bath."

Tuck kept staring at the little boy. He slept peacefully, as a baby should. At that moment Tuck vowed that Brady would have a decent home and never be neglected again.

WILMA HARPER LIVED in the projects on a cul-de-sac. Tuck parked his car and followed Opal inside the brick duplex. A neighbor and a hospice nurse were there. Wilma sat in a recliner with an oxygen tank beside her, gasping for every breath. She'd been told of her daughter's death and held a box of Kleenex in one hand, her eyes red.

In her early forties, Wilma looked twice her age. Her pallid skin, skeletal frame and sunken eyes denoted a woman who was terminally ill.

Tuck and Opal sat on a worn brown sofa. He took in the room. The walls were made of cinder blocks and painted a pale tan, which was yellowing. Linoleum squares of the same color covered the floor. Some of the floor had eroded from wear, leaving the stark concrete visible.

Opal was right. This was the flip side of a fairy tale.

"How's Brady?" Wilma immediately asked Opal.

"He's going to be fine," Opal replied, and introduced Tuck.

"This is all my fault," Wilma wailed, then sucked in a whiff of oxygen.

"No, it isn't," Opal told her. "Nicole is your daughter and you trusted her."

"I spoiled her. That's the problem."

"Ms. Harper," Tuck spoke up. "We're trying to do the best thing for Brady now."

"Yes." Wilma sniffed. "I want that, too."

"Is there a relative who might be able to take Brady?"

Wilma shook her head. "My relatives are…struggling to make ends meet. I can't think of anyone…who can give Brady the kind of care he needs."

"What about Brady's father's family?" Opal asked.

Wilma took a breath of oxygen. "After Braden's death, his parents divorced and remarried. They have new families and…I don't think they'd be willing to take him."

The hospice nurse handed Wilma a glass of water and she sipped at it, her hands shaking. "I wish I could take him. He needs me." Tears rolled from her eyes.

The neighbor, a black lady in her thirties, rubbed her arm. "Don't get upset, Wilma."

"My baby girl is dead," Wilma wheezed, and sucked in more oxygen. "Seems like yesterday she was watching cartoons and eating Fruit Loops."

"I know," the lady consoled her.

Wilma gasped for air then looked directly at Tuck. "Please find someone to love my grandson. He deserves that."

Tuck's throat felt dry. "I promise, ma'am. I'll make sure he has the best home possible."

"Thank you," Wilma whispered. "And make sure he has his stuffed dog. He carries it everywhere…and sleeps with it."

Tuck and Opal eyed each other. "What does the dog look like?" Tuck asked.

"It's blue and made out of that really soft fabric."

He stood. "I'll see that he has it." Tuck twisted his hat in his hand. "I'm real sorry about your daughter, Mrs. Harper."

Outside, Opal eyed him. "You really meant that, didn't you?"

"Sure." Tuck placed his hat on his head. "It's sad when anyone dies like Nicole did."

"Yeah, but I was talking about the dog."

"Yes, ma'am, I meant that, too." Tuck fell in step beside Opal. "I'll find the dog and I'll make sure Brady gets a decent home. He's been through enough."

"I'll put some feelers out. There are always couples looking for small children. In the meantime I guess I'd better track down the father's family."

"If you don't mind, I'll handle that."

"Mind?" Opal lifted an eyebrow. "You're like an angel sent from above. You're certainly a cut above other law enforcement officers I've worked with."

"I was left as an infant, so I know what getting a good home means."

"Well, bless my soul, aren't you something?" Opal stopped in her tracks. "You're one of a kind, Jeremiah Tucker. It's good to remember where you come from, and it's even better to give some of it back."

"Thanks, Opal. I'll call when I have any news."

He strolled toward his car, feeling better about the situation. With a little luck, he was hoping that one of Braden's parents wanted Brady.

Back at his office, it didn't take long to track them down. Bruce, the father, lived in Dallas and had married a woman with three small children. He said his wife wouldn't be willing to take on another child. He was sorry and hoped they found Brady a good home. The mother, Eileen, lived in Tulsa, Oklahoma. Her new husband had had an accident and was paralyzed from the waist down. She had her hands full and regretted she couldn't take Brady.

Tuck stared at the phone, wondering why neither had asked about Brady's recovery or his well-being. Brady was their grandchild, their flesh and blood. Yet they seemed not to care.

Tuck ran his hands over his face, hoping that Opal could find the perfect family for Brady.

Perfect.

He thought of Grace. Uptight, repressed—that was how he thought of her. How he needed to think of her, but last night was different. For a brief second she'd let down her guard and so had he. The image was playing tricks with his mind.

And it shouldn't.

His friends the McCain brothers teased him about Grace. He and Grace were the only two single people left in their group and they were often paired together, especially at weddings. His friends saw that as a sign. Maybe he needed to stop being so touchy. Maybe…

His thoughts halted as he noticed the time. It was Friday and he was late for a brother's meeting. Even though he wasn't a McCain, Tuck was included because he was Eli's foster brother and a good friend. Eli's father was Joe McCain, but Eli had never carried the McCain name because Joe denied he was Eli's father.

The McCain family had been a mess. He couldn't understand how a father could walk away from his own son, not like Joe McCain had walked away from Eli. Beau and Caleb had been the lucky ones. They had lived with their mother, but the old man had raised Jake. Now the brothers had all made peace with each other and their dysfunctional father, who had passed away years ago.

Opal was wrong. After a tumultuous childhood, the McCains had found true happiness. It did happen.

He headed for his car and Salado, which was a quaint, historic town between Austin and Waco. It was the midway point for Beau and Jake, who lived in Waco, and Caleb, Eli and Tuck, who all lived around Austin.

When he arrived at the small diner, he recognized all the cars parked in the lot. He hurried inside. It was a typical small-town café: hardwood floors, booths, red gingham tablecloths and a jukebox in a corner. A Willie Nelson tune played in the background.

"Where have you been?" Eli asked in his best grumpy voice as Tuck took a seat.

Tuck ordered a beer and told them about Brady.

"Man, I don't know how y'all handle things like that," Jake said. "I'll stick with raising cotton and corn. That I can control. Well, that is, if Mother Nature cooperates." Jake ran the McCain farm outside of Waco.

"I see a lot of it," Beau added. "Then parents who have abused their kids want them back. It's hard when you get a judge who will grant that." Beau was the lawyer in the family.

"This is turning into a downer," Eli said. "Let me tell you guys what Jesse is up to."

"We know what Jesse is up to." Tuck took a swallow of his beer. "He's chewing on everything in sight."

"That's the truth." Eli leaned his forearms on the table. "I think he might be growing fangs instead of teeth."

Jake raised his beer. "Here's to a lot of sleepless nights."

"Oh, man." Eli downed a gulp of his beer and looked at Caleb. "How's Josie?"

Caleb was also a Texas Ranger and he and Josie were expecting their first child. "She's sick as a dog in the mornings. She's taken a desk job, which I'm very grateful for. But I didn't tell her that. Can you imagine a pregnant cop with mood swings carrying a gun?"

The brothers laughed.

"I suggested that she take a leave of absence from the force until after the baby comes. That didn't earn me any points. I just worry about her."

Eli slapped him on the back. "It comes with the territory."

Beau sat twisting his bottle, which wasn't like him. He was the talker in the group.

"You're going to rub a hole in the table," Jake told him.

"What?" Beau glanced up.

"What's up with you?" Caleb asked.

"I'm almost afraid to say it out loud."

No one said a word as they waited for Beau to speak.

"Macy's pregnant."

The brothers jumped up and pumped Beau's hand, which gave way to hugs.

"Oh, man," Caleb said, smiling. "When's she due?"

"In November."

"Josie's due in October. Two McCain babies born in the same year." Caleb beamed with excitement. "Have you told Mom and Dad?"

"We told them last night."

"And Mom's kept it quiet all day?" Jake lifted an eyebrow.

"We wanted to tell everyone ourselves," Beau replied. "And, believe me, Mom's bursting at the seams to tell someone."

"This is wonderful," Jake said, hugging Beau again. "Except Katie is going to start bugging Elise and me again for a baby. When Jesse was born, we heard about it nonstop."

Eli grinned. "You know how to fix that."

"Oh, no." Jake shook his head. "A boy and a girl, we're done."

The brothers kidded back and forth. Tuck was the last to hug Beau. "Congratulations, man."

"Thanks."

Macy's first marriage had ended in divorce because her baby daughter had died from a genetic heart defect. Since Macy carried the gene, she refused to have more children. Beau and Macy had adopted Zoë, a baby of Macy's sister. But now they would have a child of their own. Tuck knew that wasn't an easy decision for them to make.

All his friends were happy with families and children. It was wonderful to see. Suddenly he saw Brady lying in that hospital bed—he had no one. Brady needed someone to love and care for him. Without even having to think about it, Tuck knew he could be that someone.

"I'd better go," Caleb said, grabbing his hat. "Josie's home by now and I can't wait to tell her."

"Me, too," Eli added. "My wife needs a break from the chewing monster."

"Remember you guys promised to come to one of Ben's Little League games," Jake reminded them.

"We'll be there," Eli and Caleb promised at the same time.

Goodbyes were said and Tuck turned to Beau. "Could I speak to you for a minute?"

"Sure." They resumed their seats at the table after the others had left.

"I know you're anxious to get home," Tuck said, now nervous about what was going through his mind.

"I've got a minute for a friend."

"Congratulations on the new baby. I'm real happy for you and Macy."

"I know and thanks. We're excited and nervous." Beau eyed him. "What's going on?"

Tuck looked straight at him. "I'd like to adopt Brady."

CHAPTER THREE

FOR THE FIRST TIME since Tuck had known him, Beau seemed speechless. "Are you sure about this?"

"Yes." The more he thought about it, the more real the idea became. "Brady needs someone and no one in his family wants him. I've always planned to take in kids, so I'll start a little earlier than I thought. Will you help me gain temporary custody pending an adoption?"

"You know I will. But think about this."

"I've thought of very little else since I saw Brady chewing on a bag of dog food." Tuck shifted in his chair. "Can you believe that? They bought food for the dogs, but not for the baby."

Beau grimaced. "Man, that's awful. I can see how upsetting it would be to find a baby in that situation. But this decision will change your whole life. Are you ready for that?"

Tuck nodded. "I know there'll be some adjustments, but I really believe I'm ready."

"Okay. I'll start on the paperwork tomorrow and call you when I'm ready to file it." Beau paused.

"What?" Tuck asked, sensing something else was bothering Beau.

"Be prepared for some hard questions from the judge."

"Like what?"

"Your job for starters. What do you plan to do with Brady during the day?"

"I haven't thought it through, but by the time the hearing rolls around I'll have a plan. Mrs. Wiggins lives down the road from me. She's a retired teacher and now keeps her small granddaughter. She might also be willing to watch Brady. I'll talk to her. And there's a small day care two blocks from my office. I'll check it out, too. I can make this work, Beau."

Beau played with the paper napkin on the table. "I have no doubt you can. You're my very good friend and I love you like a brother, but I have to be honest."

"I wish you would."

"It's very difficult for a single male to gain custody of a child, especially one that is not his biologically."

"So you're saying I don't have a chance."

"I'm saying it will be difficult and I want you to be aware of that. I'll be behind you one hundred percent, though, making sure the judge knows what an incredible man you are. And what a wonderful father you'd make."

Tuck relaxed. "Thanks, Beau."

Beau studied him for a moment. "I don't suppose there's a woman in the picture whom I don't know about."

"No."

"What happened to that police officer you were dating?"

Tuck shrugged. "It wasn't serious."

Beau lifted an eyebrow. "Is it ever?"

"Not lately."

LINDA WARREN 47

Beau leaned back in his chair. "I've never questioned your personal life or your life's choices. That's your business, but as your lawyer I'll have to delve deeper. I have to be able to argue convincingly in front of a judge that you, a single male, would be the best parent for Brady Harper."

"I understand. Ask all the questions you want."

Beau looked straight at him. "Why do you feel that taking in foster kids is exclusive of marriage and having children of your own? Your adoptive parents were married. I'm not clear on why they didn't have kids of their own, though."

"Ma had a miscarriage early in the marriage and the doctor couldn't stop the bleeding. He ended up doing a total hysterectomy."

"I'm sorry. I didn't know."

"She worked in an office for a while then Pa was asked by the FBI to help nail a firearms dealer from Mexico. When they captured the guy in El Paso, he had his five-year-old daughter with him. He'd kidnapped her from her mother in South Carolina. Pa said the little thing was frightened to death and he became attached to her. He talked CPS into letting him take her home to Ma where he knew she would get special care. Ma kept her for three days comforting her and letting her know she was safe. The mother was so grateful to have her daughter back. Ma said after that she knew what she wanted to do and they helped hundreds of kids over the years, including Eli and me."

"I've heard the stories." Beau leaned forward. "But I still don't understand completely why, to you, taking in foster kids is exclusive of marriage and having your own kids."

"The marriage thing just hasn't worked out for me." Tuck twisted his empty beer bottle, knowing he had to share parts of his life for Beau to understand him. "Have you ever seen a two-year-old who's been hit so hard that his jaw broke into four pieces and punctured his eardrum?"

Beau shook his head.

"Have you ever seen a four-year-old who's had a pot of boiling water poured over him because he wouldn't mind?"

Beau winced and shook his head again.

"Have you ever seen a six-month-old baby girl malnourished and with cigarette burns all over her body?"

Beau held up a hand. "Stop. You're going somewhere with this, so please just get there."

"Those three cases are vivid in my memory. When the grandmother in Arkansas was finally awarded full custody of the six-month-old, she didn't even resemble the battered baby that had come to live with us. Ma rocked and sang to her and doctored her burns. Eli and I did, too. She was a laughing, happy child and we were sad to see her go. But there are so many kids like that, Beau. The violence and abuse never stops. I just would feel selfish bringing more children into the world when there are so many who need someone."

Tuck looked at his friend. "I've had these goals of taking in foster children ever since I witnessed how one person can change a life. Ma and Pa did it every day. I learned everything about life from them. I feel its something I have to do. I feel it's something I need to do."

With his thumb, he peeled the label off the beer bottle. "I like being with a woman just as much as the next guy, but I haven't found anyone to change my mind—or anyone to share my goals. Eli says it's a mind-set because of the circumstances of my birth, but it's much more than that."

Beau eyed him with a strange look on his face. "You feel very deeply about this."

"Yes. Brady needs someone and I can be that someone."

"You're a better man than me. I don't think I could give up so much."

Tuck shrugged. "I'm different. I guess I've always known that."

"And you wish your friends would stop trying to change you."

"No. I know they care about me and I need that, too."

"Well, Tuck, I'm going to do everything I can to make sure you're granted custody of Brady Harper."

"Thanks, Beau. I'd appreciate that."

"And I sincerely hope that one day you find a woman to share your incredibly selfless dream."

Tuck grinned. "Ah, a romantic."

"You bet," Beau said. "I just want you to be happy."

"Helping Brady would make me happy."

Beau patted his shirt pocket, searching for a pen. "Do you have the caseworker's name? I'd like to find out all I can about Brady—to make our case as strong as possible."

Tuck handed him a pen and gave him the information. They walked out together. "I'm really happy about the baby, Beau. Give Macy my congratulations."

"I will and thanks." They shook hands and hugged briefly. "You're a rare man, Jeremiah Tucker, and I'm proud you're my friend. I'll call as soon as I have any info."

Tuck swallowed back emotions as he slid into his vehicle. He sat for a moment savoring that bond of friendship. Backing out, he reached for his phone and called Sergeant Scofield. He wanted to go by the trailer and look for the stuffed dog so Brady could have it when he woke up. The sergeant gave permission and Tuck went by the station for a key.

Darkness had fallen by the time Tuck arrived at Brady's so-called home. He saw the yellow police tape that surrounded the trailer. Getting out, he noticed the dogs were gone but the vans were still parked in the yard. There was an eerie quiet about the place.

He went up the steps and unlocked the door. As he flipped a switch, a light came on. Good. The electricity hadn't been turned off yet. A distasteful odor greeted him. It was indescribable. Death came to mind. He shook off the feeling, glancing around.

Clothes, trash, junk and broken dishes cluttered the floor. He kicked some of the mess out of the way and walked to the spot where he'd found Brady. The toy was lying in the place Brady had sat. Tuck hadn't even noticed it before.

Picking up the stuffed dog, he saw it was filthy, but that didn't matter. What mattered was that Brady had the toy when he woke up. Tuck locked the trailer and drove to the hospital. It was late, but he went anyway.

Outside the ward, a nurse stopped him. "I'm sorry. Visiting hours are over."

He introduced himself and explained about the stuffed animal. "His grandmother said he takes it everywhere and even sleeps with it. Brady will probably be less upset when he wakes up if he has the dog." He showed her the toy. "It's filthy, but I'm not too sure if it can be washed or not."

She eyed him for a second then took the dog. "Usually all stuffed animals can be washed. We have a washer and dryer here so I'll wash it and Brady will have it by morning."

Tuck hesitated. It wasn't that he didn't trust her, but nurses had a lot to do and she might forget.

"Don't trust me, huh?"

Tuck looked into her honey-brown eyes and realized she was flirting with him. She was attractive, with short brown hair and a slim figure, but tonight he wasn't interested.

"By the way, my name is Jennifer."

"It's nice to meet you, Jennifer." He motioned to the toy in her hand. "I just want Brady to have the dog."

"He will, Ranger Tucker. I promise."

"Good. I'll be back in the morning."

"I'm looking forward to it."

Tuck nodded and walked off wondering if he was losing it. A beautiful woman, a willing smile and he didn't act on it. What was he looking for? He suddenly saw green eyes and an uptight expression.

Grace.

Why couldn't he get the woman out of his head?

THE NEXT MORNING Tuck was at the hospital early. Opal was at the nurses' station so he slipped in to see Brady.

He was still lying on his stomach, but in a different direction and he had on a diaper and a gown. The dog, all clean, was tucked under his arm.

He stood there staring at this little boy whose life might become a part of his own. Suddenly he wanted that more than anything—to love him, to make sure he never went hungry and that no one ever harmed him again. He could do that. He could be Brady's father.

"Are you the officer who brought the stuffed animal?"

Tuck turned to look at a woman sitting by the next bed, where a little girl in a pink gown slept. Machines were attached to her head and her chest. "Yes," he replied, and introduced himself.

"I'm Barbara Wilcott and this—" she glanced at the baby "—is my daughter, Molly. That's very nice, what you did."

"Thank you." Tuck walked around Brady's bed to stare at Molly. Her head was bandaged and she had an IV in her arm. "How is your daughter?"

"They removed a tumor from her brain three days ago. She hasn't woken up yet. We keep waiting." Barbara brushed away a tear.

Tuck felt a lump in his throat. "How old is she?"

"Two."

"She's very lucky to have you."

Barbara wiped away another tear. "And that little boy is lucky to have someone so caring looking out for him."

Opal entered the room, preventing Tuck from responding. "I pray your little girl recovers," he said instead, and walked over to Opal.

"How's Brady?" he asked.

"He's much better. They took out his IV this morning." Opal set her purse on the floor. "He should wake up at any moment. I just spoke with the nurse and she said they'll start the refeeding process and watch him closely. The problem with kids this age who've been deprived of food is they'll binge on everything in sight. She said they'll start with formula and work up to solids, taking it slowly."

"Does anyone know how long he was without food?"

"We're guessing about three to four days. The neighbor saw Nicole with Brady about four days ago, but she hasn't seen Brady since. Nicole has been in and out, but no Brady. We think Davis cut off her drug supply and she was out looking for another fix. She found the guy who was dead in the bed in a bar. Davis came home at the wrong time, or maybe for Brady it was the right time. Just so sad." Opal shook her head.

"Yeah. But Brady's going to be okay, that's the main thing."

Opal nodded. "I got your message about the grandparents. Sad, but I see it all the time. Some can't do enough. Others just walk away, but that's okay. We'll find Brady a really good home."

"I'm thinking about adopting him." Tuck thought this was as good a time as any to tell her.

Those tired blue eyes opened wide. "You talked your wife into taking him. That's wonderful."

"I'm not married."

Opal frowned. "What?"

He knew what that frown was about. "Is there a law that says a single male can't adopt?"

"Heaven forbid, are you from another planet?"

He tensed. "I take offense to that."

"Take all the offense you want. I'm just being honest. I know you care for Brady and you've formed a connection to him. But I've been in this business long enough to know that a judge rarely grants custody to a single person, especially male."

"But it's not unheard of?"

Opal pushed her glasses up her nose. "I wish you would have told me this yesterday. I've already let people know we have a fourteen-month-old up for possible adoption. We'll get responses—" she looked directly at him "—from couples. And a judge will go for a family structure first."

"I know," Tuck admitted. "But I have to try."

Opal shook her head again. "You're a rare specimen, Ranger Tucker."

Tuck had heard that before.

Brady moaned and they turned their attention to him. He rolled over, winced as his bottom touched the bed, but he didn't cry. He sat up and stared at Tuck and Opal.

"Why isn't he crying?" Tuck asked under his breath.

"I have no idea," Opal whispered back. "He should be screaming his head off."

Brady grabbed his stuffed dog and held it close to his chest, his dark eyes watching them.

Tuck removed his hat and placed it on the nightstand. "Hi there, buddy," he said. "Feeling better?"

Brady didn't make a move or a sound.

Tuck held out his hands over the railing. "Want to get out of there for a minute?"

Brady leaned over and bit his fingers.

"Ouch, buddy. That's not nice."

"Oh, this is going to be a tough one," Opal said. "I can see that now. Usually babies who've been left alone will go to anyone, but Brady's doing just the opposite. He's fighting back at everyone."

A nurse came in with a sippy cup of milk and Tuck and Opal backed away to let her take care of him. She didn't have much better luck. Brady hit and bit her, but he took the milk.

Watching Brady, Tuck could almost feel his anger and he knew Brady's full recovery was going to take time. He'd have to learn to trust again. Tuck was patient and could help Brady—if only the court would let him.

GRACE WAS HAVING A BAD DAY—her second in a row now. It was Jeremiah's fault. Ever since he'd touched her she'd been having all these feminine feelings distracting her from her work.

Today she went shoe shopping, her passion, on her lunch break and stopped in the lingerie department at Neiman Marcus. She looked at skimpy, silk peignoirs like the ones Caroline used to wear. She'd even bought one. When she planned to wear it, she had no idea. She just enjoyed looking at it and imagining herself wearing it.

If she was really honest with herself, she'd go so far as to admit that she imagined the look in Jeremiah's eyes when he saw her in it. But being honest with herself made her appear needy and pathetic and...

She had to get Jeremiah out of her head. How did she do that? He was a man and she was a woman, so the logical process would be to have an open and adult conversation. Simple. She chewed on the inside of her lip. Then why did the thought make her feel as if she were being prepped for painful surgery—open heart surgery?

A tap at her door interrupted her agonizing thoughts. "Come in."

Nina, her secretary, walked in with a notepad in her hand. "You have a partners meeting at two and Mr. Coffey wants to speak to you beforehand." Nina, a single mother of two, was all business and Grace liked that about her. They had a good working relationship.

Grace leaned back in her chair. "Did he mention what about?"

"No. But it's either about the day care center you're opening on the first floor or he wants your support on something."

Byron Coffey was her father's age and had joined the firm soon after Steven Whitten had started it. He was the senior partner and he and Grace got along well on the surface for the sake of office morale. Byron's wife had died years ago and Byron had asked Grace out more than once. She always found a polite way to refuse. In no way was she attracted to Byron, but to maintain a positive atmosphere in the firm she couldn't tell him that.

Byron had attempted to pressure her on more than one occasion to further his own causes. She always got the impression that he thought of her as a glorified figurehead without any brains. That did not endear him to her. And he was vehemently against the day care for the firm's employees, as was her father. Grace saw it as cost-effective. Too many times cases had to be postponed or rearranged because a lawyer, clerk, aide or secretary couldn't find a sitter at the last minute. This way the babies would be nearby and parents wouldn't have to worry.

Her father had said it wasn't the firm's responsibility to provide day care. Grace saw it differently and stuck to her decision. The first time she'd ever gone against her father.

Nina looked at her pad. "There's a Lisa and Keith Templeton to see you. They said it was important. Would you rather they made an appointment and come back later or…"

"I'll see them," she said. "Give me five minutes."

"You got it."

Lisa and Keith—she hadn't seen them in years. Grace reached for her purse and quickly checked her makeup. She and Lisa had been sorority sisters and college roommates. Lisa and Keith had fallen in love in college and were inseparable. After they'd gotten their degrees, both in finance, they'd settled down to raise a family.

Grace had had lunch with Lisa about two years ago and the family part hadn't happened yet. After a miscarriage, Lisa had been unable to get pregnant again. Grace knew they were still trying.

The door opened and Lisa rushed in, a petite blonde with a sparkly personality. Keith, also blond, followed more slowly. Grace hurried around her desk and they embraced.

Lisa stepped back, perusing Grace's outfit. "Anne Klein, right?"

Grace glanced down at her herringbone suit. "Yes." If

she and Lisa had anything in common, it was fashion. In college, they'd spent many afternoons shopping together.

"Ellen Tracy," Grace responded, eyeing Lisa's ecru linen dress, pearls and heels.

Lisa held out her foot. "And Manolo Blahnik. I bought them in New York. Aren't they to die for?"

"Absolutely." Grace had a pair just like them in her closet, but she wouldn't spoil Lisa's pleasure.

Keith cleared his throat and Lisa glanced at him. "Oh, Grace, we need your help."

Grace couldn't imagine what this was about, but from the expressions on their faces she knew it was serious. They took seats and she waited.

Lisa crossed her legs. "You know we've been trying for so long to have a baby. We've tried in vitro, everything, and we've finally accepted that we're not going to have a child of our own." A look of sadness crossed her face.

"I'm sorry," Grace said, feeling her stomach tighten at Lisa's pain. "I know how much you wanted a baby."

"It's all I ever think about." Lisa smoothed her skirt over her knees.

Keith reached for his wife's hand. "It's okay, honey. Tell Grace why we're here."

"Oh." Lisa's blue eyes brightened immediately. "We're going to adopt. We have been approved at several adoption agencies, but the waiting lists are so long."

"It'll be worth it, though," Grace reminded her.

"Yes, but my mother knows a lady who works for CPS and there's a little boy that might be up for adoption. He's fourteen months old. We want to be the first ones to apply for this baby and we need your help."

"Of course. We have a very good family law department and I'll make sure that..."

"No, no." Lisa shook her head. "We want you to handle it. You're the best, Grace. I know you are. You'll fight for us."

"Lisa, I appreciate your confidence in my abilities, but our family lawyers are very competent."

"Grace, please," Keith spoke up. "We'd feel more comfortable with you."

She looked into their concerned, hopeful eyes. Could she do what they wanted? It had been a while since she'd been in the courtroom. Adrenaline began to pump through her veins and excitement filled her. Something she hadn't felt in a long time. Maybe this was what she needed to force her out of her recent malaise. They were her friends and they needed her help.

"Okay. I'll set things in motion." She reached for pen and paper. "Let me get some details."

THE NEXT MORNING Tuck got a call from Gladys Upchurch. He mentored her grandson, Micah, after his father had killed his mother. The father was in prison and Gladys had full custody of Micah, who was now twelve and going through a rough period. Micah didn't want to go to school because the kids picked on him, calling him names.

Tuck drove to the Upchurch house and took Micah to school. It gave them a chance to talk. That's what the boy needed—to talk to someone. They made plans to go to a University of Texas baseball game and Micah brightened up. Micah was a good kid; he just needed a guiding hand and to know that someone cared and would always be there for him.

After Micah went inside, Tuck thought it was time to have a talk with the principal to let him know about the problem. The principal said he'd do what he could, but it was hard to control some of the kids. Tuck knew that and had to accept the explanation—for now.

When he reached his office, Opal called. Wilma Harper had passed away. She and her daughter would have one funeral and be buried next to each other. So much heartache and sadness. Tuck hoped they'd found everlasting peace.

That left Brady.

Tuck spent every spare moment he had at the hospital. Brady's wounds were healing and he wasn't quite so aggressive, but they had a long way to go. He didn't speak, only made grunting sounds. Wilma had said he was saying words, but the staff hadn't seen any signs of that. Neither had Tuck. CPS wanted a complete evaluation of Brady so he was staying in the hospital a while longer.

Brady preferred being alone, playing alone. If anyone got too close, he became aggressive, biting and hitting. He could walk and he enjoyed the playroom, where he could play with the toys at his leisure. Tuck often sat and watched him. Occasionally he'd roll a ball to him and Brady would roll it back. Slowly Tuck was gaining his trust.

Beau called and said he'd filed the papers. Now they waited for a hearing date. Opal told him that they had another applicant file for custody. She didn't offer a name and he didn't press her. He would have to take his chances in court.

Beau called at the end of the week and wanted to meet. Tuck didn't understand why they couldn't talk on the phone, but he agreed to meet him at a local restaurant. Sliding into the booth, he noticed Beau's worried expression.

"What's wrong?"

"I wanted to tell you in person. A couple has filed a petition for temporary custody pending adoption of Brady."

A waitress arrived and they ordered coffee.

"Opal mentioned that, but she didn't give a name."

"Lisa and Keith Templeton," Beau said.

The waitress brought coffee. "Thank you," Tuck said to the waitress as she left.

"With a couple in the picture, it makes our case that much harder to win. They both have spotless backgrounds, good jobs and are respected members of the community. They don't have other children and the woman plans to quit her job to stay at home with Brady."

Tuck's stomach clenched. "It sounds too good to be true."

Beau took a sip of his coffee. "Mmm. The Templeton's want Brady badly and they've hired a very good attorney to make that happen."

"Who is it?" Tuck asked.

"Have you talked to Eli or Caroline lately?"

"No. I've been spending all my free time at the hospital and with the boys I mentor. Why? Do they know this attorney?"

Beau shifted nervously. "Yes. The Templeton's attorney is Grace Whitten."

CHAPTER FOUR

"NINA!"

Grace's door flew open and Nina rushed in. "What? Did you see another spider?"

Grace sighed heavily. "No." A grown woman and she was still frightened of spiders. But that was so far at the back of her mind that it didn't even register. She held up the document in her hand. "When did this arrive?"

"Uh...about an hour ago when you were in a meeting with Mr. Coffey." Nina frowned. "Is something wrong?"

"No." Grace sank into her chair. "Thank you. I'm sorry I yelled."

"Sure." Nina hesitated for a moment then walked out.

Grace stared down at the document. *Everything was wrong.* Jeremiah Tucker had filed for temporary custody pending adoption of a minor child, Brady Harper. How could this be?

She grabbed the phone and called Caroline. She answered immediately.

"Caroline, did you know that Jeremiah filed for custody of a little boy named Brady Harper?"

"Well, hello, Grace."

"I'm sorry. I'm a bit stressed at the moment."

"You're always stressed," her sister replied rather bluntly. "But you should see Jesse. He'd destress you quickly. He's chewing on the phone cord and he's absolutely the cutest baby in the whole world. Oh, now he's looking at me with those big blue eyes, just like Eli's."

"Caroline, please. I need to talk about this."

"Okay. Okay. Give me a minute to put Jesse in his Pack 'n Play."

Grace drummed her fingers on her spotless silver-and-glass desk. The phone was to her right with a pad and pen beside it, Jeremiah's petition lay in front of her and to her left sat a crystal Whitten paperweight her father had given her when she'd graduated at the top of her class. Suddenly it all seemed so sterile, so unemotional. Was that how people saw her?

"Now, what's bothering you?" Caroline's voice brought her back to her present situation.

"Did you know about Jeremiah adopting this child?"

"Yes. Eli told me."

"Why didn't you tell me?"

"I wasn't aware you were interested in Tuck's life."

Grace took a breath. "Caroline, this is important."

"Yes. I can hear, but I don't know what you're so upset about. Everyone who knows Tuck is aware of his plans. He's a member of Big Brothers and he's always been involved with helping kids. That's Tuck. He's very dedicated to the plight of abandoned and neglected children. It's important to him."

"I know, but why this little boy?"

"Tuck was one of the officers who found him in a trailer living like an animal. His mother and father are both dead and no one in the family wants him. Tuck has formed a connection to the boy, probably because of the circumstances of his own birth."

She squeezed her eyes shut. "Do you think he'll make a good father?"

"Of course, but I'm not sure how he plans to work things out. He has a full-time job and according to Eli this little boy is going to need a lot of attention. But Tuck is very organized and, as I said, dedicated. He'll make it work." Caroline paused. "Why are you asking all these questions?"

"Remember Lisa Gates from college?"

"Yes. You and she were good friends. I remember a lot of shopping marathons. She married Keith something."

"Templeton. They have been trying to have a child for a long time and it hasn't happened so they've decided to adopt. But it takes a long time."

"Where's this going?" Caroline asked.

"I've agreed to represent them in gaining custody of a little boy."

"So?"

"The little boy is Brady Harper."

"Ooooh."

"I just found out. I wasn't even aware that Jeremiah knew this boy." She had a strong urge to ask her older sister what to do, as she had so many times in her life. But she'd outgrown that. She'd handle this in her own way.

"Grace…" Jesse's wailing drowned out Caroline's words. "I've got to go. I think Jesse is running a little fever with the teething. Come here, sweetie." A louder wail ensued.

"Take care of Jesse."

"Grace…"

"I'll call you later."

Grace sat for a moment, wondering what she was going to do. Lisa and Keith were her friends, but Jeremiah was part of her family. For years she'd waited for him to see her as someone other than Caroline's sister. If she stayed with this case, any hopes of that happening would be over.

Loud noises erupted from Nina's office. The door suddenly opened and Jeremiah stood there, an agitated Nina behind him.

"It's okay," she said to Nina, and stood on legs that felt like wet noodles.

Nina backed out, closing the door.

Jeremiah removed his hat, showing off his neat and trim brown hair. He was angry; that was evident in his taut body and his dark eyes, which burned like chunks of coal. He stood a few feet from the door, not making a move toward her.

"Why are you doing it?" he asked. His words were clipped and short.

She didn't have to ask what he was talking about because she knew. It took a moment to find her voice. "I wasn't aware you'd filed for custody of Brady Harper." One finger touched the papers on her desk. "I just found out."

His eyes narrowed. "Would it have made a difference?" Before she could answer, he went on. "No. It wouldn't have. Ever since we've met you've had this need to stick it to me."

"What are you talking about?"

"When Eli and Caroline got married, you had to be in control of everything."

"I wanted their day to be perfect."

"I was best man and I wanted it to be a day they would remember as fun and filled with laughter. But everything had to be synchronized and go according to plan. You never listened to any of my ideas. Everything had to be done your way. You couldn't even let your guard down long enough to enjoy the dance. You were afraid I'd step on your five-hundred-dollar shoes. My God, who pays five hundred dollars for a pair of shoes?"

Each word cut into her like a sharp blow. "Jeremiah…"

"That's another thing." He pointed a finger at her. "You continue to call me Jeremiah. No one calls me that. It's like a slap in my face every time you do. Evidently you get some perverse pleasure out of it."

She was stunned. She never knew he resented her use of his given name. For a moment she was absolutely speechless.

"After Ma and Pa adopted me, I was given the Tucker name. They were so happy to have a child that they called me Little Tucker. When I started to grow, Pa said, 'Boy, we can't call you little anymore. We're going to call you Tuck. That suits you.' I felt like a king had given me a crown. I had no name, but this incredible man had given me this special gift and it meant the world to me. It still does. When you don't use it, I feel you're *condescending* to me."

Her heart fell to the pit of her stomach. "I'm so sorry. I never meant to hurt you. I like the name Jeremiah."

"See." He shook his head. "It's all about you. You don't even care what I like."

"I…ah…" She had no words to defend herself. In his eyes she was a self-centered bitch and seeing his view of her she couldn't deny it. Many of her hang-ups became crystal clear at that moment. She had to be smart, in control, organized and an overachiever because if she wasn't, the real Grace would emerge.

The real Grace? She wondered who the real Grace was.

"Brady has been through hell and he needs someone to love and care for him. I don't know anything about the Templetons and…"

"They're very nice people." She wanted him to know that.

"So Beau tells me. They sound picture-perfect." His eyes caught hers. "But there's always something wrong with picture-perfect."

"Are you saying…"

"A judge will decide," he told her. "He will do what's best for Brady and I will abide by that."

She hated that he made her feel so guilty, so weak, and her fighting spirit surfaced. "You think you're what's best for Brady?"

His eyes darkened even more if that were possible. "Are you questioning my abilities as a father?"

"I'm questioning your abilities as a single father. Brady needs security and someone who is there for him twenty-four hours a day. Lisa and Keith can provide that. Can you?"

He watched her for a moment and she resisted the urge to fidget. "So you're going to make a case of a married couple verses a single man?"

"I'm sorry, but yes."

"You know, I kind of thought you might recuse yourself to preserve family harmony. Guess I was wrong, huh?" He placed his hat on his head. "I would prefer it if you and I had no contact. If you're at Eli and Caroline's, I won't go over and I'd appreciate the same courtesy. But knowing you, Grace, I'm sure you'll do whatever you please." He turned and walked out.

Grace took a long breath and crumpled into her chair.

Nina rushed in. "Are you okay?"

Grace sat on the edge of her seat, her knees trembling. She would not let her distress show. "Yes. I'm fine."

Nina glanced at the open doorway. "That man is drop-dead handsome…and angry. What a potent combination. Who is he?"

"Someone who thinks I'm the wicked witch of Austin."

"You *are* one tough lady."

Grace's head jerked up. "Excuse me?"

"Oh…I didn't mean anything by that." Nina quickly backpedaled. "You're managing partner of this firm and you have all these men under you, men who want your job. I personally don't know how you do it. And still be so feminine."

"Great save."

Nina smiled slightly and looked down at her pad. "Your father is on line one. Aaron Canton wants to see you as soon as possible. He's a little miffed that he didn't get first chair in the Desmand case. And the

Licensed Vocational Nurse is here to go over details for the day care."

Business as usual, but she felt like running out the door and leaving it all behind. Her self-image was shattered and she wasn't sure how to put the pieces back together.

With a deep sigh, she picked up the receiver. "Hello, Dad."

"I've been waiting for ten minutes. I don't have that kind of time to waste."

She bit down on her lip. "Sorry. I was attending to something. Did you need anything important?"

"Of course or I wouldn't waste my time on a call. What's going on with you, Grace? Why are you personally handling a custody and adoption case?"

Her hand gripped the receiver. "Lisa and Keith are my friends and they asked for my help." She felt as if she were sixteen and still had to answer to her father.

"What's wrong with our family lawyers?"

"Nothing. I'm doing this as a personal favor."

"You're the Managing Senior Partner of the Whitten Law Firm and you shouldn't take petty cases. You have competent lawyers to do that. But I don't have time to get into it with you today. I wanted to let you know that I'm sending Derek Mann your way."

"Who is he?"

"He's a damn good lawyer. He'll bring some clout to the firm."

She bristled instantly. "The firm is one of the best in Texas. We *have* clout and prestige." She'd worked most of her adult life to accomplish that.

"Sweetheart, don't get upset. You're doing a very good job. I'm proud of you."

Then why are you constantly keeping tabs on me?

"I'm not looking for a new attorney," she said.

"You'll change your mind once you see his résumé. It's coming to you FedEx and you should have it today."

"Dad…"

"Just read it and we'll talk again."

"Dad." She sucked air into her tight lungs, knowing it was useless to argue with him. "I really have to go. I'll be on the lookout for the résumé."

She hung up, unclenching her aching jaw. She'd reached her limit of how much she could hold inside. Grabbing her purse, she headed for the door.

As she reached Nina's office, Nina was immediately on her feet.

"Tell Aaron I'll talk to him tomorrow and please handle the nurse."

"Yes, ma'am. Mr. Coffey wants to know if you're free for dinner tonight."

"No." She walked toward the door, needing fresh air—needing freedom.

Byron caught her at the elevator. "Oh, Grace. I just left a note with your secretary." Suave, silver-haired, Byron epitomized the sophisticated older male in his prime. He was fit, wealthy and the type of man she was sure would get her father's stamp of approval, except he left her cold. And he was much too old for her. If she was in love with him, age wouldn't matter. But she wasn't.

She punched the elevator button. "Sorry, Byron, I'm not free tonight."

"Stephen is sending Derek Mann's résumé. I thought we could go over it together."

Her father had already talked to Byron. She controlled her resentment as she stepped onto the elevator. "I'll check with you in the morning."

"Grace…" The doors swished closed, cutting off his words. She counted as she went down, down, down, not letting one thought cross her mind. Instead of going to the parking garage, she walked through the lobby and out the double glass doors embossed with the Whitten Law Firm logo in gold. As a child, she used to love to come here and see her father's name on the door. One day she would work here. One day she'd make her father proud. One day had come, but nothing she ever did was good enough.

Nothing.

She started walking down the sidewalk. She had no idea where she was going—just away. Not being an exercise-type person, by the fourth block her feet were killing her. She took refuge on a bench and realized she was at a bus stop. Removing her shoes, she rubbed her sore feet.

What a picture she must make, she thought to herself. Her skirt had ridden up her thighs as she raised an ankle to rest on her knee, massaging the sole of her foot. This was definitely a Kodak moment—Grace Whitten not impeccable and in control.

She glanced down at the heels beside her and Jeremiah's words came rushing back. *You couldn't even let your guard down long enough to enjoy the dance. You were afraid I'd step on your five-hundred-dollar shoes. My God, who pays five hundred dollars for a pair of shoes?*

For years shoe shopping had been her passion. Now she felt a sense of guilt. Maybe shoes had replaced men in her life. No man had ever made her feel as good as slipping her feet into a pair of Manolo Blahnik shoes did. And if that wasn't a depressing thought she didn't know what was, except maybe Jeremiah's words.

You continue to call me Jeremiah. No one calls me that. It's like a slap in my face every time you do.

She really liked the name. She never dreamed he hated her using it. But then she should have picked up on that the first time she'd met him. Was she insensitive? Did she not care what he thought? She'd been groomed to be independent, assertive and to speak her mind. Her father had told her many times that's what she had to do to make it in a man's world.

Suddenly she didn't like that person. She didn't like her at all.

I would prefer it if you and I had no contact. If you're at Eli and Caroline's, I won't go over and I'd appreciate the same courtesy. But knowing you, Grace, I'm sure you'll do whatever you please.

Those words hurt a little more than the rest. In the years she'd known Jeremiah she'd never seen him so angry. Evidently, he'd wanted to tell her off for some time. And she'd been wondering why he'd never asked her out. It didn't take a member of Mensa to figure that one out. Jeremiah didn't like her in any shape, form or fashion. That truth was hard to take.

People from all walks of life began to gather at the bus stop: two nurses in scrubs, a black lady helping an older man, a Mexican woman with four children and three teenagers with iPod earbuds stuck in their ears.

The bus pulled up with a roar of wheels, the doors swung open and three people got off, then the others stepped onto the bus. The doors closed and the bus rolled into traffic leaving diesel fumes behind.

On the glass building across the street she saw a woman sitting on a bench. Her pulled-back hair gave her a pinched look. She seemed unhappy, alone. For a brief moment, Grace felt sorry for her.

Then she realized she was staring at herself.

Was that her?

She put a hand up to her hair. Yes, it was her. She kept staring at the woman as if she were a stranger. That uptight, stern woman wasn't who she was inside. Or was it? That was how Jeremiah saw her, she kept thinking.

Jeremiah. Even after he'd told her how much he hated the name Jeremiah, she was still using it to herself. Was she that selfish or self-centered? A tear slipped from her eye and she quickly brushed it away. She wouldn't cry in public.

Grabbing her shoes, she started the trek back to the Whitten Building not even pausing to put them back on. She met a law clerk and a secretary in the lobby. She said hello and kept walking toward the elevators. She could feel their eyes probing her back, but she didn't care.

Within an hour it would be all over the Whitten Building that Grace Whitten was in the lobby without her shoes. By the end of the day the tidbit would find its way to her father. She didn't care about that, either.

She took the elevator to the parking garage and in

minutes she pulled into traffic on Congress Avenue.
Above the rooftops the state capitol building gleamed
in the distance. She headed toward West Austin and the
gated apartment complex where she lived. She needed
time alone. Time to come to grips with everything she
was feeling.

Entering her apartment, she took a moment to stare
at her immaculate white home. It had a sterile feel to it,
just like her office. She never noticed that before.

In the bedroom, she threw her shoes on the bed and
slipped out of her suit jacket. She folded it neatly, and
then paused. She had to break the chains that kept her
bound to this uptight, repressed person. The jacket fell
to the floor; her skirt and blouse followed.

Opening a drawer, she found a cotton T-shirt and
slipped it over her head. She took the pins out of her hair
and shook it free. She walked toward the kitchen stoically,
resolutely refusing to look back at the mess she'd made.

Chocolate—that's what she needed. And lots of it.

She found vanilla ice cream in the freezer. She
grabbed it and reached for chocolate syrup and a spoon,
carrying everything to the living room. Sitting cross-
legged on the white sofa, she cradled the half gallon of
ice cream in her lap, squirting chocolate syrup all over
it. Gulping down two spoonfuls, she paused to stare at
herself in the pane of the French doors leading to her
small patio.

She frowned. Why was she seeing herself everywhere today? The frown dissolved into a smile. This
was her, the real Grace, disheveled blond hair around
her shoulders and a chocolate-induced gleam in her eye.

She didn't look excitedly happy, but she looked at peace with herself. To fight her deep-seated attitudes she had to keep this person alive. There was something cathartic about letting go, and it was something she intended to do more often.

And it had nothing to do with Jeremiah Tucker.

Or what he thought of her.

CHAPTER FIVE

TUCK SAT AT HIS KITCHEN TABLE wondering what had gotten into him today. He hadn't meant to say all those things to Grace. It wasn't like him to be that cruel and it bothered him. He'd stepped over the line so far he wondered if he could salvage anything of their relationship—whatever that was. For Eli, he had to try.

They were part of the same family and families worked out their problems. That's what Ma and Pa had taught him. Tomorrow he'd apologize or he wouldn't be able to live with himself.

He ran his hands over his face, seeing the hurt in Grace's eyes. He'd never intentionally hurt anyone in his life and he didn't like the feeling. But for a brief moment it had angered him that Grace had taken the case. She didn't take child custody cases. She only worked on the high-profile ones, so why had she gone out of her way to take Brady's case? There was only one clear answer to him—because Tuck was involved. That made sense to him at the time, but now he felt like a fool. Grace wouldn't go out of her way to intentionally hurt him. He was sure it was a business decision.

He sighed with regret as he remembered some of her words. She hadn't known he was involved in the case.

When she'd said that, he should have backed out of the room and left. But he hadn't. For some reason he wasn't sure about, he'd wanted to wring her pretty neck and words came tumbling out. Now he felt rotten about the whole thing.

But he wasn't giving up his fight for Brady. That was one thing he was very resolute about.

Out of the corner of his eye, he caught a movement and saw Eli and Caroline pushing a stroller up his driveway. They must have walked down the blacktop road. He quickly opened the screen door and Eli rolled a sleeping Jesse inside.

Caroline paused to kiss Tuck's cheek. With blond hair and green eyes, Caroline favored Grace a great deal. But Caroline was soft, caring and impulsive while Grace was hard, driven and methodical.

"Jesse's having a bad day," Caroline whispered. "He fell asleep when we got halfway here. Hopefully, he'll sleep for a while."

Eli pushed Jesse into the den and turned the stroller to face them, then went to get a beer out of the refrigerator. "Anybody want a beer?"

Caroline sighed, taking a seat at the table. "It's a good thing you're not married, Tuck. Eli treats your place like home."

"I'll have a beer," Tuck replied. "And this is Eli's home."

"See, he doesn't mind." Eli placed a beer in front of Tuck and handed his wife a bottle of water.

Caroline looked at Eli, one eyebrow raised. "You just assumed I wanted water."

Eli removed his hat and sank into a chair. "You're

nursing. That's all you drink is water and milk. And I was certain you didn't want milk."

"But you could have asked."

"Okay. What would you like to drink, Caroline, love of my life?"

"Water. Thank you for asking."

Eli rolled his eyes. "I'll never understand women."

Caroline laughed and their words faded away as Tuck's inner thoughts intruded. Understanding was about being sensitive to someone else's needs and feelings. He'd completely blown that concept today with Grace. He hadn't given her a chance to explain her side of the situation.

"Tuck. Tuck?"

He jerked up his head to stare at Caroline. "Grace didn't know you'd filed for custody of Brady Harper. She feels bad about it."

He shifted uneasily. "It's a difficult situation."

"Have you thought about how you're going to handle a baby with your job?"

"I'm working on it." He studied his beer can.

"You know I love you dearly," Caroline said. "You're our best friend. You're always there when we need anything. I've always admired your desire to help children, but have you thought that Brady might need a mother?"

Tuck knew the big but was coming. Caroline was known for speaking her mind. This one caught him a little off guard, though.

"Evidently you do."

"Well, yes." Caroline glanced at Eli, then back to Tuck. "After what Brady's been through, he needs someone to love and care for him full-time."

"You don't think I can do that?"

Caroline got up and wrapped her arms around Tuck's neck. "I think you're a wonderful person, but you have a full-time job and Brady needs to build trust again in someone he knows will be there for him. He needs a mother."

"A lot of women work and leave their babies in day care," Eli spoke up. "And stop hanging on Tuck."

Caroline gave Eli a sharp glance and threw up her hands. "You guys are missing the point. Brady's mother has let him down terribly. He now needs to build a nurturing relationship with a woman. He needs a mother."

"Tuck can give him everything a woman can," Eli stated stubbornly.

"No, he can't," Caroline insisted just as stubbornly. "The first bond a baby makes in life is with his mother. Brady needs to form that bond again. As I said, it's all about nurturing and women do that. Men don't."

"Jesse does just fine with me," Eli pointed out.

"Well, Eli, Jesse will need nursing as soon as he wakes up. Let's see if you can do that."

"I can give him a bottle, Caroline."

Caroline placed her hands on her hips. "It's not so much about the nourishment received while nursing but the act itself that encourages the bond. It's just not the same holding a baby and giving it a bottle."

"A lot of women choose not to breast-feed. Are you saying they're not nurturers?"

Caroline's green eyes flared. "No, I'm not. There's more to nurturing than breast-feeding."

"Since Brady's not breast-feeding, I…"

"Time-out." Tuck did the time-out sign with his hands. "I don't want you two arguing about this."

A wail pierced the long pause and Caroline went to Jesse, lifting him out of the stroller. "Hey, sweetie." She kissed him. "Are you hungry?" Caroline glanced at Eli. "Would you like to try to nurse him?"

"Sometimes you can be hard-nosed," Eli replied.

"Like my sister?"

"I didn't say anything about Grace."

"Stop it," Tuck ordered. "I'll handle the custody hearing and you two stay out of it."

Jesse's cries broke through his words. Eli and Caroline hardly ever argued or disagreed and he didn't want to be the cause of any dissension between them.

"I'm going to nurse Jesse." Caroline headed for the bedroom.

"I'm behind you one hundred percent," Eli told Tuck, taking a long swig of beer.

"I know, but I don't need you guys to take sides. This will be decided by a judge."

"How's Brady doing?" Eli asked.

"He's better, but he's not talking or responding to people. They're still running tests on him and Brady's not leaving the hospital until a complete evaluation is done. That way the Templetons and myself will be aware of what Brady's problems are and what kind of care he will need." He swished the beer in his can. "The Templetons have their first visit in the morning. I got a call from Beau a little while ago."

"Are you okay with that?"

"I want what's best for Brady. That's my bottom

line." Tuck took a swallow of beer. "And stop arguing with Caroline over it."

Eli stood, grinning. "Think I'll go help Jesse nurse."

In a little while, the Coltranes loaded up and headed back to their house—all lovey-dovey, the way Tuck wanted them to be.

Tuck stared at the phone and thought about calling Grace to apologize. But he knew he needed to do that in person.

GRACE DIDN'T SLEEP MUCH, and by dawn she knew what she had to do. She showered and dressed, slipping into a black pantsuit and green silk blouse. She brushed her hair and let the waves hang loose around her shoulders. It was a start in breaking the restraints she'd placed upon herself.

It was a start in finding the person within.

She slid her feet into a pair of Prada sling-backs. Shoes weren't her passion. They were her weakness. And until she found something to replace them, she was allowing herself that indulgence.

By eight she was in her office ready for a meeting with Byron, and then she met with Aaron and soothed his wounded ego. Both men kept staring at her and she ignored their obvious glances at her change of hairstyle.

She checked on the progress of the day care and met with the Licensed Vocational Nurse who was going to run it. At one she was back in her office for a meeting with Lisa and Keith.

Lisa was bubbling over with excitement. "Brady is so beautiful," she gushed. "He has these big brown eyes. I wished they were blue, but that doesn't matter. We sat with him for about an hour in the playroom. I helped him put a puzzle together and it was fun just watching him run around the room. He hit me once when I tried to put the puzzle away. The therapist said he does that a lot. Brady has so much to overcome, but we're willing to help him, aren't we, honey?"

"Yes, honey, we are." Keith gripped his wife's hand.

"I'm glad things went so well," Grace said. "The hearing will be set as soon as they have all the results from Brady's tests."

"The caseworker told us that a Texas Ranger has also filed for custody." Keith looked concerned.

"Yes." She clenched her fingers tightly. "I wanted to talk to you about that. He's Jeremiah Tucker and he's Caroline's brother-in-law."

"You mean…"

"Yes. He's a part of our family and I now have a conflict of interest."

"Oh."

"I've assigned Ann Demott to your case. She'll do a very good job."

Lisa wrinkled her nose. "I'd feel so much better with you."

"I want you to have the best representation possible and since I know both parties that wouldn't be fair to you."

"I understand." Lisa stood. "But I don't have to be happy about it."

Grace stood, also. "I'll walk you to Ann's office. She's waiting for you."

Afterward Grace felt an enormous relief. She would not personally be involved in the proceedings. If Jeremiah lost, she wouldn't be the bad person. Something about the road less traveled came to mind. That was certainly a road she didn't want to travel.

GRACE WORKED LATE, as always. Driving home, she kept thinking about the little boy whom Jeremiah wanted to adopt. On impulse, she turned and drove to the hospital. She hadn't planned to, but she suddenly wanted to meet Brady Harper.

The nurse on duty wasn't too friendly. "I'm sorry, visiting hours are over."

"I'm Grace Whitten and my firm is representing the Templetons, who have filed for custody of Brady Harper."

The girl gave her a so-what look.

"If it's not too much trouble, I would like to meet the little boy."

"Ranger Tucker put him down about thirty minutes ago. I'm sure he's asleep."

"May I just take a peep at him then?" Grace wasn't sure why this was so important, but something she couldn't define was spurring her on.

The girl seemed to consider it, and then walked around the station to Grace's side. "This way, but please be quiet. There are other children in the ward, too."

"I will." She followed the girl across the hall to a semidark room with baby beds. A nurse was attending to a baby on the other side of the room. A woman sat in a straight-back chair asleep by another bed where a small girl lay sleeping. The woman's head was on a pillow propped against the baby bed. Grace glanced at her for a moment, wondering how she could sleep like that.

The nurse stopped by a bed. "This is Brady...oh, he's awake."

A little boy sat in a corner clutching a stuffed dog, his gown tangled around his hips. His head had been shaved and Grace saw the medicated sores. She was mesmerized by the big brown eyes staring back at her.

"Brady, what are you doing awake?" the nurse asked him gently.

Brady didn't move or even blink. He kept staring at Grace.

"He's met so many new people lately. I think it's a little overwhelming for him. He doesn't know who to trust."

Grace saw the empty baby bottle lying beside Brady. "Maybe he's hungry," she suggested, reaching in for the bottle.

Brady made a dive for it, jerking the bottle away before Grace could touch it.

"He's very territorial," the nurse said. "I guess he's had to fight for everything. It's just so sad." She took a breath. "We only give him a bottle at night. I'll get him a little bit more formula and maybe he'll go back to sleep."

Grace leaned slightly into the baby bed. "Hi, Brady." Even in the semidarkness she could see his long dark eyelashes. "My, you have very long eyelashes. See—" she blinked one eye then another "—mine are short and light brown. Maybe we could trade. Would you like to trade eyelashes, Brady?"

One eye blinked. She was almost positive. Leaning closer, she watched him, but he didn't do it again. She wasn't sure he'd even done it in the first place.

The nurse brought another bottle. "Do you mind if I give it to him?" Grace asked.

"No, but be aware he doesn't take it like a normal child."

Grace took the bottle from her and handed it to Brady. He snatched it from her, retreating to his corner, his eyes watching her.

"Wow. That was fast."

"Yes," the nurse replied, glancing at her watch. "I have to give a doctor a report. Maybe when I come back, he'll be ready to go to sleep."

"Do you mind if I stay here?"

"No. Just don't try to take him out of the bed."

"Sure." Grace placed her purse on the floor, never taking her eyes off Brady's wary ones. She leaned over the railing again and patted the mattress. "Wouldn't you like to lie down? I have a nephew and he likes it when I rub his back. Would you like me to rub your back, Brady?"

No response. But he scooted closer to her, sucking hungrily on the nipple.

She reached out and touched his leg. He pulled it back.

"Lie down, Brady, and go night-night." This time he frowned at her.

"Rock-a-bye, Brady," she began to sing softly. After a couple of choruses, Brady lay on his side then turned onto his stomach. Grace pulled the blanket over him and rubbed his back slightly. He slapped her hand away.

"Rock-a-bye, Brady," she continued to sing, watching his precious little face.

When she stopped, he opened his eyes wide, so she kept on singing. Finally those gorgeous lashes fluttered against his cheeks.

"Night, Brady," she murmured as his beautiful eyes stayed closed. When she walked out, she met the nurse. "He's asleep," Grace whispered. At the nurses' station, she asked, "How is he?"

"His wounds are healing. There's a large infected wound on one butt cheek that's going to take some time, but it's those inner wounds we're worried about." The nurse held out her hand. "My name is Jennifer and I was on duty when they brought him in." They shook hands. "It's hard to tell how long he went without his diaper being changed, but his skin was raw and infected. Poor thing had to have been in so much pain."

"But he's not now?" The thought of Brady being in any type of pain disturbed Grace.

"Maybe some. We keep a very loose diaper on him to prevent any pain we can. And we keep the sores medicated and we change his diaper frequently. Brady's been through a traumatic experience, but he has a real friend in Ranger Tucker. Tuck is here first thing in the mornings. He comes on his lunch hour and he comes after work and stays to put Brady to bed."

Grace noticed she called him Tuck. How close were they?

"They said your clients were here this morning," Jennifer went on. "But I haven't seen them tonight."

Grace slung the strap of her purse over her shoulder. "Thank you for letting me see Brady. I appreciate it."

"As you can tell, I'm partial to Tuck and I will be testifying for him."

"Yes. I can see that. Good night, Jennifer." Grace

quickly walked away before she smacked Jennifer with her purse. She wasn't a violent person, but she was suddenly filled with a desire to pull Jennifer's hair out by the roots.

She needed chocolate, the more the better.

Rounding a corner, she spotted a vending machine. Digging in her purse, she found her wallet and pulled out a dollar. She inserted it into the slot and made her choice. Oreo cookies, for sure.

The machine took her money and gave her nothing. Damn. She beat on the glass with her fist. Nothing. She pulled off her shoe and gave it a good whack. The machine groaned and spit out three bags of Oreo cookies.

She sank to the floor, leaning against the machine. Did she just hit the machine with her shoe? Her expensive shoe? She examined the leather and discovered the shoe was fine.

And so was she.

Letting down her hair had released a new Grace. She was sitting on the floor, probably a dirty floor. Still she made no effort to get up. She was taking tiny baby steps, even though they seemed gigantic to her. But they were steps she was willing to take, needed to take.

Ripping open one bag, she removed a cookie and twisted off the top, licking the icing in the middle. When she and Caroline were kids they had perfected a routine of eating an Oreo and dunking it in milk. Sometimes they'd race to see who could eat a cookie the fastest. Caroline always won because she wasn't afraid to get milk all over her. Grace ate fastidiously, not wanting to get crumbs or milk on her clothes.

Even at that age, she was repressed.

What had made her that way?

Her thoughts went back to her childhood. When Grace was born, Stephen Whitten had wanted a son. From as early as Grace could remember, her father had said, "You're my son, Grace. I know you'll make me proud."

And she had tried to be that son in every way that counted. She excelled in school and she didn't rebel or get in trouble like Caroline. Her father didn't like it when Caroline got dirty, so Grace stayed extremely clean and neat. Caroline's room was a disaster area. Grace's was immaculate.

Although Caroline rebelled at times, she still tried to fit the mold her father had planned for his girls. Caroline got her law degree, but after a year in the Whitten Firm she bolted for freedom. She pursued her love of photography and was now a great photographer. Their father was not pleased, but Caroline stuck by her decision.

On the other hand, Grace had become the chosen daughter, the good daughter. She'd told Caroline many times that she was happy in her career. Lately that wasn't true. So much of her life was based on material profits, gains and wealth.

But at what price to her personal well-being?

She thought of the lady asleep by her sick child in Brady's ward. Grace wondered if she slept there every night. Did she ever leave her child? Grace pulled up her knees, munching on an Oreo. Real love. That's what life was all about—being there for another person no matter what.

Grace wanted that—to experience a love that strong.
She heard a noise and glanced up to see Jeremiah
staring down at her.

CHAPTER SIX

TUCK TURNED THE CORNER and stopped dead in his tracks. He'd gone to watch one of his boys, Pablo Martinez, wrestle. He was on the wrestling team in school and Tuck never missed a match. Pablo's mother had found her husband in a motel with another woman and she'd waited in the parking lot, running over both of them with her car. They died from their injuries.

Pablo now lived with his grandparents and he was filled with a lot of anger. Tuck got him into wrestling and it helped to work off his negative energy in a positive way. His grandfather encouraged him and that helped, too. Pablo was going to make it, despite his parents.

Afterward he congratulated Pablo and treated him and his grandfather to supper. Pablo was excited about his win and Tuck had stayed out longer than he'd planned. He wanted to check on Brady one more time before he went home. Since Brady wasn't used to a routine, he slept sporadically. Just in case Brady was awake, Tuck strolled to the vending machines for animal crackers. Brady loved them.

Tuck blinked. He must be seeing things. All day he'd been trying to get in touch with Grace, even went by her office, but he kept missing her. Now…could that be

Grace? A woman sat on the floor, her back against the machine and her blond hair hung to her shoulders in disarray. She looked like Grace, but the Grace he knew would never be caught with her hair down doing something so out of the ordinary.

She looked up and he knew it was. "Grace."

"Uh…hi…Jer…Tuck."

The moment she said his name something happened inside him. The annoyance he'd felt toward her vanished. That's what it came down to—her respecting him enough to use his name.

Removing his hat, he sank down beside her, propping his back against the vending machine. "What are you doing here?"

"Eating Oreo cookies. Want one?" She held out the bag to him.

He positioned his hat on his knee and reached into the bag.

As he took a bite, she said, "There's a special technique to eating an Oreo."

"Really?" He finished the cookie in record time.

"But you need milk."

"Wait a sec." He swung to his feet, walked to the nurses' station and asked for milk. Jennifer wasn't there but another nurse gave him a carton without question. He often brought Brady milk with animal crackers.

He eased back down by Grace, placing his hat beside him and showing her the milk.

"Magic." A smile lit up her face and his chest tightened.

He opened one corner and she shook her head. "Not big enough for dunking."

He pried opened the lid fully. "How's that?"

"Great. Now watch." She twisted off the top, licked the icing in between, dipped the top in milk, took a bite, licked the center again and dipped the rest of the top. Lick, dip and eat, over and over. He was captivated by her tongue. Licking the last crumb from her lips she added, "That's how to eat an Oreo."

He stared at her chin.

"What?"

"You have milk right there." He pointed to her chin and he restrained himself from licking it away.

"Oh." She wiped at it with her hand, getting some on her blouse.

"Now you have it on your blouse." He reached into his pocket for a handkerchief and handed it to her.

"Thank you." She wiped at her mouth and her blouse. "I'm usually not so messy."

"I know."

Their eyes met and emotions he couldn't define hovered just below the surface—emotions he wasn't ready to define. He cleared his throat. "Now let me show you how a man eats an Oreo." He reached for a cookie, dipped it into the milk, popped it into his mouth and ate it in one bite. "Simple, easy and no mess."

"But not as much fun."

"No." He watched her lips, coughed and took a swallow of milk. "I tried to reach you several times today."

She brushed at the crumbs on her slacks. "Did you? What about?"

"I wanted to apologize for barging into your office and saying what I did." He raised his knees, staring down at his cowboy boots. "I was angry and upset. I knew that filing for custody of Brady was a long shot. I guess I just didn't expect you'd be the one to make sure that didn't happen."

"I…"

"Don't say anything. You have a right to represent anyone you want. I was the one who was out of line."

Grace couldn't believe how much the apology meant to her. His opinion mattered. His feelings mattered. And she rather liked sitting on the floor, milk and cookie crumbs on her clothes, talking to Tuck. Making that leap from Jeremiah to Tuck had been the easiest thing she'd ever done. She wondered if she had called him that from the first moment she'd met him, what type of relationship would they have now?

"What happened to your shoe?"

His question threw her for a second, and then she realized her shoe was still in her lap. "The machine took my money and I whacked it a couple of times with my shoe."

He lifted an eyebrow. "You hit the machine with your *shoe?*"

"Crazy, hmm?" She shrugged. "What can I tell you? I wanted chocolate."

He rested his forearms on his knees, his eyes on her face. "So when you need a chocolate fix, it's okay to scuff up your shoes?"

She winced. "Okay. I need to apologize, too. I'm sorry I've been such a pain. Seeing myself through your eyes was a big eye-opener. If we ever dance again, I won't care if you step on my shoes. That's really very silly."

"Grace." He stretched out his long legs and folded his arms across his broad chest, his eyes holding hers. "I haven't stepped on a woman's shoes since I was thirteen years old."

She recognized a sexual undertone in every word and welcomed the warmth that flooded her body from the top of her head to the tips of her toes.

"I like your hair like that," he said unexpectedly.

She touched her hair, feeling almost giddy. "Thank you. I've had it like this all day and although I've received some startled glances, no one said a word."

"Maybe they didn't know what to say," he commented.

"Maybe." But it felt extremely good that someone had mentioned the change in her appearance. At the moment, she didn't resemble Grace Whitten of the Whitten Law Firm.

"What are you doing here, Grace?" He asked the same question he'd asked earlier.

"I came to see Brady." There was no reason to lie.

Tuck rose to his feet and reached out a hand to her. She placed hers in his and he pulled her to her feet. She hopped around on one foot until she slipped her other foot into her shoe.

He watched her for a moment. "Let's call a truce," he said. "For our family's sake and our own, we'll abide by the judge's decision without any ill feelings."

She should tell him that she'd recused herself from the case, but for some reason she didn't. Her firm still represented the Templetons and she had to support them professionally. Personally was another matter.

They'd just had a very nice conversation and had

started the process of getting to know one another. Trust had to be built and earned, not just given. If they had a future, it would happen naturally.

She nodded. "That's fine with me. And if you're at Eli and Caroline's, am I allowed to visit, too?"

He picked up his hat from the floor and placed it on his head. "Of course. That was uncalled for."

"Good." She held out her hand. "Let's shake on it."

He stared at her hand then raised his eyes to hers. "We're family, so we should hug on it, don't you think?"

She was taken aback, but only for a second. Pushing her hair behind her ears, she replied, "Yes," then stepped into the circle of his arms and wrapped hers around his waist.

His chest was solid, his heartbeat strong and the sensation that enveloped her was something she'd never felt before, something that had been missing from her life— the touch and feel of a man. Her feelings for Tuck were as strong as the arms that held her. She admitted that for the first time. That's why his words had hurt so badly. That's why she'd changed her appearance and her ingrained habits about neatness and order. That's why she'd attacked a vending machine. Tuck mattered to her. But now they were set on a course that would test their relationship. Sadly, she wasn't sure if she mattered to him at all, except as Caroline's sister.

She forced herself to step back. "I wish you all the best in the custody hearing."

"I just want Brady to have a good home."

"We all do." She picked up her purse and the empty milk carton, her eyes catching his. "Good night, Tuck."

"Night, Grace."

She walked away, resisting the urge to look back and also resisting the urge to brush the dust from her clothes.

Another baby step.

TUCK STROLLED down the hall to Brady's ward. Jennifer sat at the desk. "How's Brady tonight?" he asked.

She smiled a welcome. "You're back."

"I just went out for a bite. Nurse Dunbar said Brady's not sleeping well."

"He's used to doing his own thing and suddenly there are so many people around him that he's confused. He was awake a little while ago, but Ms. Whitten, the Templeton's attorney, stopped by and got him back to sleep."

"Grace got him to sleep?"

Jennifer's eyes opened wide. "You know her?"

"My brother is married to her sister."

One eyebrow arched. "Now that's interesting."

"Yes. It is, sometimes."

"She seems like a high-maintenance type of woman so I was a little surprised when she asked to give Brady his bottle."

"She has a nephew and she's good with him, too."

"You could have fooled me. I thought she was a little on the uppity side."

Words rose in his throat to defend Grace. He smiled inwardly. Grace didn't need his defense. She could take care of herself. "I'll just check on Brady," he said instead. "And I'll be very quiet."

"If you don't get custody of that little boy, then there's something wrong with this world."

"Thank you, Jennifer."

He caught all of Jennifer's signals, but she didn't trigger a response in him. He must go for high-maintenance, uppity women because he could still feel Grace's body against his. Her scent, a delicate lilac, still teased his senses.

Entering the room, he thought it was ironic they were pitted against each other. But they didn't have to be enemies. Tonight proved that to him. He'd seen a side of Grace he hadn't seen before and he wanted to get to know her better. Though in light of everything going on, he couldn't see that happening.

Barbara was asleep in her chair and he wondered how long she could continue to do that. For as long as necessary, he was sure—that's what loving parents did.

He straightened the blanket around Brady, careful not to wake him. Brady deserved devoted, loving parents and Tuck intended to stay in the game until that happened.

WHEN TUCK GOT INTO HIS CAR, his cell rang. It was Beau.

"Hey, Tuck. I got a call from Ann Demott."

"Who's that?"

"She's the Templetons' new attorney."

"What?"

"Grace has recused herself. The Whitten Law Firm is still handling the case, but Grace is no longer personally involved."

"Oh." He wasn't sure how to respond to that. He'd just seen Grace and she hadn't said a word. Why, he wondered?

"I guess Grace realized it was best for the family."

There was a slight pause. "She's not as bad as you think she is."

"I never said Grace was bad." He was immediately on the defensive.

"Really? I always got the impression you'd rather be audited by the IRS than spend any time with Grace."

"Well, your impression was wrong." He could actually feel Beau smiling. "And stop smiling."

"How do you know I'm smiling?"

"I know you, Beau McCain. You're a natural born peacemaker trying to keep everyone happy."

"You could be right." Beau laughed. "Now let's get down to business. I have other news."

"What?"

"The hearing has been set for next Thursday at two o'clock in the judge's chambers."

"That was quick."

"CPS is pushing for a quick decision from the judge. They feel Brady needs a stable environment as soon as possible so we have to have our ducks in a row. How are you coming with help for Brady while you're at work?"

"I plan to take four weeks' leave so Brady can be well-adjusted before I'm gone all day. Mrs. Wiggins has agreed to keep Brady at my house. She's no longer keeping her granddaughter. I hadn't realized that."

"That's great. The judge will look at that favorably."

"But not as favorably as a married couple where the wife is willing to stay home with Brady?"

"No, I'm sorry, Tuck. That's going to be a hard one for us to beat. But I never give up until that gavel bangs."

"Thanks, Beau. I knew from the start this was going to be tough."

"How is Brady doing?"

"Physically he's healing quickly, but mentally is another matter. He's still not responding to anyone."

"I guess that's what CPS is worried about. They want the caregiver in place so Brady can feel at ease to form that bond. It will happen. Jake went through the same thing with Ben."

"I know some of the story, but not all of it."

"Ben was three years old when Jake found out about his existence. Ben's grandmother, who had custody of him, had passed away. Not able to understand why his grandmother was gone, Ben shut down completely. Jake's name was on the birth certificate and that's why the authorities contacted him. As newlyweds, it was rough for Jake and Elise. They suddenly had a baby they weren't expecting who had developmental problems. It took a lot of patience, but they made it. You'd never guess now that things had been so rough at the start."

"No, and, Beau McCain, I bet you were right in the middle of it."

"When it comes to family, you bet I am. I'll be in touch before Thursday to go over some details."

"Thanks, Beau."

Beau would give the case his all, but Tuck was afraid it wasn't going to be enough. The outcome didn't look good and he had to be prepared.

As he drove home he wondered about Grace. Why hadn't she told him she was no longer on the case? Because it didn't matter. Her firm still represented the

Templetons and her loyalty was with them. What about her personal feelings? Did she feel he'd make a good father?

Turning off the freeway, he decided he was thinking too much about Grace. But tonight had been one of those experiences that he would remember always.

She'd called him Tuck.

CHAPTER SEVEN

THE WEEK PASSED SLOWLY for Grace. She knew the Templeton case was on the docket for Thursday and they had gone over it in the weekly meeting. She didn't offer Ann any advice and Ann didn't ask for any. Ann felt the case was a sure win. Grace didn't respond to that, either.

To say she was torn was putting it mildly. Her heart was clearly going in a different direction than her mind or her firm's best interest. But since she'd had the talk with Tuck by the vending machine, her heart was not on business.

Her mind was, though.

On Wednesday, she went by the hospital to check on Brady. Tomorrow his future would be decided and she wanted to make sure it was the right one. Telling herself to stay out of it didn't seem to work.

The beautiful Jennifer wasn't on duty but another nurse told her that Brady was in the playroom with the Templetons. She stood outside the door watching Brady, Lisa and Keith interact. Lisa and Keith sat at a child's table with a big puzzle on it. Brady stood trying to fit the pieces together, seeming oblivious to the two adults.

Lisa said something to Brady and he didn't respond. She touched his shoulder and Brady pulled away, concentrating on the puzzle for a second then darting around the room, his socks making no sound on the tiled floor.

Brady was so beautiful with his big eyes and sweet face that Grace couldn't take her eyes off him. Brady's whole life was ahead of him. All he needed was the right people to nurture and guide him. Were Lisa and Keith those people? She had to be sure about that.

For Tuck.

And for herself.

Brady ran by Lisa and she reached out to catch him, holding him in her arms. Brady wiggled for a second to get away, but Lisa held on. Suddenly he laid his head on her shoulder. Grace's breath caught in her throat.

"I guess everyone was right," a familiar voice said from behind her.

Grace whirled to face Tuck, her pulse racing at his tall figure. She swallowed. "About what?"

"Caroline and others have said that Brady needs a mother. He needs nurturing and care from a woman so he can trust again." His eyes were on Brady and Lisa and the pain in those eyes tore through Grace.

"Brady has a lot to overcome and it's going to take time," she offered for lack of something to say.

"Yeah, and he needs someone with him twenty-four hours a day."

She was taken aback by his response. "Does that mean you're withdrawing your petition?"

"No." He glanced at her. "A judge will still have to make the decision concerning who's best for Brady. But when Brady grows up, I want him to know there was a man who never gave up on him."

That was the most caring thing she'd ever heard and tears stung the back of her eyes. She couldn't make a fool of herself in front of him.

"You didn't have to take yourself off the case," he said abruptly. "I'm sorry I mentioned that."

Her hand tightened on the strap of her purse. "I felt it was the right thing to do."

He stared at Brady and Lisa. "Sometimes doing the right thing is hell." After saying that, he walked off down the hall.

Grace's chest contracted painfully and she wanted to go after him, to reassure him. But it wasn't up to her.

Glancing back to the room, she saw Brady push Lisa away. She caught him again and he hit her. Grace winced. That wasn't good. Brady had a lot of anger inside him and his recovery wasn't going to happen overnight.

As Grace left the hospital, she thought of going to Tuck's but she knew he wouldn't welcome her presence. And he probably wanted to be alone before the big decision tomorrow.

So she went home to her neat, quiet apartment.

NOT MANY THINGS made Tuck nervous, but he had to admit he was on edge about today's proceedings. Shaving, he nicked his chin. He spilled coffee on his slacks and had to change. When he spilled his coffee a second time, he realized he was as nervous as he'd ever been.

And the day had barely begun.

He met Beau at the courthouse and Beau explained what was going to happen. Tuck nodded. He just wanted it over with.

They met the Templetons and their attorney in the judge's chambers. Opal Johnson and Harvey Beckman from CPS were there. A doctor and a therapist were there, too. They found seats in front of the judge's desk.

They stood as the bailiff introduced Judge Nora Farnsworth. She took her seat and everyone resumed theirs. Each attorney presented their reasons why their client was the best person to gain custody of Brady Harper. The doctor spoke of Brady's injuries and his recovery. The therapist talked about Brady's mental health and the care and attention he needed for a full recovery.

"I have read all the facts, listened to the witnesses and in most cases I would take more time to review this case." The judge closed a file and addressed everyone. "But CPS, Mrs. Johnson in particular, has stressed that Brady Harper needs stability now. So many people around him is confusing him more." The judge adjusted her glasses.

"Ranger Tucker, I'm very impressed with your devotion to this child, as is Mrs. Johnson. I have depositions from just about every nurse on the pediatric ward praising your devotion and constant vigil at Brady's bedside. For a single male that is very unusual and I realize that you've formed a connection to the boy."

Tuck felt a big but coming and he didn't have to wait long.

"But I have several reservations. Number one is your job. As a lawman, it is very high risk and time consuming. Number two is your single status."

"Your Honor." Beau was on his feet. "I sent the court several cases where a single male was granted custody of a minor child. Just because a man is single doesn't mean he can't successfully raise a child."

"Yes, Mr. McCain, I read your documents and I am thoroughly impressed with your research. But Brady Harper is different. He's not biologically linked to Ranger Tucker and Brady has problems that will require a lot of attention. Even at fourteen months, he has a lot of anger issues. He needs to know that someone is always going to be there for him. That trust, that bond, has to be built day by day."

"Your Honor…"

"Sit down, Mr. McCain. I'm ready to rule on this case.

"In light of Brady's physical and mental state, I see no recourse but to place him with the Templetons, where he will have a full-time mother and father. Brady will need that structure to grow strong and healthy."

"Damn," Beau said under his breath.

Tuck's breath wedged in his throat like a wad of cotton and for a moment he had trouble breathing. The verdict was what he was expecting, but he never realized it would hurt this much.

"Thank you, Your Honor." Ann Demott rose to her feet. "When will the Templetons be able to take Brady home?"

"His wounds haven't healed completely and I'm also concerned about his mental state. The therapist feels Brady has locked himself away into a safe corner of his mind and it will take a lot of patience and love to reach him. I would like the Templetons to spend most of each day with Brady so he can get to know them and start the bonding process. The therapist feels strongly about this, as do I. Brady is in familiar surroundings and to take him out of the hospital now would be disastrous. This has to be done slowly. In two weeks, I'll review the therapist's reports and make a ruling on when the Templetons can take Brady home. I hope all goes well. This little boy deserves a second chance."

"Thank you, Your Honor." Lisa smiled brightly and hugged her husband.

"I hope you realize the enormous task ahead of you," the judge replied.

"Yes, Your Honor, we do," Keith said.

Tuck stood, needing to say something. "Your Honor, may I please have some time to say goodbye to Brady? I don't want him to feel that I've abandoned him."

"Ranger Tucker, considering Brady's mental state, I agree. I want this to go as smoothly as possible for Brady." She signed a document then looked at Tuck. "Ranger Tucker, I hope you understand I'm doing what's best for Brady Harper."

"Yes, Your Honor."

And that was it. The Templetons would raise Brady. He swallowed back any resentment he felt. His bottom line was still Brady's well-being.

Everyone rose as the judge left the room. Tuck saw Eli and Caleb standing at the back, and to the right stood Grace. His heart leaped. For a brief moment he thought she was here for him, and then he realized she was here for the Templetons. They were her friends and her firm represented them.

For some reason that hurt.

Opal gave Tuck a hug. "I'm sorry, but I told you. Don't worry, though. One day I'll find the perfect child for you."

"Thanks, Opal."

"Even if you are single," she whispered under her breath and walked away.

Tuck smiled slightly as Eli and Caleb strolled toward him.

"Sorry, man," Eli said.

"Me, too," Caleb added.

"Thanks," Tuck replied, feeling the need to be alone. Out of the corner of his eye he saw Grace speaking to the Templetons. Was she congratulating them?

"We're meeting Jake at Metz's Park to shoot some hoops then we're going out for a juicy steak." Caleb was talking, but Tuck's attention was on Grace. Her hair was loose around her shoulders again, making her green eyes vibrant and her features soft and appealing. She was beautiful. Why had he never noticed that before?

And why was he noticing it now?

"Tuck?"

He swung his focus to Caleb. "It's not even three in the afternoon. I'll be fine, guys. I appreciate your being here, but go back to work."

Eli shook his head. "No can do. Jake's on his way and he's dropping Elise and the kids at my house. Macy and Zoë are already there and Josie will arrive after work. It's all planned."

Tuck took a moment to absorb this. It felt good to be included as one of the McCains and no way was he letting them down. He needed to burn off some restless energy and what better way than to fool around with friends who knew what he was going through.

"Okay," he said and picked up his hat, placing it on

his head. As he did, his eyes caught Grace's and she walked over to him.

Being perceptive guys, his friends moved away to give them some privacy.

"I'm sorry," she said, and he got the feeling she really meant it.

"I knew it was a long shot, but I had to try." He shoved his hands into the pockets of his slacks, feeling nervous again and he didn't know why.

"Brady will have a good home."

"I'm counting on it." He tried to smile and failed.

They stared at each other and he wasn't sure what to say, so he said the only thing he could. "Bye, Grace." Walking toward his friends, he felt this was goodbye in more ways than one.

Without warning, a pang of regret hit him.

GRACE FELT BAD FOR TUCK and she couldn't get his hurt expression out of her mind. So she spent the rest of the afternoon in her office, working, staying busy to keep from thinking about Tuck.

She had three messages from her father, all irate that she wasn't taking calls, all about Derek Mann. After returning the calls, she sat in deep thought. Her father was nervous and she had to wonder why. She had taken over the firm so why was he stepping back into the picture? He was a U.S. Congressman and not affiliated with the Whitten Law Firm anymore. Or that was the picture he presented to his constituents and his adversaries. What was going on?

She flipped through the impressive résumé of Derek

Mann. He'd attended law school at Baylor University and had received a law degree from University of Houston. He graduated in the top ten percent of his class. After that, he clerked for some impressive judges in Texas and Washington. The last year he was a partner in a big-name firm in Boston. Why did Mann want to come back to Texas? And what did he have to do with her father?

Pushing a button on her phone, she said, "Nina, I'd like to see Chuck as soon as possible."

"Yes, ma'am, I'll let him know."

Chuck Wallace and his father, Charley, were the firm's main private investigators. Sometimes they hired outside investigators if they needed extra help on a case, but Charley Wallace had been on the payroll since her father's days at the firm. She'd hired Chuck three years ago and she knew she could trust his discretion. Charley was very loyal to her father and she wanted to avoid questions she felt she didn't need to answer.

Her cell buzzed. It was Caroline.

"Are you okay?"

Her hand gripped the phone. "Yes. Why wouldn't I be?"

"You don't have to appear tough with me, Grace. I know this day was hard for you."

Her sister knew her better than anyone. "Yes," she admitted. "I felt bad for Tuck. He really loves Brady." That's what bothered her the most—Tuck's feelings for Brady were real, sincere. But then, she reminded herself, Lisa's and Keith's were, too. And those feelings would grow once they got to know Brady. They would make great parents. She really believed that.

There was a long pause on the other end. "You called him Tuck."

"Yes" was all she could say.

"We're having a girls' night at my house," Caroline said. "And you're invited."

"Caro, I'm busy." She didn't want to intrude. Everyone was married and had kids or were expecting. She'd feel out of place.

"The guys are consoling Tuck and you're coming. Do you hear? No suit, either. I'm making double-fudge brownies and I have ice cream."

"Caro…"

"And Jesse would like for you to come. He misses his Auntie Grace."

Grace sighed. "You're so good."

"See you later."

Grace clicked off with a thoughtful expression. She was glad Tuck had company tonight. At least he wasn't alone. Or with Jennifer. Where did that thought come from? It came from the right side of her brain where jealousy was alive and well. She definitely needed a night out.

She checked her appointments as Nina buzzed.

"Yes?"

"Chuck's here."

"Send him in."

A man in his thirties with disheveled hair and a worried expression entered. Chuck lived on antacids. There was always a roll in his shirt pocket. She noticed the bulge along with his pens and notepad. An ex-police officer, Chuck was injured in the line of duty and Grace was more than glad to have him as a member of the Whitten team.

"You wanted to see me?" Chuck asked.

"Yes. Please have a seat."

He complied, sitting on the edge of a chintz chair. Chuck reminded her of a man always ready for action. He was never relaxed.

"I would like a job done, very discreetly, very professionally," she told him.

"Yes, ma'am."

"And this is between you and me. No one else is to know, not even Byron or your father."

"Yes, ma'am."

She pushed a file toward him. "I want to know what's not in here."

He picked up the file and flipped through it. "Very impressive," he commented.

"Yes. It's too impressive. I want to know everything about Derek Mann, his grades in high school and college, how he got all those distinguished jobs and why he wasn't satisfied with them. I want to know what that résumé is not telling me."

Chuck stood. "Yes, ma'am, I'm on it."

"And, Chuck…"

"I know." He held up a hand. "You can trust me."

"Thank you."

THE GUYS HORSED AROUND on the old asphalt basketball court until they were short of breath.

Eli jumped and made his famous three-pointer, then

put his hands on his knees. "You know what?" he said in between deep breaths. "Running around on asphalt in cowboy boots isn't as much fun as it used to be."

Jake sank to the pavement with a groan. "I think we're getting older."

They gathered on the court in a circle.

"Y'all might be, but I'm not. I'm the youngest," Caleb said with a smirk.

Jake playfully pushed Caleb into Beau. Beau pushed Caleb back into Jake. After going back and forth a couple of times, Caleb stuck out both hands to ward off his brothers. "Okay, okay. Age is just a state of mind."

"Yeah." Eli nodded. "In your case it might be a state of good health."

They all laughed.

Tuck had the ball and he twisted it around in his hands, feeling its firmness.

"Are you okay?" Caleb asked in a concerned voice.

Tuck looked at his friends. "Yes. I'm fine." And he was. How could he not be with friends around him?

"I think it infringes on your civil rights to be denied custody because you're single." Beau still wasn't convinced. "I might do some research just to make sure some lines haven't been crossed."

"No," Tuck said. "I want Brady to have this chance at a life."

"I'm not convinced that the Templetons are the better people to raise him," Beau kept on.

"I'm not, either," Eli said. "No one should have the right to say a man can't raise a child because he's single or has a high-risk job."

"Well, I don't want to get beat up here." Jake drew up his knees. "But I've been through this. I thought I could raise Ben alone and I was fully prepared to. Once Elise entered the picture Ben just blossomed under her nurturing and care. I could see it happening. It made me feel good and bad at the same time. I wanted to do it all for my son, but I'm telling you a baby needs a mother. I'm not saying the Templetons are better for Brady. I know Tuck would have made the better parent, single or not."

"In my opinion Tuck is the better parent. He just got penalized for his life and that sucks." Caleb spoke his views. "I admire any man who wants to raise a child alone. That takes courage. Me, I guess I'm a wimp because I want to do everything with Josie."

Beau punched Caleb on the shoulder. "Youth and rose-colored glasses."

"Really, brother Beau?" Caleb squinted at Beau. "I seem to see a pair perched on your nose. It wasn't always like that, though. About a year ago we were sitting on another basketball court when you were going through a midlife crisis."

"Mmm," Beau murmured. They sat silent as they remembered the trials and heartaches they'd been through together. "I still believe Tuck is the better parent to raise Brady," Beau finally added.

"Me, too," Eli said. "And nothing will change my mind about that—not even my beautiful wife."

"I'm not giving up on this case." Beau made his position very clear.

"Beau…"

Tuck didn't get to finish his objection. Caleb threw

his arm over his brother's shoulders. "We're gonna nominate ol' Beau for sainthood one of these days."

"Hear, hear," Jake said as they rose to their feet.

Eli patted Tuck on the back. "Let's buy Tuck the biggest Texas steak we can find. Maybe a gorgeous motherly type will wait on us, and how does that country song go? 'I woke up married.' Maybe Tuck will wake up married and solve all his problems."

"Or create more," Tuck replied, laughing as they made their way to their vehicles.

Climbing into his car, he felt so much better. His friends' support had done the trick. He'd learned a lot today. Maybe he needed to make some changes in his plans, his life. Maybe he couldn't do everything on his own. Maybe, like his friends, he needed a woman to complete him.

That thought had always annoyed him before.

Tonight, though, he saw green eyes.

And again, he wondered why.

CHAPTER EIGHT

FIVE WOMEN SAT around the kitchen table eating hot double-fudge brownies with vanilla ice cream melting over the decadent treat. Talk of babies filled the room—babies, husbands and marriage. Grace swirled her spoon through her scoop of ice cream, trying not to be annoyed, trying to fit in. But she couldn't stop the mental notebook forming in her mind. Two moms with children, one mother with a child expecting another, one woman expecting her first baby and one single, uptight, almost virgin.

Grace licked ice cream from the spoon. Was there such a thing as an almost virgin? Maybe she was a slightly used virgin. Either way, she was totally frustrated with her life. Caroline, Elise, Josie and Macy were all happy and in love with the men of their dreams while Grace was the powerful, single career woman. For her, that didn't compute anymore. She wanted to feel that crazy-in-love sensation, talk about diaper changing, breast-feeding and a man who made her life complete. She wanted a life, not just a career.

She shifted uneasily. Being around this much happiness was making her head spin. It had been a rough day. No matter what she was doing, thoughts of Tuck kept intruding. She hadn't planned on going to the hearing today, but found she couldn't stay away.

"Grace, I love your T-shirt." Elise's voice reached her.

"Oh. Thank you." She swallowed a mouthful of brownie and looked down at the front of her shirt. "Caroline said for me not to wear a suit and I found this in my dresser. I can't remember where I bought it or why. I think someone gave it to me." On the front of her white T-shirt was written in red letters I'm a Good Kisser.

Caroline gave a long, put-out sigh. "I gave it to you. And, Grace, when I said no suit, I didn't mean starched jeans and an ironed T-shirt. Nobody irons a T-shirt."

"Next time you'll have to be more specific." Grace didn't bat an eye at her sister's teasing.

"Don't pick on Grace," Macy said. "She always looks wonderful and I think we should all have ironed T-shirts just like Grace's. We can wear them on nights like this when we're just being women. On the back we could put That's How I Got My Man.

"I love the idea." Josie swallowed a mouthful of chocolate.

"We'd have to leave the back of mine blank," Grace said.

"Poor, poor pitiful Grace," Caroline chided. "This isn't like you. Where's that strong, professional sister of mine?"

"I'm not sure." With her spoon, she made more trails in the ice cream.

She could feel Caroline's eyes on her. "Grace, it's not your fault that Tuck didn't win custody today."

Grace laid her spoon on her plate. "Then why do I

feel like it is?" She did. That was the problem. She couldn't shake that feeling.

"Listen to me," Caroline continued. "You stayed out of the proceedings. You didn't have to do that, but you did. There was no way Tuck could have won this, especially since there's a woman involved who can stay at home with Brady. Lisa and Keith were just the better choice." Caroline took a drink of milk. "Now don't get me wrong. I love Tuck like a brother but in this case, Brady needed more than Tuck could give him. He needed a mother."

"I tried to tell Jake the same thing." Elise brushed back her champagne-colored hair. A professor of American Literature, Elise was as beautiful as she was brilliant. "I reminded him how he thought he could raise Ben alone and how much easier it was when we worked together as husband and wife. But he was very adamant that in this case Tuck was the better choice. We agreed to disagree."

"Caleb and I had the same conversation." Josie's dark eyes flashed. Grace often thought that Josie with her Spanish and American ancestry was one of the most stunning women she'd ever met. "I had to remind him of the difference in a mother's role and a father's role. He agreed up to a point, but he stuck to his belief that Tuck was best for Brady."

"In our house we don't have that discussion anymore." Macy joined in. A strawberry blonde with naturally curly hair, Macy epitomized kindness and goodness. As a nurse, she cared for people with all her heart, and that caring extended to animals, as well. "Beau is one of those men who can do both roles effortlessly. What can I say? He's special." She smiled, her blue eyes twinkling. "But sometimes he can be just plain stubborn. He believes Tuck is the better parent and nothing will change his mind, not even me."

"Maybe because he's right." Grace heard the words and realized she'd spoken them out loud. Everyone watched her closely. In that moment, she made a decision. She wasn't going to defend herself. It was the way she felt.

"Da-da, Da-da." Zoë came running, chanting her favorite word and saving the moment. Zoë looked up at Macy. "Da-da."

Macy lifted Zoë into her lap. "The second she hears Beau's name she thinks its time for her daddy to come home."

"Da-da," Zoë repeated, reaching for Macy's spoon. Macy fed her the rest of the ice cream then pushed the plate out of harm's way.

Macy kissed one fat cheek. "Sweetie, can you tell everyone how old you are?"

Zoë held up one finger, smiling. "Un."

"Whose girl are you?"

"Da-da, Da-da, Da-da."

Grace watched the little girl's animated expression. She clearly loved her daddy. Her big blue eyes sparkled and the strawberry-blonde ringlets bounced on her head. She sat in Macy's lap, her head beneath Macy's chin; it was hard to believe that Zoë wasn't Macy's biological daughter. They looked so much alike. But a bond had been formed that had nothing to do with biology, even though Zoë was Macy's niece. Their bond had to do with the heart and the many facets of love.

A cry punctured the silence. Ben and Katie came running. At five, Katie was an absolute doll with blond hair and brown eyes. "Caroline, Jesse is crying," Katie informed Caroline.

"Thank you, sweetie," Caroline replied, getting to her feet.

Ben leaned against his mother and Elise kissed the top of his head. "Would you like some ice cream?"

Ben shook his head. "We…we…" As Ben struggled to find the words, Elise stroked his hair. "We have popcorn." With dark hair and eyes, Ben favored his father. Grace watched the love on Elise's face and it had nothing to do with biology, either. It came from the heart.

"Ben, let's go watch the rest of the movie." Katie raced back to the den.

Caroline cradled a fussy Jesse as he rubbed his face against her blouse. "Okay, big boy, give mommy a chance to get her blouse open."

Grace was always amazed at how fast Caroline could lift her blouse and unsnap her bra cup. In a split second, Jesse latched onto a nipple. They all watched as if it were one of the wonders of the world.

"I can't wait," Josie said in a breathless voice.

Macy locked her arms around Zoë. "That's what it's all about—life-giving nourishment. Nurturing. That's a woman's role."

Caroline kissed her son. "We'll never get our husbands to believe that."

"Yeah, but that's okay," Macy said. "We love them anyway."

"Hey, buster." Caroline jumped. "No chewing, please."

She lifted Jesse to her shoulder and patted his back. "He always does that when he's had enough, but since he's teething he's started chewing sooner and sooner. I hope he's getting enough milk."

"Look at his size," Macy said. "I think he's getting enough. If he isn't, he'll let you know real soon."

"About two o'clock in the morning," Elise remarked.

"Let me have him." Grace got to her feet. "I'll put him down for the night."

"Ah, sisters are wonderful, even if they wear ironed T-shirts." Caroline handed over her son.

"Thank you very much." Grace gathered her nephew in her arms, glad to escape to Jesse's room. All the marital bliss was about to suffocate her.

She gave Jesse a bath and Katie and Ben had to help. Clean and dry, Jesse drifted off to dreamland.

"I wish we had a baby at our house, don't you, Ben?" Katie asked, watching Jesse.

"Yeah," Ben answered, also watching Jesse.

Grace touched Katie's cheek. "Then you wouldn't be the baby anymore."

"Oh."

Grace took Katie's and Ben's hands and they walked back to the breakfast room. Clearly, Katie was giving the baby idea more thought. Grace knew that she was Jake's baby girl and obviously Katie had second thoughts about giving up that title.

For the first time Grace realized she liked kids and she liked being around them. For years she'd thought just the opposite. Facing thirty-five was changing everything about her.

Or maybe it was something else.

A man she couldn't stop thinking about.

THE MEN ARRIVED HOME. Grace said goodbye and quickly left, having had all of the marital happiness she could handle for one night.

Driving by Tuck's she saw his lights were on. Without a second thought, she pulled into his driveway. His ranger car and his silver truck were parked under the carport. Knocking on his door, she waited with her breath lodged in her throat like a cube of ice.

The door swung open and Tuck stood there in his slacks, socks and a T-shirt pulled out of his pants. Her heart rate accelerated.

"Grace," he said in surprise, and the warmth in his voice melted the blockage in her throat.

She swallowed. "May I come in?"

"Sure." He held open the screen door and she walked in.

Sam reared up on her jeans, wagging his tail. She froze, but realized this was a pivotal moment. What she did now would set the tone of their future relationship. Taking a breath, she reached down, picked up Sam and held him in her arms, forcing herself to lightly stroke him. This wasn't a normal reaction for her, but she wasn't sure what normal was anymore.

Tuck's eyes widened, but he didn't say anything.

"I wanted to tell you again how sorry I am about today."

"You know, Grace, you keep saying that and soon I'll start to believe it."

"Please do." Her eyes held his. "We just had a lengthy conversation about this at Caroline's."

"And the women believe the right decision was made today?"

"Yes."

He scratched his head. "Actually, the guys had the same conversation—all believing just the opposite."

"Venus and Mars." She managed a slight smile.

"Something like that." His eyes narrowed. "Are you seceding from your planet, Grace?"

"Maybe." They were flirting and she relaxed, enjoying his company.

"Before you make that momentous decision, how about a beer?"

"Sure." She wasn't fond of beer, but she'd probably drink quinine if he'd asked her. And that really wasn't like her. She was used to saying no, making decisions based on her ideas and beliefs. This time she made the decision on how she felt about him, a purely feminine decision.

She placed Sam on the floor and resisted the urge to wipe her hands on her jeans.

Tuck turned from the refrigerator with two beers, his eyes on her hands. "Go ahead, wash your hands."

She glanced up. "It's okay. Jesse threw up on my shoulder then he got me thoroughly wet giving him his bath so washing my hands seems moot at this point."

He set the beers on the table. "I get the feeling you're going through some sort of metamorphosis. You can freeze water, but it's still water."

"I don't know what that means."

"It means you can't suppress who you really are.

You're a fastidious person. I am, too. So wash your hands and we'll both be happy."

She went to the sink and washed her hands, not having a clue what that bit of conversation was about. Maybe she couldn't change who she was inside. She just wanted to be comfortable within herself again.

Drying her hands on a paper towel, she joined Tuck. He sipped his beer, forearms resting on the table, Sam at his feet.

She slipped into a chair. "Where's Dee?"

"She's mostly an outdoor cat. She comes in when she wants to."

Grace took a swallow of beer and stared down at the names carved on the old oak table, a long rectangle that could easily seat ten people. She ran her fingers over a name. "What are these?" She'd noticed them before on her rare visits to his house, but she never had the courage to ask how the names had gotten there.

"Names of children my parents took in. If you stayed for any length of time, you got to carve your name in a place of honor. That's what Pa said. Once your name was on the table, you always had a home."

"Where's yours?" She searched the table's surface. John, James, Dan, April, Beth, Billy, Mike, Judd, Brian, Gail, Nancy, Jimmy, Frances, Hector, Maria, Will, Janis, Cari, Doris, Matt, and the list went on. But she didn't see Tuck or Eli.

"I'm sitting in Pa's place and Ma sat to his right. Eli sat next to Ma and my place was next to Pa, so my name is to your right."

"Here it is," she said excitedly, running her forefinger over his name.

"I remember the day we did that. I must have been about four. Pa held my hand and said, 'This is forever, boy. Forever.' And it was. I may not know my birth parents, but God gave me the best He had."

She heard the love in his voice and she was spellbound, wanting to know more.

"Does it bother you that you don't know who your parents are?"

He stared down at the table in silence and she wondered if she'd stepped over the line.

"Sometimes," he finally answered. "I didn't know there was a stigma attached to adopted kids until I was in my teens. Some parents didn't want me dating their daughters because they didn't know where I came from. They concluded that since I was abandoned, my parents had to be undesirables with low moral character."

"It doesn't matter now." She wanted him to know that. "Everyone knows the type of man you are, selfless and giving."

"Thank you," he said, studying the beer can. "Some people don't understand why I have this dream to help children." He ran the palm of his hand over the table. "But when I look at these names, I know what I have to do. What I was meant to do." He took a swallow of beer. "You probably don't understand that."

"I understand it perfectly."

"Really?" His eyes caught hers. "That's why your law firm represented the Templetons and believed in the nurturing ability of a two-parent family instead of a single male?"

She didn't shift under that burning gaze. "You said you'd abide by the judge's decision without any ill will."

"Yes, I seem to remember saying that." He got up, crushed his can with one squeeze of his big hand and threw it into the trash can under the sink. He turned to look at her, his hands on his hips. "What are you doing here, Grace?" Suddenly, all that easy friendship was gone.

By the look in his eyes she knew she had to be completely honest. She had to lay her feelings on this table of honor and see if there was any magic left in it. She stood, gathering thoughts in her head. What she said now would sustain or destroy their tenuous relationship.

"Ever since I've known you I seem to accomplish the amazing feat of putting my foot in my mouth whenever I talk to you. When I get nervous, my mouth goes into overdrive. And you make me nervous. I've worked around men most of my life, but you reach a part of me no one ever has, my feminine side. For four years I've hoped you would ask me out." She took a breath as the truths poured out of her mouth.

"I've finally realized that's never going to happen. You've made it very clear how you feel about me, but I kept hoping until I saw the look in your eyes in my office. You really dislike me. And I didn't feel very good about myself, either." She looked directly at him. "If I had known you were involved with the Brady Harper case, I would never have taken it."

"And now?"

She blinked. "What?"

"Do you feel the Templetons are better for Brady?"

"What difference does it make?"

His eyes darkened even more. "It matters to me. How do *you* feel?"

She glanced at the table. "I feel that Brady's name should be on this table."

He walked toward her. Her hair was in disarray, a smudge was on her cheek and a stain covered her right shoulder. Yet, she'd never looked more beautiful. His eyes centered on the T-shirt. I'm a Good Kisser.

"Is that true?"

"Of course. I wouldn't lie about that, but the judge has ruled and there's nothing else to do."

He realized she was talking about Brady. He was talking about the message on the T-shirt. He felt as if he'd just been sucker punched in the most pleasant way. Never, not for one second, did he ever think she might be attracted to him. The first inkling he'd had was when he touched her breast that day in this kitchen. There was something between them. He'd felt it then and he felt it now.

He pointed to her breasts. "I meant the message on your shirt."

"What?" She frowned, glancing down. "Oh."

He lifted an eyebrow. "Is that true?"

"You'll never know, Jeremiah Tucker," she said with a gleam in her eyes. "Good night."

He caught her before she reached the door, sliding his arms around her and pulling her close to his body. "I don't have boots on. Let's dance."

"What? There's no music."

"We'll make our own."

Tuck turned her round and round, hearing music somewhere in his head. Pulling her closer, he molded her body to his. Sam jumped up and down, barking at them. Neither heard the yelping dog. They were in step with a different sound, the music of falling in love.

Tuck stopped moving and cupped her face, taking her lips softly, gently. She moaned and he deepened the kiss, tasting, discovering everything new and exciting about Grace.

Her hands curled around his neck into his hair and he was totally lost in a sensation that blocked all his reasoning. He wanted her, just like that day in his kitchen. He wanted her as he'd never wanted a woman before. That scared him. He was losing something he always had—control.

Taking a long breath, he rested his forehead against hers. "You'd better go while you still can."

"Maybe I don't want to." Her dreamy, husky voice wrapped around him.

"Mmm." He ran his tongue along her lower lip.

The ringing of the phone was like a douse of cold water.

"Damn. I have to get it. It might be important." He released her and moved toward the phone. Out of the corner of his eye, he saw her slip out the door. "Grace…"

He restrained himself from going after her, realizing they needed time. Suddenly his world was looking a whole lot better.

That T-shirt was right.

CHAPTER NINE

GRACE WENT TO SLEEP with a smile on her face, but by morning the smile had disappeared. Was she going to be like hundreds of other women, waiting for him to call? Sadly she wasn't too clear on the rules of dating. But she'd read enough magazines to know that one kiss didn't guarantee he'd call—even though it was one hell of a kiss.

Last night had been magical, like something out of a movie. She could be heading for a heartache, but she didn't care. Excitement simmered in her veins and she felt young and a little crazy.

She quickly dressed in a black sleeveless dress and a black-and-white matching jacket. Brushing her hair, her hand paused. She wasn't going to spend the day waiting for a phone call. *It was a kiss, Grace. Get over it.*

At least they'd reached an amicable peace. She wouldn't obsess about what happened next. She'd be too busy.

In her office, she went over her schedule. The meeting with Derek Mann was at two. She needed to talk to Byron before then. She had reservations he might be able to explain.

Nina buzzed through. "Ms. Whitten, Chuck is here."

"Send him in." This was excellent timing—she

needed something concrete to substantiate her doubts, or facts to put them to rest.

As she waited she stared at the phone, wondering if Tuck was going to call. So much for not obsessing. How was she going to keep her mind on business?

The door opened and Chuck walked in. His rumpled clothes looked as if he'd slept in them. He laid a file on her desk. "Everything in that file is false. Derek Mann's career was bought and paid for by Emmett Cavanaugh." Right to the point—she liked that about Chuck.

Grace opened the file. "You mean the East Texas oil tycoon and billionaire?"

"The one and only." Chuck eased onto the edge of a chair.

"What's the connection?"

"Stepson. Clarissa Perez Mann married Cavanaugh twenty years ago when he was fifty-two and she was thirty-two. Her son was fifteen at the time."

Grace closed the file. "Give it to me in a nutshell."

"Derek was always in trouble. His father is out of the picture, serving time for a failed armed bank robbery. Clarissa is a very beautiful Latina and Cavanaugh was captivated with her. He wasn't crazy about the son but they came as a package deal. Derek failed all through Baylor, but he managed to graduate with stellar grades, same in law school. Cavanaugh's money is all over the campus. Can't prove anything, but it doesn't take a rocket scientist to figure it out."

Chuck reached for the antacids in his pocket and popped a couple into his mouth. "The last year of law school there was a wild party with drugs in his apartment. He was arrested for rape. The charges were quickly dropped and Mann was moved rather abruptly to Houston. You can guess how he got a law degree. My sources tell me Cavanaugh paid someone to take the bar for him. After that, Mann got some pretty impressive jobs with judges who owed Cavanaugh favors. At the last job, in Boston, Mann beat up a young woman rather badly. Again, the charges were dropped, but he no longer has a job at that firm. That's been a pattern. Seems no one is immune to the big bucks. It bought Derek Mann a rather impressive career." Chuck waved a hand, munching on antacids. "Look at the photos in the back of the file."

Grace gaped at the face of a battered young woman. The left side of her face was black, blue and purple. Her eye was swollen shut.

"That's what he did to a young clerk in the Boston law firm. She's now living in Florida in the lap of luxury and Cavanaugh is trying to get Mann to Texas, closer to his mama."

Grace leaned back in her chair, never expecting anything like this. "How did you get this information?"

Chuck rubbed his hands together. "Mostly by asking. My friend at the police station knew an officer in Waco who worked the rape case. I can't prove much of anything. The records are gone, but where you find Cavanaugh's money being spent in a big way, you'll find Mann in some sort of trouble. Mann's bad news."

"Thank you, Chuck." She leaned forward. "I really appreciate this."

"No problem." He stood. "If you need evidence, it's

gone, especially in Texas. Boston had some, like those pictures, mainly because an officer held on to them."

"I don't have to prove it in a court of law," she told him. "I just needed to know."

Chuck nodded and walked out.

Her father's motives became clear now. There had been a lot of changes in Washington and evidently his seat in Congress was in jeopardy. Emmett Cavanaugh's support and backing could assure Stephen of a win. But at what price?

Grace did not want Derek Mann in her law firm. And it was *her* law firm. She had to make that perfectly clear.

Talking to Byron was out of the question now. She knew without a doubt that Byron was in on her father's plans. Pity he didn't see fit to tell her. Anger curled through her stomach. Because she was a woman and his daughter, Stephen thought he could use and manipulate her to his benefit, as always. The meeting this afternoon was going to be very interesting. She was so glad she'd gone with her gut and checked out Mr. Mann.

Her cell buzzed and she jumped. She was so deep in thought that it startled her. She clicked on, not looking to see who it was.

"Good morning, Grace." The deep voice filled her ear and all her anger dissipated.

"Good morning." *He'd called.*

"You left in rather a hurry last night."

"I didn't want to appear too obvious."

She could feel him smiling and her pulse raced.

"Are you free this evening?"

"Yes." She'd waited four years for this invitation. No

way was she being coy or using an excuse to look at her schedule. She'd rearrange, reschedule or whatever it took to spend time with him.

"Good. Would you like to go out for dinner and dancing at a real Texas honky-tonk? And I promise music this time."

"Doesn't matter," she found herself saying. "I liked the music we had last night."

There was a long pause on the other end of the line. "I guess you have to work today?"

She laughed a sound that warmed her whole body. "Yes."

"Me, too. I'm on my way to see Brady, to say goodbye. I don't know if he'll understand but I still have to do it."

"I'm so sorry."

"I know, and that means a lot. I'll pick you up about seven. Is that okay?"

"Wonderful."

Grace clicked off and held the phone to her face for a moment. He'd called and she couldn't believe how good that made her feel.

TUCK SAT AT THE SMALL TABLE in the hospital playroom watching Brady stack building blocks. The sores on his scalp were healing and Tuck hoped the scars on his soul were, too.

"Hey, buddy, could we talk for a minute?"

Brady looked at him with big eyes.

Jennifer walked in. "Snack time." She placed animal crackers and apple juice on the table.

"Thank you," Tuck said. "Double shift today?"

"Yes, a nurse called in sick." Jennifer shook her head, watching Brady and Tuck. "There's something wrong with that judge's thinking."

"We all want what's best for Brady," he told her.

"Yes." Jennifer didn't say another word and quietly left.

Brady sucked on the straw in the apple juice while Tuck opened the crackers. Brady suddenly tried to yank them out of his hand.

Tuck held them out of Brady's reach, pointing a finger at him to get his attention. "No," he said sternly. "Be nice and I'll give you one."

Today it worked. Brady didn't hit or slap him, but waited patiently for the cracker. Tuck gave it to him and he munched away.

"Would you like to have a tea party, buddy? No, well, I don't think guys have tea parties, anyway. Katie has tea parties." *But you'll never know her.* "And Beau and Zoë have tea parties." *You'll never know them, either.*

Tuck handed him another cracker. "Soon you'll have new parents who will love you and they will never hurt or abandon you. You'll live in a nice home, have all the toys you want and never go hungry again." He felt the thickness in his throat and swallowed it back. "I won't be coming back, Brady. I hope you understand that I'm not abandoning you. I would never do that. I hope someday someone will tell you that I hung in to the end. You won't remember, but I will."

He swallowed again. "This is goodbye, buddy."

Brady held out his hand for another cracker and Tuck's heart almost pounded out of his chest. That one simple action showed Tuck that Brady was hearing and interacting in his own way. He placed several crackers in Brady's outstretched hand. Brady poked them into his mouth.

"Goodbye, Brady," Tuck said and rose to his feet.

Brady ran and grabbed a ball and rolled it to Tuck.

Tuck winced inwardly. *Brady, don't do this. Not today. I have to be able to walk out of here.*

With his foot, he rolled the ball back. He was grateful when Jennifer appeared. He raised his hand in farewell at the door before he walked away.

Brady just stared forlornly after him, hugging the ball tightly to his chest.

Tuck poked the elevator button with a hand that shook slightly. At that moment he knew that Lisa and Keith Templeton could not love Brady more than he did.

That was a reality he had to live with.

GRACE AND BYRON were meeting before the interview with Mann to go over his résumé and their interview strategy. She was ready. Her father hadn't called all morning and Grace thought that a little strange considering what she knew. Maybe Stephen had just promised Cavanaugh an interview for his stepson. But Grace knew better than that. The political scratching of one's back required a lot more than perfunctory gestures.

It didn't matter. She was fully prepared to handle the situation.

She opened the door to the boardroom and stopped short. Her father sat at the table with Byron. So that's why he hadn't called. He was here in person.

Stephen got up and kissed Grace's cheek. "Hi, sweetheart."

She didn't return the kiss. "What are you doing here, Dad?"

He shrugged. "Your mother wanted to see Jesse and I thought I'd come into the city to make sure the interview goes smoothly."

Grace laid her briefcase on the table. "And you doubt my ability to do that?"

"Oh, no, sweetheart."

"Then what are you doing here?"

A look passed between Byron and her father.

"I think you're unaware of the clout and the prestige Mann will bring to the firm."

"I'm very aware of what Mann will bring to this firm. I did my homework, Dad. You taught me that." She snapped open her briefcase and the sound resonated around the room. Pulling out Derek Mann's folder, she threw it onto the table. Several photos of battered girls slipped out. "Let's talk about Derek Mann."

Another look passed between Stephen and Byron.

"Stop looking at Byron. He's your lapdog and will do your bidding, even attempt to warm me up for this atrocious farce."

"Sweetheart, you're upset."

"Yes, I'm upset that you're trying to manipulate me. You have nothing to do with this law firm anymore, so I'm asking once again, what are you doing here?"

"Grace…"

"I make all hiring decisions on what I feel is right for this firm. *Me*, Dad, not you, I make decisions based on facts and performances. Using those criteria, Derek Mann is not even on the page."

Stephen was silent for a moment, but Grace knew her father never admitted defeat. He was known for his bulldog tendencies, especially when his career was at stake. "This is important to me, Grace."

"Then tell me the truth."

"Things are changing all over the country. People want change. I'm just doing what I've always done, fighting to keep my position in Congress. I thought my daughter would be glad to help."

"Maybe she would be if you had treated her like an adult and told her the truth."

"I'm telling you now." His chin jutted out. "So Mann's a little off the wall. He can be controlled. Cavanaugh assured me of that."

She looked at this man who was her father. She'd idolized him, wanting to walk in his footsteps. But today she got a glimpse of her hero with feet of clay. Truth was an evasive tactic politicians used to their own advantage. Most of the time no one saw through it, but Grace had a clear view now.

Stephen knew her weakness—his approval. Everything she'd done in her life she'd done to obtain his approval and he'd used it for his own ends. She was his puppet, keeping the law firm running just the way he wanted.

Those responsibilities were the chains that bound her. Those were the chains making her so restless, so unsure of her life. She'd had a glimpse of what life was all about, a little boy who needed love and a man's kiss that made her feel alive.

Without a second thought, she drew out a piece of paper from her briefcase and began to write, talking as she scribbled. "I will not hire Derek Mann. I will not jeopardize the reputation of this firm and I certainly will not jeopardize the safety of the women working here." She handed the paper to her father. "If you're so set on hiring Mann, then you'll have to do it yourself. I resign and turn the firm back to you. I'm done." Grabbing her briefcase, she headed for the door.

"Grace, come back here," her father shouted, but she kept walking.

She didn't go to her office. There was nothing there she needed. She took several cleansing breaths and let them out, feeling liberated, feeling free. Jumping into her car, she drove away. Everything she'd worked for, everything she'd thought was her life was behind her.

GOING TO HER APARTMENT was out of the question. Her parents would eventually show up there, trying to make her change her mind, trying to make her see reason, as she was sure they would put it. Everything had to be sacrificed for her father's career. That was the Whitten mantra, but not anymore. She would not sacrifice her integrity.

It had taken her years to get to this point. The dutiful, good daughter had rebelled. Caroline had done it years ago, but it had taken Grace a little longer. She had to be her own person now, find her way. She was starting over. Being unemployed would terrify most people, but discovering the real Grace hidden inside was suddenly her most important priority. Fortunately, she had a healthy bank account and she intended to use it wisely.

Without realizing it, she found she was driving south on the I-35. She passed the round Holiday Inn and Fiesta Gardens before she crossed the bridge over Town Lake. She took an exit and stopped, got out and sat on a bench, watching the easy movement of the water. This peace, this quiet was what she needed. The wind tossed her hair and she breathed in the scent of the fresh outdoors. People were headed for the walking and biking trails, but she hardly noticed them.

Her cell kept buzzing. She finally checked the callers. Her father—five times. Her mother—four times. And Caroline—three. She didn't want to worry her sister so she called her back.

"Grace, where are you?"

"I'm fine, Caroline."

"Tell me where you are and I'll come so we can talk. Mom will stay with Jesse. Just you and me, like old times."

"I don't need to talk. I know what I'm doing."

"Grace, your life is that firm. You can't just walk away from it."

"I really thought it was and I really thought Dad trusted my abilities to make it one of the best law firms in Texas."

"He does."

"No. I'm a puppet for him. He still controls everything from Washington. I finally can see I'm just a figurehead like everyone said from the start."

"Grace, Dad is worried sick. He even has Charley looking for you. You and Dad can work this out. I know you can."

"How many times did you try to work it out with Dad?"

There was a slight pause. "That's different. I'm stubborn."

"So am I."

"Grace…"

"There's a big world out here and for once I'm going to live my life my way. I don't need Daddy's approval anymore. I haven't been happy for a long time, Caro, and that's what I want…to feel happy with my life and myself. I'll be in touch."

"Grace…"

She clicked off and sat staring at Austin in the distance. Everything was the same, yet so different. If her father had Charley on her trail, then it was only a matter of time before he found her.

TUCK WAS DRESSED for the evening in his starched jeans, white shirt and dress cowboy boots. He called them his dancing boots and he intended to dance the night away.

He splashed a bit of aftershave on his cheeks and winced at the scent. Damn, that was strong. Sam barked at the smell.

"Don't like it, huh?"

Sam barked again.

He grabbed a washcloth and wiped it off. "How's that?"

Sam sprinted for the kitchen. "What…?" Then he heard Eli's voice and followed Sam more slowly. Eli sat at the table bouncing Jesse on his knees, the diaper bag on the floor. He glanced up as Tuck entered the room.

"Whoa." One eyebrow shot up. "You must be going out."

"Yep. I have a date."

"Well, Jesse and I were hoping you needed some company, but I can see that you don't."

"Caroline tired again?"

"No. The Whittens are at my house and all hell is breaking loose. Grace resigned from the Whitten Law Firm today."

Tuck's head jerked up. "What?"

"I'm not clear on all the details, but evidently Stephen and Grace had a disagreement over hiring some lawyer. Grace resigned and walked out. Stephen has the company P.I. looking for her."

"You mean no one knows where she is?"

"No. I didn't offer to help. I figure Grace can take care of herself."

"Why do you talk about her in that tone of voice? She does have feelings and she's very vulnerable."

Eli frowned. "Uh…I…what did you say?"

Clearly he'd thrown Eli for a loop with his response, but he didn't have time to explain. He reached for his dress Stetson and placed it on his head. "I've got to go. Stay as long as you want."

"Tuck…"

He kissed Jesse and walked out.

His one goal was to find Grace.

CHAPTER TEN

BACKING OUT of his driveway, Tuck glanced at his watch. Six-thirty. In the turmoil of her day, had Grace forgotten about their date? He'd thought of very little else. What had happened to make her walk away from everything she'd worked for? With a little luck, Grace would be at her apartment getting ready.

She wasn't.

In his car, he called the highway patrol station where Tuck's office was located. "Stan, I need a favor."

"Tuck, don't you ever quit working?"

"My date's run out on me and I need to find her."

"You single guys have all the fun."

"Seriously, Stan, I need to find this woman. Her name is Grace Whitten and she drives a white Lexus. Put it through the system and see if you can bring up her license number. Alert the patrol and let me know if they spot her car. Don't stop her, just let me know."

"You got it. I'll be in touch."

"Thanks, Stan." He clicked off wondering where Grace could have gone.

And why she hadn't called him.

GRACE HAD NO IDEA where she was going. When she looked around, she saw she was near the hospital.

She wondered about Brady and if Tuck's goodbye had affected him, or if he even understood. It was none of her business, she kept telling herself. She was no longer with the Whitten Firm. Somehow, that didn't stop her from turning onto the street leading to the hospital.

Grace approached the pediatric ward, nodding to the woman at the desk. "Hello, Jennifer."

Jennifer glanced up. "Ms. Whitten. You just missed your clients."

"Oh?"

"They put Brady in his crib and they've gone for the evening. Mrs. Templeton said they'd be back at ten in the morning."

"Brady's down for the night?"

Jennifer looked at the clock on the wall. "Hardly. It's barely six-thirty, but Mrs. Templeton said she wanted to get him into a routine of going to bed early."

"I see." But she didn't. And Grace was sure this wasn't what the judge had meant by providing Brady with stability.

"May I see him, please?"

Jennifer arched an eyebrow. "Why?"

"I want to see how he's doing. Do you have a problem with that?"

Grace expected a comeback, and she got it. "I have a problem with the whole situation. Tuck said goodbye to Brady this morning and Brady's been violent ever since. Brady may not respond or understand much, but he knows he's never going to see Tuck again."

"What do you mean by violent?" Grace was trying to keep her cool, to get some answers.

"He's hitting and biting again. He'd stopped the biting, but today he's taking a piece out of everybody. Mrs. Templeton hung in there. I have to give her credit for that. I personally think she was exhausted and that's why they went home so early."

Grace thought about this for a moment. "I assume you are keeping a record of all of this."

"Oh, you bet I am."

"Good. I'm going to check on Brady."

"Suit yourself."

"I will, and thank you."

She walked across the hall and opened the door to the ward. The woman sat by her little girl's bedside, flipping through a magazine. Another baby, not even a year old, lay in another bed. Brady sat in his bed, holding his stuffed dog.

"Hi," she said to the woman, and moved toward Brady.

"Be careful," the woman warned. "Brady's not in a good mood today."

"I heard." She walked to the crib. "Hi, Brady."

Brady rose to his feet and started toward her, a gleam in those dark eyes.

Grace held up a finger. "Don't even think about biting me," she told him, smiling. "I have sensitive skin and it would hurt." She leaned in slightly. "And you want to hear a secret? I don't take pain very well and I'd cry. Big tears would roll down my cheeks." She tilted her head sideways and made a sad face. "Don't make me cry."

The corners of Brady's mouth twitched and he sank to the bed.

"My, those eyelashes are much longer in the daylight, Brady. And I think we really need to trade. You can have my stubby ones and I could have your gorgeous ones. What do you think?" She blinked her eyes several times.

Brady reached up and touched his eye with one finger.

"I've never seen him do that before," the woman said. "He's interacting with you."

Grace held out her hand. "Hi, I'm Grace Whitten."

The woman shook her hand. "Barbara Wilcott. You're one of the lawyers for the Templetons."

"Yes."

"Lisa was with Brady most of the day and she had a rough time. Maybe you need to give her some tips."

Grace smiled. "I have a small nephew so I've learned to speak their language. Lisa will get the hang of it."

"I suppose."

She glanced at the baby in the bed. "How's your little girl?"

"I don't know. They removed a brain tumor days ago. We're waiting for her to wake up. It's taking so long, though."

That sad voice tore at Grace's heart. "What's her name?"

"Molly."

Molly's head was completely bandaged and Grace stared at the cherub face. "She's so pretty."

"Yes. She's my baby. I have three boys at home."

"Who takes care of them?" Grace realized that was none of her business, but the words had slipped out.

"My mom is helping my husband. It's been a rough time."

Grace looked at the tired lines on Barbara's face, the worry in her eyes. But she also saw the selfless, unconditional love. Her clothes were rumpled, her hair uncombed but her heart was solid gold.

Grace felt she had to do something to help Barbara. That feeling came out of nowhere and it surprised her. It didn't stop her, though.

"Why don't you go to the cafeteria for a good meal and I'll sit with Molly."

"Oh, no, I don't leave her. I only go to the bathroom and the nurses let me use the one in this room. I have to be here when she wakes up. I don't want her to be afraid."

"Then I'll go down and get you something."

"I don't want your charity," Barbara snapped, her face slightly flushed. "I'm sorry…I…"

"It's okay." Grace immediately knew the problem. Barbara didn't have any money to go to the cafeteria. Molly's medical bills had probably drained them financially.

"If my husband has time, he'll bring something. If not, the nurses always bring snacks. Don't worry about it."

"Oh, but I do." Surprising herself even more, Grace held up a foot encased in a Manolo high heel. "I paid six hundred dollars for these shoes. So, you see, I'm a little crazy. And at the moment I'm feeling selfish, self-centered and out of touch with what's really important in this world."

Barbara looked back at her, shocked.

"I'm going downstairs to buy your dinner." She held up a hand as Barbara began to protest. "It's not charity. It's a token for women like you who have their goals and priorities straight. If you feel the need to repay me, maybe you can keep an eye on Brady and help Lisa as she tries to become his mother. Because I have a feeling you've written the book on motherhood."

"Oh, I'd be happy to."

Grace nodded and headed for the door. The cafeteria was serving chicken spaghetti with green beans, garlic bread and a salad. Grace bought the works and topped it off with chocolate pie and iced tea.

Carrying the food down the hall, she met Jennifer. "You can't carry food into the ward."

"How does Barbara eat?"

"She eats mostly sandwiches. We allow her to do that."

She could see Jennifer was going to be hard-nosed about this. "Is there a room with a table where she can eat a decent meal?"

"It's at the end of the hall on the other wing and I can tell you she's not going that far."

"There has to be a table somewhere."

Jennifer hesitated for a second. "There's one for the nurses behind the nurses' station."

"Perfect."

"But it's only for nurses."

Grace looked her in the eye. "Barbara hasn't had a decent meal in days. Are you going to deprive her of that?"

"It's against hospital policy."

Grace wasn't listening. She walked around Jennifer and into a lounge with a refrigerator, microwave, small sofa, four chairs and a table. "Perfect," she said, and placed the food on the table.

Jennifer watched from the doorway. "You know, you're very pushy."

"Actually, I'm known for it." She threw the plastic bag into the garbage. "I'm pushy and bossy, but I get results. Remember that."

Grace walked past her to the ward without another word.

Barbara was straightening Molly's sheets, though they were already perfectly straight.

"Your dinner is in the nurses' lounge," Grace told her.

"Oh, thank you, but I can't leave Molly."

"The lounge is across the hall in a small room, within shouting distance. I'll watch Molly. If she moves a muscle, I will shout for you. I promise I'll watch her closely."

"It's across the hall?"

"Yes. Now go. Your food is getting cold."

"I…"

"Tell you what—I'll leave this door open." She took Barbara's magazine and stuffed it beneath the door. "Now, even if I say your name, you'll have no problem hearing me."

"You're a very unusual person," Barbara said.

Grace knew she didn't mean that in a bad way because she was smiling. Actually smiling. She gently pushed Barbara out the door and sat in her chair, staring at Molly.

"You can't keep this door open." Jennifer stood in the doorway. "It will disturb the other children."

Grace took a deep breath and glanced around the room. Brady stood at his railing, watching everything.

The other baby lay quietly, hooked to machines. "What's wrong with that baby?"

"His father threw him against a wall. He's brain-dead. The hospital is waiting for orders to pull his feeding tube."

"Oh my God." Grace felt a tremor run through her. *Oh my God!*

"We try to maintain quiet and order, Ms. Whitten, for everyone's benefit, even if you don't see that."

"I'm sorry I disregarded your rules, but Barbara Wilcott needs a break. Ten minutes, Jennifer, that's all I'm asking."

Something changed in Jennifer's expression. "That's nice what you did for Barbara, but in ten minutes this door will be closed."

"Thank you."

Grace settled into her chair. Brady watched her. She waved at him but he didn't respond. Her gaze kept going to the little baby, so still, so alone. How could someone do that?

Molly slept so peacefully, like an angel. Suddenly tears stung the backs of her eyes—the emotional overload had finally hit her. But she knew this moment, sitting in this room with these children, was very meaningful. Everything else paled into insignificance.

And that was probably the most real feeling she'd ever had.

GRACE SLID INTO HER CAR and glanced at her watch. *Seven o'clock!* She'd completely lost track of time. She needed to call Tuck. It seemed she'd been waiting her whole life for this date and she couldn't miss it. Damn. She fished her phone out of her purse. What was Tuck's cell number? Think. Think. She didn't know it. Double damn.

Wait. He'd called her this morning so it would be on her caller ID. She flipped open her phone and searched her calls. Yes. There it was. She quickly punched in the number.

She started her car and drove out of the parking lot. "Hi, Tuck," she said when he answered. "I haven't stood you up if that's what you're thinking. I'm just running late."

"Where are you? I can meet you."

"I'm headed toward I-35. Oh, no."

"What is it?"

"A highway patrolman is following me."

"Is he stopping you?"

"I don't…no, he's passing me. Whew, that was close."

"Where are you?"

She gave him her location.

"You can meet me at The Broken Spoke." He gave her directions. "It's a country dance hall—best dancing in Austin. Wait for me in the parking lot."

"Okay." She followed his directions and soon pulled into the graveled parking lot of The Broken Spoke—a big red barn with a large oak tree out front. And, of course, there was a wagon wheel with a broken spoke resting against the tree. Wagon wheels also adorned the long front porch and each side of the sign at the top of the building.

There was a very old broken-down bus with a Lone Star Beer sign painted on the side. Next to the bus was an ancient oil rig. She'd never been here and she had no idea what the bus and rig were about.

The marquee advertised the name of a band playing tonight. The place looked rustic and couples were going in, arm in arm. They were all dressed in jeans and boots. She had on a dress. Oh, well, she'd make the best of it. She wasn't missing this date. She grabbed her purse, searching for her makeup.

Flipping on the light, she studied herself in the mirror. She looked tired, worried and a little excited. Her face was flushed and her hair resembled a bush, the wind doing a number on it at the lake. No one seemed to notice this at the hospital.

A car swung into the spot beside her. Charley, the firm's P.I., got out. He'd found her. She pushed a button to roll down her window.

"Good evening, Ms. Whitten." Charley bent to speak to her. In his early sixties, Charley was balding and about twenty pounds overweight. "Your father would like to speak to you."

"Charley." She heaved a deep sigh. "We're not going to play games. I've spoken to my father and he knows how I feel. If he wants to continue the conversation, then I'll be at my apartment in the morning. But tonight that conversation is not happening." She touched the button and the window went up.

Charley saluted and went back to his vehicle. Her nerves were frayed. The emotional roller coaster she'd been on was about to slam into a solid wall and she felt powerless to stop it.

Grace saw Tuck drive into a parking spot and she quickly brushed her hair and applied lipstick. On a night when she wanted to be beautiful, she was a mess.

She watched as Tuck swung out his long legs and locked his car. Pocketing the keys, he strolled toward her. He moved in a sexy, loose-limbed sort of way. His shirt stretched across wide shoulders and his Stetson fit perfectly on his dark head, giving him a mysterious appeal. Her stomach tightened.

As he slid into the passenger seat, a tangy male scent filled the car. She swallowed.

"You okay?" he asked.

"I could really use a glass of wine."

NEON BEER SIGNS, country music and laughter greeted them. Grace realized she was in a real Texas honky-tonk, another new experience. Pictures of celebrities from baseball player Bob Gill to singer Dolly Parton and patrons covered the walls.

Straight ahead was a dining room with a bar. She could see pool tables there, too. They sat at a table close together so they could hear each other above the chatter. It was a packed house tonight. She ordered a glass of Merlot and Tuck ordered a longneck. After a couple of sips, she relaxed. Looking into Tuck's dark eyes she relaxed even more.

Tuck ordered chicken-fried steak and she selected a grilled chicken breast. During the meal they talked. She told him about her father and he understood her decision to resign. Then she told him about Brady and he was surprised.

"I think Jennifer is going to have me barred from the hospital."

"I doubt it."

She wondered about his relationship with Jennifer, but she didn't ask. It didn't matter.

She took a sip of wine. "I keep thinking there should be sofas in the ward or recliners so mothers could get some rest. If Caroline was there with Jesse, it would be totally unacceptable that she'd get no rest."

"Grace, it's an indigent hospital. There aren't any luxuries. And if, God forbid, Jesse needed medical care, he would be in a state-of-the-art hospital with all the amenities because Caroline and Eli have insurance and they could afford it."

"I know, but I feel something should be done." She straightened her napkin in her lap. "I might look into it. I'm going to have a lot of time on my hands."

"Do you have any idea what you're going to do?"

"No. Right now I'm just feeling my way through." She wiped her mouth and laid her napkin on the table. "The dinner was delicious but now I just want to dance." They went through a door by the bar into a long dance hall with a stage at the back of the room. The band was playing "It's Five O'clock Somewhere" and the crowd was singing along and shouting the punchline.

They took a table on the side of the dance floor and Grace slipped off her jacket and laid it on the back of her chair.

Tuck set their drinks on the table and took her hand, grinning. "Let's dance." His feet were already moving to the beat of the music.

As they reached the floor, the band eased into a slow George Strait two-step. "I won't tell you what my shoes cost," she said above the noise.

"Good idea."

"And I don't care if you step all over them."

"I think you have a shoe fetish."

She giggled and went into his arms as if she belonged there. One hand rested on his neck, the other was held firmly in his. Her body molded to his perfectly, sensuously. She felt every muscle, every sinew of his hard body. Her frayed nerves eased and she slid into the most wonderful feeling of her life—that feeling of knowing she'd found the man for her.

Tuck kissed the side of her face. "Feeling better?"

"Yes. Much." The other couples on the floor seemed to fade away.

"You smell wonderful."

"So do you." She moved her head to smile at him.

"Sam didn't like it. He ran into the other room."

Her smile broadened. "What does a dog know?"

She locked her hands around his neck and he tightened his around her waist.

"We're talking too much," he whispered into her ear.

"Definitely." She moved against him to the beat of the music. As she turned her head, their lips met in a slow, aching kiss. The music played on, but Grace didn't hear it. All she heard was the beat of her heart against his, a magical sound that bound them together for this moment in time.

CHAPTER ELEVEN

THE NEXT MORNING Grace had coffee ready when her doorbell rang. She took a deep breath and opened the door. Her parents stood there. And to her surprise, so did Caroline. She didn't think her sister would leave Jesse this early in the morning, but then she remembered it was Saturday and Eli was at home.

It was hard to keep her mind on business because she was floating about three feet off the ground. Last night had been wonderful. They'd shared a long kiss before she got into her car and drove home, alone. It was tempting to ask Tuck to her apartment, but they both knew it was too soon.

Her family walked into her living room without saying a word. She poured coffee and passed it around, not caring they were drinking coffee in her spotless white living room. Well, that wasn't completely true, but she was forcing herself to be okay with it. She was still taking tiny steps. Each one was getting easier and easier, though.

Stephen sipped from a china cup, his eyes on Grace. Like a dutiful daughter, she waited for him to speak.

"I think you owe me an apology for running out yesterday. Byron had to handle the interview with Mann."

She ran her thumb and forefinger over the handle of her cup, feeling the dutiful daughter suddenly disappear. "If you came here for an apology, you're not going to get one."

Her father frowned. "What's wrong with you, Grace? You don't seem to care about your family anymore."

She carefully placed her cup on the silver tray, trying to maintain control without losing her temper. "Family has nothing to do with this. Your political career does."

"That's my life, Grace, and I expected my daughter to step up to the plate and do what she had to in a difficult situation."

"You expected wrong, then." She met his eyes squarely. "When you had your heart attack, you said the only thing that mattered was seeing your girls' faces one more time. You said that in the scheme of your life, we were all that mattered. Was that a lie?"

"Of course not. And I resent…"

Joanna placed a hand on her husband's arm. "You promised not to get upset."

Stephen shrugged off her hand, his eyes on Grace. "You've had this dream career handed to you on a silver platter and this is the thanks I get. I feel like you've stabbed me in the back."

Grace stood, some of her control slipping. "Maybe that's it. The job was given to me—*for a reason*. I didn't earn it. And lately I've felt the pressure of that. Please understand I'm not happy doing your bidding anymore. Byron can easily take over. I need some space and time to do my own thing." She took a long breath. "I will not be coming back to the firm. That's my final decision."

Stephen got to his feet. "I expect this kind of behavior from Caroline, but not from you, Grace."

"I'm sitting right here, Dad!" Caroline had been silent up until now.

"You know what I mean."

"Sadly, yes, I do." Caroline rose. "And for what it's worth, I wouldn't hire this guy, either."

Stephen's eyes bulged. "I can't believe my ears. What type of daughters have I raised?"

"Daughters with integrity, pride and ethics," Grace replied. "We got those qualities from our father, but he's forgotten those essential, important characteristics."

"How dare you…"

Joanna stood by her husband, rubbing his arm. "Stephen…"

He shook off her hand. "Stop mollycoddling me, Joanna. Sometimes you treat me like a child."

"Maybe because sometimes you act like one," Joanna shot back. "Have you ever thought that we raised intelligent, discerning women and that they're right about Mann? He's vile, and I'm telling you for about the hundredth time we can win this election without Cavanaugh's money."

"You don't know what the hell you're talking about," Stephen shouted.

"Fine." Joanna reached for her purse. "I'm going home. I'll call a cab from the street." She glanced at Caroline's and Grace's stunned faces. "I'm sure my daughters can take care of themselves because that's the way *I* raised them—independent and strong, able to stand up for the things they believe in." With those words, she headed to the door.

"Joanna, don't you dare walk out that door."

Joanna kept walking; the door snapped shut behind her.

"Joanna!" When Stephen realized she wasn't coming back, he quickly went after her.

Grace and Caroline stared at each other in shock. Their mother never stood up to their father. She was the quintessential politician's wife, and always acquiesced to Stephen's wishes.

"We need chocolate," Caroline said, and headed for the kitchen.

Grace kept staring after her parents, not wanting to be the cause of a rift between them. But she wasn't going back on her decision, either.

Caroline came back with a half gallon of Rocky Road and two spoons. She had a strange look on her face. "There's a glass, two spoons and a fork in your sink," Caroline said. "And there's trash in the trash can."

For anyone else that statement would sound very stupid, but not for Grace. She was known for not leaving dirty dishes in her sink, or anywhere else for that matter. And she emptied her trash daily. It was important to her to be clean, tidy, neat—perfect. But not anymore.

"There are clothes on the floor in the bedroom, too," she told her sister.

"You're joking." Caroline ran into the bedroom. "Oh my gosh, you're having a nervous breakdown."

"I am not," Grace said. "Bring that ice cream back in here."

They sat cross-legged on the sofa eating ice cream

out of the carton like when they were kids and their parents were away and the nanny was asleep.

"You made the right decision," Caroline said in between mouthfuls. "Just in case you needed to hear that."

Grace licked her spoon. "I didn't know if I had enough strength to stand up to Dad, but it was quite easy. There was no way I'd hire Derek Mann." She took a bite, savoring the almond and chocolate taste. "I was hoping Dad would trust my judgment. Wrong."

"Yeah, what planet are you living on?"

Venus and Mars. Her eyes grew dreamy.

Caroline watched her. "So what's going on with you?"

Grace stuck her spoon in the ice cream. "I've been visiting the pediatric ward and it has opened my eyes."

Caroline licked her spoon, watching Grace. "How has it done that?"

"There's this one woman who sits with her daughter, who had a brain tumor removed. The little girl hasn't woken up yet and Barbara wants to be there when she does. She has three more children at home, so she doesn't spend money on food for herself. Her kids might need it." She paused. "I've never seen that kind of love before."

"That's a mother's love."

"I know, and then there's the flip side. Brady, and what his mother did to him. There's another baby in a crib who is brain-dead. His father threw him against a wall."

"Oh, no!"

"It's heartbreaking and eye opening to see all this." Grace twirled her spoon in the ice cream. "I spend a fortune on shoes and clothes. Barbara and her family are barely getting by and what I spend on shoes alone they could live on for a month. That makes me feel selfish and worthless as a human being, and as a woman."

"When I talked to you yesterday, you said you weren't happy."

"No, and I haven't been for a long time, but when I'm on the pediatric ward I feel alive and needed." She licked her spoon. "I know exactly how Tuck feels. He saw abused kids come through his home as a child. How could he not want to help? It's second nature to him."

Caroline paused in taking a bite. "You're calling him Tuck now?"

"Yes. It's something I should have done from the start."

Caroline swallowed a mouthful. "I get the feeling things have changed between you and Tuck."

Grace couldn't stop the smile that spread across her face. "We went dancing last night."

"What?" Caroline sat up straight.

"We had a great time. We didn't argue at all."

"Oh, honey, please take it slow," Caroline advised. "Tuck's a wonderful man, but he's not the marrying kind. He has plans and dreams in his head and there's not much room for a woman. He's the most self-sufficient man I know and that includes my darling of a husband."

"We're just getting to know each other. It's been nice." She heard the wistfulness in her voice.

Caroline lifted an eyebrow. "Thinking of sleeping with the enemy, huh?"

Grace grinned. "Maybe."

"Good for you." Caroline pointed her spoon at Grace. "You need some excitement in your life. I want to know all the details."

"Oh, please." Grace rolled her yes. "We're not sixteen."

"No." Caroline laughed. "Thank God for that."

Grace joined in the laughter, releasing the last of her pent-up emotions.

Caroline sobered. "You do realize Dad is going to keep pressuring you. He'll make up with Mom and he'll continue to try to get you back at the Whitten Law Firm."

"I'm aware of his tactics. I can handle it."

"I'm always here for you," Caroline said.

"I know that." Grace raised her spoon. "To sisters."

Caroline tapped her spoon against Grace's. "Sisters first—sisters always."

That had been their slogan when they were kids and it still held true today.

AFTER CAROLINE LEFT, Grace sat for a long time thinking about her life. She wasn't rushing into anything. She would take this time to get to know herself and find out what she wanted out of life. From now on everything she did would be her decision.

She thought about what Caroline had said about Tuck not being the marrying kind. Well, maybe she wasn't, either. But she was willing to explore her options.

Later that afternoon, she headed to Tuck's. He'd told her last night to let him know how the meeting with her father turned out and she wanted to do that in person. She drove into his driveway and saw he was at the barn, leaning on the corral watching a small boy riding a horse.

As she stepped out of her car, the spring day embraced her with a freshness that cleared her mind. She took a deep breath and the scent of budding trees and green grasses filled her lungs, boosting her spirits.

The wind ruffled her hair and she made no move to brush it back as she walked toward him. He wore jeans and a chambray shirt. Her heart wobbled at the sight of his tall, masculine figure.

Tuck watched her sashay toward him in tight-fitting jeans, her hips swinging with an easy rhythm. His lower abdomen tightened. A few days ago he was angry as hell at her. Today he couldn't take his eyes off her.

All day he kept remembering the taste of her lips, the feel of her body against his. His eyes had strayed to the road several times looking for her white car. He couldn't believe how much he wanted to see her.

"Hey, Tuck. Look at me," Dillon shouted.

Tuck turned his attention to the boy. "You're doing great. Use the reins to turn her just like I taught you."

Dillon pulled on the reins and the horse turned. "This is fun."

"Watch what you're doing," Tuck instructed.

Her perfume wafted to him a moment before he looked into her green eyes. He was beginning to associate that scent with her and it did crazy things to his senses. His head spun at the brightness in her eyes. The talk with her father must have gone well because she didn't look upset. She looked wonderful, almost glowing.

"Hi." She smiled, and his heart fluttered like a bird about to take flight.

"Hi," he replied. "How did it go?"

She shrugged. "Not good. He doesn't understand my position and I don't understand his. We're at an impasse."

"So you're unemployed?"

"Yes, but I'm okay with that."

He watched the light in her eyes. "I can see that."

"Hey, Tuck," Dillon called.

"Come here." Tuck motioned to the boy, who guided the horse closer to the fence.

"Dillon, I want you to meet Grace."

Dillon raised a hand. "Hi, Grace."

"Hi, Dillon."

"I'm riding."

"Very well, too."

"Take the horse to the barn," Tuck said. "It's time to rub her down and feed her."

"Yes, sir," Dillon responded and slowly made his way into the barn.

"Is he one of the boys from Big Brothers?" she asked, and he sensed her nervousness.

"Yes. His father died from a drug overdose two years ago."

"Oh, how sad."

The only way he knew to put her at ease was to tell her about Dillon. "His mother, Sheila, wants a strong male role model in Dillon's life so I spend a couple days a month with him or whenever he calls. But he'll be leaving soon."

"Why?"

"Sheila's been estranged from her family since she ran away and married Lanny Gibbs against her parents' wishes. They live on a farm in Kansas and her mother passed away about six months ago. Sheila's sister tracked her down and it opened the lines of communication again. Her father asked her to come home and Sheila jumped at the invitation. She's getting a second chance. And so is Dillon."

Sam whined at Grace's feet and without having to think about it she reached down and picked him up.

"I guess you know that's a trick of his," Tuck told her.

"Yes. I figured that out." She stroked Sam until he was almost purring.

"Let's go see what Dillon's doing," Tuck suggested.

"I'd better go," she replied. "I'm sure you have plans."

"You can't join us?"

"No." She shook her head. "That wouldn't be fair to Dillon. This is his…"

Tuck reached for her hand and pulled her toward the barn. "Come on." They walked into the barn. Dillon was undoing the saddle straps and Tuck helped him remove the saddle. Dillon ran for a bucket of feed and held it so the horse could eat, then Tuck handed Dillon a brush and together they rubbed down the horse.

"You stay here with Grace and I'll put Dolly back in the pasture." Tuck led the horse away, thinking it would give Grace and Dillon time to get acquainted. That was the best way to get to know the boy.

"Okay," Dillon replied, and sat on a bale of hay.

Grace was unsure of what to say or do. This was a kid who'd been traumatized and whom Tuck had reached out to, one of many. What could she say to him? Words eluded her and she wished she'd called first. She clutched Sam a little tighter.

"I'm nine, almost ten," Dillon said proudly.

"Oh, my, you're getting so old." Grace stared into his shining blue eyes and her nervousness eased. She eyed the bale of hay and wondered what kind of germs it held. She also wondered what kind of tiny furry creatures made this old barn their home— maybe even spiders. With strength born of sheer determination she walked over and sat by Dillon, refusing to squirm.

Another tiny step.

Dillon tipped back his cowboy hat and his blond hair poked out from underneath. "I know. I tell my mom that all the time." Dillon looked at Sam in her lap. "He likes for you to pet him."

"Yes, he does." Grace scratched Sam behind his ears and felt comfortable doing it. But that urge to wash her hands was very strong.

"I like Tuck," Dillon said suddenly.

"Is something wrong?" she asked, zeroing in on his sad expression.

"Do you ever have good and bad feelings at the same time?"

"Sure."

"My mom and I are moving to Kansas to live with my grandpa. I'm happy about that 'cause my mom won't have to work so hard and I'll get to drive a tractor. But I'm sad 'cause I'll never see Tuck again. He's better than a daddy. He's my best friend. I'll miss him."

"You can call him," Grace said. Any awkwardness she felt suddenly vanished in her desire to ease Dillon's sadness.

"That's what Tuck told me. It gets really cold in Kansas.

I can't wait to see snow." Dillon shifted gears quickly, as most kids did. He was sad at the thought of losing Tuck, but Grace knew he would adjust quickly to his new life.

"Who's ready for pizza?" Tuck asked, strolling into the barn.

"Me." Dillon jumped up.

"How about if we invite Grace to go with us?" Tuck spoke to Dillon, and Grace knew Tuck was letting Dillon make the decision so she'd feel comfortable.

"Sure," Dillon answered without hesitation. "I bet I can beat you at video games."

"You're on," Grace said, smiling.

They first went to the movies and saw a family film, eating a bucket of popcorn. Pizza was next on Dillon's to-do list. Grace watched Tuck and Dillon play video games then Dillon insisted she play.

The moment was surreal. She glanced around at the families with kids, laughing, giggling, having fun. She, Grace Whitten, stood in sneakers and jeans with her hair disheveled. She had never felt happier in her life.

Her eyes caught Tuck's and he smiled. Her heart skipped in the most pleasing way. So much had been missing from her life, but looking into his eyes she was sure she had found the pot of gold at the end of the rainbow.

IT WAS LATE when they took Dillon home. Sheila, Dillon's mother, worked two shifts as a waitress on weekends and didn't get off until eleven. Tuck told her that he never took Dillon home unless Sheila was there.

Dillon and his mom lived in government housing and Tuck pulled up to the curb of an apartment complex.

Streetlights gave a shadowy view of the old brick two-story buildings.

"I had a great time," Dillon said, leaning over the seat. "I'm glad you came, Grace. I so beat you at Hoop Fever."

"Yes, you did." Grace smiled.

A young woman came out of one of the downstairs apartments. She was thin and didn't look more than eighteen, but Grace knew she was older.

"Oh, there's Mom. Bye, Grace."

"Bye," she called.

Tuck followed Dillon up the sidewalk and shook hands with Sheila. He squatted and Dillon hugged him, holding on tight. Grace swallowed a lump in her throat. Each day she understood Tuck more and more—the selfless love and devotion he gave to kids like Dillon.

And to Brady.

A moment of guilt pierced her, and she wondered if Tuck had forgiven her for her part in the Templetons' winning custody of Brady. Tuck didn't hold grudges; she was sure of that. But still, she wanted to hear him say the words—that he didn't blame her.

Tonight they had to talk. She had to know how he felt about her.

CHAPTER TWELVE

THE SILENCE on the drive home was nice, pleasant. Grace knew Tuck was thinking about Dillon and that he'd soon be leaving. Tuck gave so much of himself to these kids that she wondered if there was any room for a woman in his life. He truly was a special person—she was just beginning to see how special. Not many men could do what he was doing.

Tuck stopped at a red light. There was something sensual about riding in a pickup at night with a man. A man she was attracted to. The cab smelled of coffee, leather and pure masculinity, which was reinforced by a pair of spurs dangling from the rearview mirror.

"I know there's a story behind those spurs."

"Pa gave them to me when I got my first horse. He said, 'Son, I'm giving you these spurs, but a real man doesn't need spurs. All he needs is a gentle hand and a kind heart.' No way was I going to use those spurs after he told me that, so I hung them in my room. When I got my first truck, I hung them on the rearview mirror and that's been their resting place ever since." The light turned green and Tuck drove on.

"Why do you think he gave them to you then?"

"Because I'd been asking for them. I saw cowboys

wearing them in some old movies that Pa used to watch. I wanted to be a cowboy, but I'm sure Pa was trying to teach me one of life's many lessons—a gentle hand and kind heart wins every time."

"That's the way you are with Dillon."

"The way I try to be with all the boys I mentor."

"Dillon is sad he'll never see you again."

"I know, but I'll call him often. He'll adjust."

"But you'll miss him."

"Yes, but that's life."

She licked her lips. "Like Brady?"

He drove into his carport. "Yeah, like Brady." He turned off the ignition. "Want to come in for a while? I have Oreo cookies."

She wanted to talk about Brady, but now her mind was on other things. "I never turn down an Oreo."

Climbing out of the cab, they went into the house. Tuck flipped on lights as he went. Sam scurried from the den, sliding on the hardwood floor in his haste to reach them. Dee followed more slowly.

Sam whined at her feet.

"Will you stop that, you big baby," Tuck scolded, opening a cabinet. Sam wagged his tail, evidently knowing what Tuck was doing. He opened a couple of boxes of flavored snacks and handed Sam and Dee a treat. They gobbled them up. "Now back to bed, guys. It's late."

As if understanding every word, Sam and Dee trotted to the big dog basket in the den and curled up inside it together.

"They sleep together?" Grace had to ask.

"When Dee's in the house, they do. They don't know they're supposed to be enemies."

"Oh." Grace nodded. "Caroline took pictures of the two of them. I remember her showing them to me."

"She gave me one. It's in my bedroom." He opened the refrigerator. "Now for the milk and an Oreo or two."

She kicked off her sneakers and sat cross-legged in a chair, feeling relaxed and at home. The thought shocked her, but only for a moment.

Tuck brought the loot to the table. Removing his hat, he sailed it toward a wooden hat rack. It landed perfectly on a hook.

"Wow. I'm impressed. You're so talented."

He popped off the top of a plastic milk container. "Sometimes I make it and sometimes I don't," he said, pouring two glasses of milk. "It doesn't take talent, just luck."

Opening the bag of cookies, Grace asked, "Did you buy these especially for me?"

"Yep." His dark eyes twinkled. "I sure did, ma'am. My Ma taught me good manners and to always feed a lady."

She giggled as she twisted off the top of an Oreo. The sound was scintillating to Tuck's ears. He'd never heard her laugh so carefree, so young at heart. Her tongue darted out to lick the sweet filling and he watched, captivated. If anyone had told him a month ago that Grace Whitten would be sitting in his kitchen eating cookies and milk and looking sexier than he'd ever seen her, he would've asked what they were drinking.

"It's very quiet out here. No traffic noises," she commented, dunking a cookie.

He dunked a cookie and took a bite. "Sometimes I'll have a kid who has a real bad attitude, hates cops and life in general. I bring him out here and something about the outdoors, the peace and the serenity gets to him. It calms him down enough to see that I'm not a bad person."

"Do you mentor a lot of boys?"

"I have Micah Somers, Pablo Martinez and Dillon. Micah's twelve and lives with his mother's mother. His dad beat his mom to death in front of him. He's filled with a lot of resentment and sadness, rightly so. But he's into sports and he's really good at it, especially baseball. We go to a lot of sporting events. His grandmother worries about him so she likes to have a lawman around to keep him on the straight and narrow." He took a swallow of milk.

"Pablo's fourteen and also lives with his grandparents. His mother is in a Huntsville prison for killing his dad and his dad's girlfriend. Pablo had a lot of anger and he just wanted to hurt somebody. I got him involved in wrestling and he's now on a team in school. I just offer guidance, encouragement and steer him in the right direction."

He ran his thumb over the rim of his glass. "I told the supervisor of Big Brothers that I wouldn't be taking on any more boys because I was planning to adopt Brady. Since that's fallen through, I guess I need to call her back."

"Could we talk about that?"

His eyes met hers. "What about it?"

She took a deep breath. "Do you blame me for losing Brady?"

He shifted uneasily, bringing those raw emotions to

the surface and admitting the truth to himself. "You had nothing to do with my losing Brady. I have a high-risk job and I'm single. That's why I lost Brady." He meant every word. At first, he'd been upset with her, but something about sitting on the floor in the hospital eating Oreo cookies enabled him to see Grace in a new way, as a woman who cared.

Grace moved restlessly in her chair, feeling a release that was hard to describe. "Have you ever thought of getting married?" The words slipped out of their own volition and she couldn't snatch them back.

"A couple of times," he answered, to her surprise.

"What happened?" She nibbled on a cookie, waiting with bated breath.

Tuck stared at the milk carton. "Our goals in life were different. The moment I mentioned taking in foster kids, the relationships changed."

"So you decided to go it alone?"

"Yeah, but that's not working too well." He swallowed back the rest of his milk.

She sat up straighter and dived into treacherous waters. "Do you think you have this need to help children because you feel your parents would want you to? I know you love doing it," she added hastily. "But I have to wonder why you'd give up having a life, having your own kids, to do so."

She braced herself for a sharp retort, but he didn't say anything for a moment, then he shook his head. "I don't know, Grace. All I know is that I have to do it." His eyes darkened. "I guess you had to have lived in this house and witnessed all the kids who came through here needing shelter, needing someone to care."

"Have you ever thought of having kids of your own?" She was pressing her luck now, but he didn't seem upset.

"Sure, when I was younger." He picked up the milk container and carried it to the refrigerator. "And if I'm honest I'd have to admit that when I look at Jesse, I wonder how it would feel to look into the face of my own child. That's a selfish male reaction. I know it would be the same as looking at Brady or Dillon."

She carried the rest of the cookies to him. "Do you know that you're a wonderful man?"

Putting the cookies in the pantry, he asked, "Care to back up those words, ma'am?"

She lifted an eyebrow. "How?"

"Dancing." He grabbed her hand and pulled her into the den. The big-screen TV and stereo system were in a wall unit. Tuck poked buttons and a beautiful slow waltz wafted around the room. He moved the area rug back, flipped off the light and darkness surrounded her. The light from the kitchen streamed through, but otherwise they were enclosed in a world all their own.

In a corner, a grandfather clock chimed the midnight hour as the music played. "I think you have a thing about dancing," she murmured, almost afraid to speak in case it broke the magical spell around her.

"I do," he replied. "I love to dance." His arms slipped around her and she wrapped hers around his neck, pressing her body into his. They moved slowly to the beat of the music and Grace shivered.

"You're trembling," he whispered against her hair.

"I think I'm a little afraid of what's happening between us." She hadn't realized what she was feeling until she heard herself say the words.

"What's happening?"

"I don't know. Maybe that's what I'm afraid of."

They moved in unison to the music as close as two people could get with their clothes on. "Tell me what you're feeling," he said.

She took a deep breath. "I never want to leave your arms," she admitted honestly, laying her head on his chest.

"And I don't want you to," he replied just as honestly.

"So what do we do?" she asked, pressing closer, needing to feel every inch of him.

"Let me kiss you one more time."

She raised her head. "What…" The words were smothered beneath his lips. As he deepened the kiss, she gave herself up to him and the sensations he was awakening in her.

Finally, he broke the kiss and rested his face in the curve of her neck. "I say let's take a chance and explore these new feelings. Let's see where they'll take us. Are you game?"

It wasn't a declaration of love. She'd be lying to herself if she said she didn't want to hear those words. She wanted a relationship with Tuck, though, and this is where it started. It was her decision.

"I'm game."

He raised his head and ran his forefinger over her bottom lip. "Are you sure? You've been going through an emotional upheaval. We can…dance…later."

She stepped back and threaded her fingers through her hair. "That's not exactly the response I expected."

"What did you expect?"

"I expected you to rip off my clothes in eagerness."

"Grace, I'm forty-two and I've never ripped off a woman's clothes. I never needed to."

She winced. "Sorry. Can you tell I'm new at this?"

"I think you've been watching too much television. Making love is about mutual need and gratification. It's about respect, caring and…"

"Tuck, please make love to me."

He held out his hand. "Come here. Let's slow dance in the dark."

She drifted back into his arms, not sure if her feet were touching the floor.

"Relax, Grace. Relax," he breathed against her face, and she felt herself floating into a world of pure pleasure. The music played on, but all Grace heard was the wild beating of her heart in her ears, all she felt was his breath in her hair and his muscles imprinted against her body.

She trembled again and Tuck took her hand and led her to the bedroom. Moonlight streamed through the windows, the only light in the darkened room. He gave her a slow, lingering kiss and her knees almost buckled.

"After tonight, our relationship will change," he whispered, his words thick.

"I know," she said as she undid the buttons on his shirt.

Her hands splayed across his bared chest and desire filled him—along with disbelief. He wanted to sleep with the enemy. For years that's how he'd thought of her, although lately he saw a desirable woman he couldn't get out of his head—a woman soft, warm and pleasing. Things were happening too fast, though. He needed to stop. They had to talk.

Whenever he'd had doubts, he'd never had a problem stopping. Tonight he couldn't. He wanted her more than he'd ever wanted anyone. Her lips touched his skin and all rational thought left him.

He slipped her T-shirt over her head, threw it on the floor and unsnapped her bra. He touched her breasts, stroking, caressing as they removed the rest of their clothes. He struggled with his boots. It only took a few seconds, but it wasn't fast enough.

Skin on skin, they fell backward to the bed. She giggled and something akin to a laugh left his throat. He held her against his body, loving her soft, silky skin and his reaction to it. His body erupted with desire, need and unadulterated passion. He kissed her lips, her throat and her breasts, then trailed his lips down to the smoothness of her stomach. A moan escaped her as his tongue traveled farther.

Her hands eagerly sought the hardened muscles of his body. With fingers stroking and tongues tasting, they discovered new and exciting sensations.

When Tuck knew he had reached his limit, he reached for a condom in the nightstand and quickly sheathed himself. His hand shook with an eagerness he hadn't felt in years.

She reached for him and as his lips met hers, he slid between her legs and into a vortex of pleasure he only thought he knew about. Her body welcomed him with a warmth and need that erased all thoughts.

As his body exploded into a spasm of pleasure inside her, he heard her sigh raggedly, "Oh, Jeremiah."

Her body trembled and shuddered as they danced the dance as old as time.

There would never be a moment like this again—their first time.

He raised his head to look into her passion-filled eyes and caught his breath at the sheer beauty of her face. Kissing her swollen lips, he whispered, "You can call me Jeremiah any time you want."

She smiled and her eyes sparkled like emeralds.

Grace touched his face, her fingers feeling the stubble on his jaw. She floated somewhere between reality and fantasy. They were both damn good. She never knew sex could be like this. It was a lot more than sex, though. To her, it was love and she wanted to say the words to him, but she knew he wasn't ready.

She wondered if he ever would be.

She wouldn't think about that tonight. She would just enjoy this wonderful man and the way he made her feel.

Like a desirable woman.

Pulling her into his arms, he reached for the comforter and covered them. Snug in his embrace she understood what giving herself to one man totally and completely was about. It was wonderful, fabulous and nothing she'd ever do again would match it.

Now she knew why Caroline smiled all the time. Grace would be smiling now, too. She knew the secret and she savored this moment out of time. This moment that belonged to her and Tuck.

To her and Jeremiah.

GRACE WOKE UP to a wet kiss and bad breath. Opening one eye, she was relieved to see Sam licking her face.

"Get down, boy," Tuck said, raising up on one elbow. Sam hung his head and turned to jump off the bed.

Grace grabbed him, unable to withstand that pitiful face. "It's okay." She stroked him and scooted up in bed.

Tuck watched her. "Do you realize that a few weeks ago you couldn't stand for him to touch you?"

"I'm changing," she replied, and glanced at the rumpled bed, his warm eyes and tousled hair. For a second she forgot her train of thought as desire swept through her stomach. "I've had these rules and this structured behavior that I adhered to. I had to have discipline and order in my life so I could achieve the goals I had set for myself."

"Or goals your father had set for you?"

"Yes." She pushed her hair behind her ears. "I've finally realized that. I was very unhappy and I found that letting down my hair released a whole new me. I think she's always been there, but I've been afraid to let her out because…"

"You wanted your father's approval." He finished the sentence for her.

"Yes. The Mann situation was the last straw for me. I could see Dad didn't care about my opinions. I was just a figurehead like my colleagues had whispered behind my back."

His forefinger lifted her chin and she stared into the warmest eyes she'd ever seen. "It's more than that. Under your leadership the Whitten Firm has become a powerful, prestigious law firm."

"You think so?" Fishing for compliments wasn't her

thing, but it was pure feminine vanity that made her ask the question.

"I know so. Grace Whitten is the force behind the success—you're a lot more than just a figurehead."

"You wouldn't be saying that to have sex with me?" Teasing wasn't a part of her personality, either, but she had to tease or burst into tears at his praise—something she thought she would never hear from his lips. "Not that you have to do that," she added quickly. "All you have to do is touch me."

His eyes darkened. "And all you have to do is say my name."

"Tuck or Jere…" The word was smothered under his mouth. She threw her arms around his neck and the kiss went on and on. She wiggled farther down in the bed to feel his body against hers.

Sam yelped.

"Oh, Sam."

"He's fine," Tuck said, cupping her face and staring into her eyes. "What do you think? Did we do the right thing last night?"

"Yes. We're two consenting adults. What happens next is up to us."

He needed to hear her say that. In the cool light of day he was having second thoughts. Last night was magical and that wasn't a word he would normally use. However, magic was a favorite theme of the books Caroline sent to read to Jesse when he kept him. There was power in magic—the power to believe, to believe in love.

He'd shared more emotions with Grace than he had been willing to share with any other woman. At times he felt vulnerable that she could so easily make him forget his life's goals. All he wanted was to make love to her. Nothing else mattered.

This morning everything mattered. He didn't want a casual relationship with Grace. He wanted a life with her and that frightened him to death.

She was going through changes and she had her own life to sort out. They had jumped the gun, but he didn't regret that.

He stroked her arm. "Do you want to talk about it?"

She kissed his jaw, his ear and her lips trailed down his neck. "I'd rather not talk at all."

"Women always want to talk." He closed his eyes and savored her lips on his skin.

"Mmm." She straddled him and he looked up, her blond hair tickling his face. Her eyes were dreamy, laden with desire. He pulled her down to him and nothing else was said for some time.

Later they took a shower together and those three magical words were never spoken. She didn't seem to need them.

And he wondered why.

He had never needed to say them before, but he wanted to say them to her. So many things held him back. Their lives and goals were so different. Only time would tell if their feelings were strong enough to sustain a future.

In the meantime, he would believe in magic.

CHAPTER THIRTEEN

"Tuck, are you awake?" Eli's voice came from the kitchen. "Can I borrow some milk? I'll replace it as soon as I get into town."

"I may have to change my locks," Tuck said, reaching for an oversize towel as they stepped out of the shower. He wrapped it around Grace, taking his time. "Damn. I never thought I'd regret having Eli next door."

With a hand towel, he towel dried her hair. "I'd better go to the kitchen before he comes back here." His tongue licked water from her shoulder and she had trouble concentrating. "Do you mind if he knows about us?"

"Us" sounded almost as good as "I love you"—almost. She swallowed, leaning into him and loving the feel of his wet, naked body. "No, we're adults, not teenagers."

He grinned a gorgeous grin that she was beginning to associate with him. "I feel like a teenager." His lips caught hers in a slow, lingering kiss.

"Tuck."

He groaned. "I'll be right back." After one more, quick, tantalizing kiss, he did a fast dry-off and hurried into the bedroom. Grace unashamedly watched his long, lean legs and slightly rounded buttocks. He looked as good from the back side as he did from the front.

Slipping into jeans, he winked at her. "I'll get rid of him—fast."

She strolled into the bedroom and sank onto the bed, feeling warm enough to burst into flames. This was better than anything she'd ever imagined and she hoped they could make the feeling last outside this room.

Sam crawled into her lap and she stroked him. "You really like this, don't you?" Sam licked her hand and she resisted the urge to laugh. Here she sat in a rumpled bed holding a dog. Was there something wrong with that picture? Most people would say yes. That wasn't Grace Whitten.

But it was. The new Grace Whitten.

Glancing around, she took in the rustic country bedroom. The wooden engraved headboard was an antique and reached almost to the ceiling. The bed linens were a golden tan, as were the drapes. Simple, neutral colors. There was so much warmth in the room that she could actually feel it.

A photo of Tuck's adoptive parents stood on the nightstand. Picking it up, she looked into their faces. The man, tall and lean, had his cowboy hat at a slight angle, a gleam in his eyes. He looked strong, capable and loving. His arm was around the woman, who leaned against him, one hand on his chest. Grace stared into her blue eyes and all she saw was good—a good woman, wife and mother.

She got up, walking around the room barefoot on the hardwood floor, holding Sam. On the dresser was the photo of Sam and Dee that Caroline had taken. But the photos on the wall were the ones that held her attention.

Pictures of the Tuckers and their foster children covered almost every inch. Grace could almost pinpoint the before and after photos. The smiling kids had been touched with the Tuckers' love. The pictures of scowling kids were taken when they had just arrived.

She touched one photo of Tuck and Eli with two little boys. Tuck appeared to be about ten or eleven, the boys about four. Eli was older and stood in the back. Tuck held the boys' hands, smiling, as if to let them know they were welcomed.

Staring at the photos, she sensed all the sacrifice and love that had been given selflessly to kids in need. For the first time she fully understood Tuck's desire to give back a small portion of what all these kids had been given.

And her love for him grew that much more.

TUCK BUTTONED HIS JEANS as he hurried into the kitchen.

"Hey, Tuck," Eli said as he spotted him. "We're out of milk. Mind if I borrow some?"

"No. No problem." He ran a hand through his damp hair.

Eli opened the refrigerator. "What's Grace's car doing here?"

Tuck took a breath. Once he said the words he couldn't take them back. "She spent the night."

Eli grabbed the milk and closed the refrigerator. "Here? Oh, she's hiding from her parents and she didn't want to bother us?"

"Not that I'm aware of."

Eli frowned at him. "If her car's broken down, I can take a look at it."

"Her car is fine."

"Then…"

Grace sashayed into the room in one of his old T-shirts, her hair damp, hanging down her back, and Sam held tightly in her arms. "Good morning, Eli."

Eli looked from Grace to Tuck. "What's going on here?"

Tuck took his brother's arm and led him toward the back door. "If I have to tell you that, then you need to go home and get reacquainted with Caroline."

Grace burst out laughing as the door closed. "Did you see his face?"

"He's in shock," Tuck said, smiling.

They stared at each other and both sobered. "Are you okay?" he asked softly.

"I'm wonderful," she replied.

"Good." He kissed her cheek on the way to the refrigerator. "Hungry? I make a mean batch of scrambled eggs."

"Ravenous."

"You can put Sam down or he's going to forget he has legs."

"He's such a sweetie," she said, placing Sam on the floor.

Tuck opened a can of dog food and dumped it into a bowl. "Here." He took the bowl to the utility room and Sam scurried after him.

Grace placed her hands on her hips. "I'm devastated."

"Sam's fickle. Food is his number one love."

"But he's so sweet."

Tuck eyed her from the doorway. "That shirt looks

better on you than it does on me. I'm trying very hard not to get sidetracked." He looped his arm through hers. "Come. You can help me with breakfast."

Together, they made breakfast, laughing and joking. Grace sat at the table, munching on toast. "I saw all the photos in the bedroom."

"When I had the bedroom redone, I didn't have the heart to take them down."

"There's a lot of history in this house. I love that bed."

He took a swallow of coffee. "It belonged to Ma's grandmother."

She ran her finger over a name on the table. "Do you think your mother might have been one of the girls who stayed here as a child?"

"Pa was a Texas Ranger and he did a thorough investigation at the time. He said every lead was a dead end and I was a gift from God. I was meant to be their son."

"But you still wonder?"

He ran both hands through his hair. "The older I get, the more I think about it. Who was she? What had driven her to give me away? My parents were the best, but I'd still like to know those answers to fill the empty place in my heart and in my mind."

Tuck had never said those words to anyone, not even Eli. Yet it felt so easy to tell her.

She slipped onto his lap, wrapped her arms around his neck and rested her head on his shoulder. "You do realize it doesn't matter to anyone, especially me."

Their lips met in an explosive kiss and it took a moment for them to realize someone's cell phone was buzzing.

"It's not mine," Tuck said raggedly.

Grace ran her finger down his straight nose. "That means it can only be one person."

"Caroline," they said in unison and laughed, knowing Eli had had enough time to inform his wife where her sister was.

Grace hopped off his lap, grabbed her purse and fished out her phone.

"Grace, it's Dad." Suddenly her world came roaring back and she wanted to close the phone, breaking the connection. But she had to deal with her past before she could have a future.

"Yes, Dad, what is it?" she asked, sitting in a chair, her eyes on Tuck and his concerned face.

"Could you please meet your mother and me for lunch?"

"Why?"

"I would like to talk. No pressure."

"We did that yesterday."

"This is different. Things have changed and I'd rather talk to you in person than on the phone. Is one o'clock okay?"

She took a deep breath. "Okay." He gave her the name of the restaurant and she clicked off.

"Your father wants to see you?" Tuck asked, watching her.

"Yes."

"You seem upset."

"I don't understand what has changed in a day."

Tuck carried dishes to the sink. "He wants you back at the helm of the Whitten Law Firm."

She placed her phone on the table. "I know."

"So you have to decide what you want."

"I know." Her eyes caught his and she was as honest as she knew how to be. "I don't want to lose what's happening between us."

"You won't. Just be honest with yourself and with me. You've put a lot of time and effort into the success of the Whitten Firm. That'll be hard to walk away from, but you'll know in your heart if it's right. It won't change a thing between us."

She was reassured and buffered by his words. He respected her as a businesswoman and whatever decision she made wouldn't affect their relationship. That was good. They would build on the emotions they'd discovered last night and soon she'd be able to tell him that she loved him.

"I'd better go to my apartment and change." She hurried to the bedroom, made the bed and dressed, then stared at all the photos. Her hand touched the photo of Tuck, Eli and the two boys. She would love to have a child with that face and those big brown eyes. For the first time she realized just how much she wanted that. She also realized that she was the marrying kind. Was Tuck? Caroline had said that he wasn't, and he had admitted as much. But could love change his mind?

With a deep sigh, she walked out of the room.

TUCK WATCHED HER drive away with a lump in his throat. For a brief moment in time they had connected, but now he wasn't sure what was going to happen. They'd made no promises or vows and that's the way he had always liked his relationships with women. Grace was different, though. He could dance with her for the rest of his life.

He went back into the house and it seemed empty without her. He walked down the hall to his bedroom. On the top of his neatly made bed lay his T-shirt, folded perfectly—in typical Grace style. His heart constricted and he eased onto the bed staring at the wall of photos.

He didn't remember half the kids on the wall. Maybe he should have taken them down when Ma had passed on. But he hadn't. Now he wondered why. Why was he clinging to the past? He took a long breath. Maybe he'd kept them as a reminder, especially when someone like Grace touched him and filled his heart with dreams other than his own.

He buried his face in his hands, his elbows on his knees. Every time he made love to her he wanted to say those magical words, to believe they could have a life, a family. What was the right decision?

His parents, the kids on the wall and Grace battled inside him.

The man in him recognized that his motives were changing.

He'd always been very sure about his goals, even breaking up with two women who saw life differently than he had. How would Grace react if he asked her to share his dream? He didn't know, but he felt an ache in his chest at the thought of letting her go.

He stood. Maybe it was time to let go of the dream, or just postpone it. Could he do that? Could he do that for Grace?

Again, he wasn't sure, but he was willing to give it time. Time to make sense of everything he was feeling.

Time to find out what love was all about.

GRACE WALKED into the restaurant five minutes early, but her parents were already there. A maître d' showed her to their table and her parents stood.

Joanna hugged her. "Darling, you look wonderful. I love that suit."

"Thanks, Mom."

She hugged her father briefly and sat down.

Stephen stared at her. "I wish you wouldn't be so angry."

She placed her napkin in her lap. "I wish you wouldn't treat me like a child."

"Darling, please listen," Joanna begged, and Grace relaxed at the entreaty in her mother's voice.

"I don't understand what's happened since yesterday. My decision is still the same."

"A lot has changed," Stephen said. "I…" He was interrupted by a waiter. "We've already ordered. What would you like?" Her father looked at her.

She handed the waiter the menu. "I had a late breakfast. I'll just have a house salad and tea please."

The waiter nodded and walked away.

"Your mother and I had a long talk last night." By his tone, Grace suspected the discussion wasn't to his liking. "We've decided we don't need Cavanaugh's money. We trust the voters." Grace knew that was the last thing he wanted to do, but evidently her mother's opinion had won out. "If I win, I'll retire after another term. If I lose,

I'll retire sooner. Your mother and I plan to become more involved in our girls' and grandson's lives."

She folded her hands in her lap. "So you're not hiring Mann?"

He moved restlessly. "That wasn't ever my decision." He coughed. "I'm sorry I sprang Mann on you like that. I was desperate and afraid of losing everything I'd worked for. Desperate men do desperate acts."

"Thank you, Dad. I appreciate the apology."

The waiter brought the food and the conversation stopped. She noticed her father was eating grilled salmon where normally he would order steak. Since his heart attack, Joanna was on him constantly about his diet. Seems her mother was winning the game these days.

As she poured dressing over her salad, Grace wondered what this meeting was really about. Was it just to apologize or did her father have something else up his sleeve?

They talked about family and Joanna gushed on about Jesse. Finally, Stephen wiped his mouth and laid his napkin on the table.

"I apologize for interfering in the firm. I was so out of line and I really realized that when your mother reminded me that Mann would be working with you, near you. I suddenly had a clearer picture of the situation. My career is not worth one hair on your head being harmed."

"Thank you, Dad." Tears welled in her eyes at this revelation.

"You've done an astounding job and I hope you'll reconsider and come back to *your* law firm, because it is yours and not mine anymore. Sometimes I tend to forget that."

Yesterday she would have jumped at this sincere apology, but today was different. She'd spent the night in the arms of a man she loved and she was unsure if she wanted to spend the rest of her life in a job that didn't make her happy. She didn't need to prove anything to her father anymore. She didn't need his approval.

Grace was smart enough to know she still had stars in her eyes, so she knew it was best to take it slow—to make the right decision for her. She'd devoted ten years of her life to the firm, building it, promoting it and making it the best. Maybe she wasn't ready to walk away. People depended on her.

She dabbed at her mouth and clutched her napkin in her lap. "I do have some conditions."

"Conditions!" Stephen's eyebrows jerked up in disapproval. Normally she would instantly backtrack, anything to remove that look from her dad's face. Today she stared straight back at him, unrelenting and unflinching.

"What are they, darling?" Joanna asked, very smoothly.

Grace held up one finger. "Number one—we're not hiring Mann. I think we're clear on that now. Number two—the day care stays. Number three—you will stay out of the firm completely and not use it for political gain. Number four—do not call Byron behind my back. Number five—I will not be spending fourteen hours a day at the office."

"That's your decision, but you love that firm and you love being a lawyer. It's been your dream since you were a little girl."

"That's just it. I'm not a little girl anymore. I'm a

woman and I've had very little time to explore that part of my nature."

"Of course, darling, we understand." Her mother touched her arm. "And you don't have to explain this to your father or me."

"I just want you to be happy," Stephen said.

Grace stood. "Thank you."

Joanna jumped up and tucked Grace's hair behind her ear, just as she had when Grace was a child. "I'm so proud of you," she said. "Both you and Caroline. You're strong, independent women."

"Sometimes a little too strong." Stephen spoke his two cents.

"But, darling—" Joanna kissed his cheek "—that's the way you wanted them to be." She dropped her voice to a deeper tone. "Strong enough to make it in a man's world."

"That's not funny, Jo."

"No it isn't, so pay the bill and let's go see our grandson. I told Caroline we'd come by for a visit before we left town."

Stephen fished his wallet out of his pocket and laid his credit card on the table. The waiter immediately whisked it away. Stephen pushed back his chair.

As he stood, he held out his hand. "Congratulations on opening your old man's eyes."

She shook his hand, then remembered what Tuck said about families hugging. On impulse, she hugged him. "I wasn't trying to be difficult."

He squeezed her tight. "I seem to remember Caroline saying that once."

"Yes." She drew back. "I think we're a lot like you."

He nodded. "I really want my girls to be happy."

"Then stop interfering in our lives."

"That's hard when you love someone."

Joanna linked her arm through her husband's. "But he's going to try very, very hard."

Grace kissed them goodbye and walked out into the bright April day. The sun warmed her skin and her mood. She was going back to work, but this time on her terms and in her own way. She didn't have to prove anything to anyone but herself. Then she would decide what she wanted to do for the rest of her life. She had a feeling she already knew.

All she could see were dark eyes calling her home. A home that had a table with names carved on it and a wall of photos that touched her heart.

CHAPTER FOURTEEN

TUCK SPENT THE DAY doing what he always did on Sundays—housework. He did the laundry, changed his bed and washed Sam's, then he vacuumed and made a list of things he needed from the grocery store. He put his work clothes in a bag for the cleaners and set it by the back door so he wouldn't forget it in the morning.

He hated every minute of the tedious, boring chores. It crossed his mind that if he had a wife she would help run the household. That wouldn't be bad. Suddenly he could envision Grace here and that was a startling revelation. He didn't push it away as he normally would. Maybe his mind-set was changing. Maybe Grace was changing his way of thinking. Glancing at his watch, he saw it was mid-afternoon and Grace hadn't returned.

Although, he hadn't asked her to, had he? He should have, but he didn't want to pressure her. She was feeling her way now and he recognized that. There'd probably never been two more mismatched people than the two of them. But they'd found each other. Grace carried a lot of responsibility with the Whitten Firm and he couldn't see her giving that up for good. And he would never ask her to.

He walked into the small bedroom he used for an

office. It used to be his and Eli's room until they moved upstairs. He was in the process of redoing it for Brady. His computer was now in his room and soon he'd have to put his office back together. Brady wasn't going to live here.

He sucked in a deep breath, went into his bedroom and sat at his computer. He was working on an embezzlement case and had all the evidence to turn over to the district attorney. A woman who had worked thirty years for a large company had steadily been depositing over a half million dollars into a bogus account.

The owner had finally become suspicious and talked with the district attorney, who asked the Texas Rangers to investigate. In the morning, Tuck would turn in his findings and probably by tomorrow evening the woman would be arrested. He hoped the theft was worth it because prison was not a place for a sixty-year-old woman. What made people do such crazy things?

He stood and flexed his shoulders, needing exercise. Grabbing his hat, he headed for the corral. He glanced at his watch again. Grace hadn't called or come back. He had expected her to. He'd really wanted her to.

GRACE DRESSED IN JEANS, sneakers and a mint-green blouse and headed for Tuck's. He hadn't asked her to come back, but last night they both had been feeling the same thing. There was no question in her mind that their feelings were real. She had to see him.

To tell him she was going back to work.

As she drove up she saw him on a horse, galloping toward the barn. Her heart skipped a beat. Dressed in jeans and a chambray shirt, his hat was pulled low over his eyes. She quickly got out of her car.

Sam barked at her feet. She picked him up, her eyes on Tuck.

He saw her and leaned down to open a gate. She set Sam on the ground and started to run. As she reached him, he removed his boot from the stirrup and held out his hand. Without a second thought or a single word, she put her sneaker in the stirrup and placed her hand in his.

With one pull, she was on back of the horse, her arms locked around his strong waist. Usually the smelly, sweaty horse would unnerve her, but today it didn't bother her. She was with Tuck and she'd never felt more safe or alive.

They galloped through a pasture then into a valley of spring grasses and steadily climbed a steep, rocky hill. Oak branches brushed against her, but she clung to Tuck, loving the strength of his back and the easy rhythm of the ride.

At the top of the hill, Tuck stopped the horse and they dismounted.

"Oh, my," she said, gazing at the valley below. She could see Tuck's house, Caroline and Eli's and miles of the Texas Hill Country. "This is spectacular."

"It's my favorite place," he said, and they sat side by side in the grass. "I came here a lot as a kid. I was king of the world and superhero all rolled into one."

She watched the excitement on his face. "You were happy as a kid."

He nodded. "There was a lot of sadness, too, because of the abused kids. But Ma and Pa had a way of making us feel safe and secure. They were incredible people."

She heard the love in his voice and she didn't have to ask if he loved them. It was evident in everything he said and did. He loved them so much he was willing to give up having a life of his own to continue what they had started.

"Look." He pointed. "Your parents are getting into their limo."

"I can almost see the relief on Eli's face," she said. "Caroline's, too."

They watched the car pull out of the drive. "How did the meeting go?" Tuck asked.

She told him everything that had been said.

"So you're going back to Whitten's?"

"Yes." She plucked a blade of grass and twisted it around her finger. "I started a lot of things I have to see to fruition, especially the day care. But my time is my own and the office will not be my whole life, as it has been in the past."

"I didn't know if you were coming back here or not."

She lifted an eyebrow. "You didn't ask me."

"I didn't want to put any more pressure on you in case…"

She touched his lower lip. "In case I decided last night was a mistake."

"Something like that." His tongue licked her finger.

Her lower abdomen tightened in uncontrollable need. "Kiss me and let's see."

He bent his head and caught her lips in a mind-blowing kiss. Her hands found their way into his hair, knocking off his hat. Groaning, he pressed her down into the grass and nothing was said for a while.

Kissing her cheek, her neck, her collarbone, he breathed, "We have to stop. I don't have a condom."

She knew he would never risk an unwanted pregnancy. That wasn't part of his plans, nor hers. But she felt a moment of disappointment that he was so in control. She recognized the insane feeling as a purely female reaction.

He rolled to his back, staring up at the dimming sky. Dark clouds were chasing away the sun as it slowly sank in the western sky. She rested her head on his chest and they lay in the peace and the quiet of a lazy spring afternoon.

"What did you do while I was gone?" she asked, making circles on his shirt with her forefinger.

"Housework." He made a face.

"Poor baby."

"And a lot of thinking."

"Really?" She raised her head. "Guys actually do that?"

He tugged her hair in retaliation. "Yes, guys are capable of some deep thinking. Or, at least, I am."

"What were you thinking about?"

He sat up. "My life. Showing you the table and looking at the wall of photos made me realize that I'm clinging to the past. I've changed nothing in the house but the master bedroom. Everything else is the same as when Ma and Pa were alive. I'm living in the past." As he said the words, he knew they were true.

He drew up his knees. "You asked if I felt the need to take in children because it was something Ma and Pa wanted me to do. I guess that's true. I don't want anyone to ever forget the sacrifices they made, especially me. So I keep the legacy alive but…"

She linked her fingers with his and he gripped them tightly. "But what?"

"It's their legacy, not mine." He took a deep breath, hardly believing he was saying the words out loud, hardly believing that he was allowing himself to say them. But with Grace it was so easy. "I'm living their life. It's time I started living my own. I know in my heart that's what they would want."

"What do you plan to do?"

"I'm going to start refurbishing the farmhouse. I need to make it mine—my home, not my childhood home."

"Have you changed your mind about taking in children?"

"I'm not sure. All I know is that I'm looking at life a little differently."

He gazed into her eyes and saw the hope. He knew they had to talk about their relationship. "With everything in me I want to ask you to be a part of my life, but we both know that's premature. I'm going through a life-changing decision and I'm not sure it's the right one. Only time will tell. And that's what we need—time. I suggest we take one day at a time being honest and true to each other and see what happens. What do you think?"

She smiled. "I think you'd better kiss me."

"Yes, ma'am, my pleasure." He took her lips gently, tenderly, binding them together in a way no one would understand but them.

Raindrops peppered their bare heads. "Damn." Tuck jumped to his feet and pulled her up, grabbed his hat and plopped it onto her head, then they sprinted for the horse. Slowly they made their way down the hill, the rain steadily growing heavier. When they reached the valley, Tuck kneed the horse and they flew across a coastal pasture. Grace buried her face against him, trying to hold on to his hat but the wind whipped it from her fingers.

"Tuck."

"Don't worry about it."

The horse splashed through puddles as they made a beeline straight for the barn. As hard as they tried, they couldn't outrun the rain. By the time they reached the barn, they were both soaking wet.

Tuck quickly unsaddled the horse and let him loose in the corral, then they made a dash for the house, laughing like kids. They stood in the utility room, their hair plastered to their scalps as water dripped onto the floor. Sam barked at them but they didn't pay him any attention.

Tuck grabbed a towel off the dryer and began to dry their clothes, but they were too wet. "We have to get out of these wet things."

She shivered. "I'm freezing."

"Quick, start stripping."

Within seconds their wet things were in a heap and they were naked. Tuck vigorously rubbed her hair then her body. One stroke led to sensuous movements that had nothing to do with drying. He pulled her against his damp body and kissed her deeply. With groans, moans, turns and twists they made it to the den, then down the hall and into the bedroom.

Tuck wanted to take it slow, but he forgot slow the moment he saw her naked body. Through heated kisses, sensuous caresses and mind-tripping emotions they made love, then cuddled together in the bed at six o'clock in the evening.

GRACE RAN HER FINGERS though his hair, loving the feel and texture of it. The threads of gray at his temples made him look that much more handsome.

"If you keep doing that, we'll never leave this bed," he said in a drowsy tone.

"That's okay with me." She trailed her finger down his straight nose to his full lower lip. She loved touching him and she loved everything about him. They hadn't said the magic words and surprisingly she was okay with that. They both had decisions and choices to make—life-changing decisions. Time would tell if their lives were meant to be together. In the meantime they would get to know each other and the future would unfold the way it was meant to be.

She only hoped she had the strength to handle whatever that was.

"Are you hungry?" he asked.

"Starving."

He crawled out of bed and handed her a T-shirt then slipped on a terry cloth robe. "I make a mean grilled cheese. C'mon." Taking her hand they walked into the den.

Sam met them, whining at Grace's feet.

"Poor baby," Grace cooed, picking him up. "We've been neglecting him."

"He's a con artist," Tuck remarked, continuing on to the kitchen. As he got cheese out of the refrigerator, he watched Grace cuddling Sam. Sam never did that with him. Grace was good with dogs and babies. Jesse's eyes lit up whenever he saw her. He wondered if she ever thought about having children of her own. All women did, didn't they?

He'd never thought Grace had motherly instincts, but his whole perception of Grace had changed—drastically. She'd make a great mother.

Grace put their clothes in the washing machine and then cut up apples to go with the sandwiches. They sat in comfortable silence, eating.

"This grilled cheese is delicious," she said, licking cheese from her fingers.

"It's Ma's secret recipe. Every kid who came here loved them."

"I can see why."

He took a bite of a quartered apple. "Have you ever thought of having kids?"

"Sure. All women do. But I firmly believe in marriage first, then baby. I'm still looking for my Prince Charming or—" she made quotes with her fingers "—'Mr. Right.' I'm told I'm pushy and bossy and men don't go for that type of woman."

"They just don't know you."

Her eyes opened wide. "You think so?"

"I know so."

She nibbled on an apple. "So are you a candidate for my Prince Charming?"

"Definitely." He grinned. "We're alike in so many ways. I never realized that before."

"How are we alike?"

"We both have very strong father figures in our lives and their approval means a lot to us."

"Yes. And it's time we learned to deal with the feelings about our fathers."

"We've made a start."

"How else are we alike?" she asked.

"Neatness—yours is over the top, but lately you have it under control."

She rolled her eyes. "Sometimes. Right now I want to wipe the table and spray bleach on the floor where Sam licked the crumbs from my sandwich, then mop the whole floor. It's just an urge, though. It used to be important to me to be organized and neat. It meant I was in control. But I don't need to be in control every minute, every day of my life. I kind of like running and laughing in the rain and not caring about the mess on the floor. It makes me feel more human, more feminine."

He watched her animated face and felt a catch in his throat. Her hair was in disarray around her face, her eyes sparkled and her expression was dreamy. Could she be more beautiful? He didn't think so.

"So how are we different?" she asked.

He thought about it for a minute. "Let me put it this way. You're like an expensive imported bottle of champagne. Me, I'm a domestic beer made in Texas."

Smiling, she slid onto his lap and wrapped her arms around his neck. "That doesn't mean we can't find some common ground."

He kissed her gently. "I think we already have."

She rested her head in the crook of his shoulder. They sat that way for a while.

"Tomorrow I have to turn in some evidence on a case then I'm off the rest of the week. Caleb's taking over for me. We planned this in case I got custody of Brady. And I'll take over for him when their baby comes. When I leave the courthouse, I'm going to see an architect about remodeling the house. I'd like to add on, maybe make the master bedroom and bath larger, add a bathroom upstairs and maybe a game room with a pool table."

"You've really thought about this."

"I have to start living my own life."

"I know what you mean." Her voice sounded melancholy.

"Another way we're alike," he murmured against her face and took a moment to breathe in her scent. "Now's a good time to start," he added, getting to his feet and leading her into the bedroom.

For a moment he stared at the pictures on the wall then went into the other bedroom for a plastic storage box. He'd bought several to store things away so Brady could have the room. Now he had another use for the box.

He began to take the pictures down and place them in the container.

"No." Grace grabbed a photo. "You have to save the ones with you in them."

"Grace…"

"Humor me."

"There are tons of other photos in albums."

"Okay." She handed them back, all but one. "I like this one and I think you need to keep it."

He glanced at the photo of him and Eli with the Cochran boys. "Okay."

She kissed his cheek. "Thanks. What are you going to do with the rest of the photos?"

"Store them for now. Tomorrow I'll start to clean out the attic. Ma's and Pa's clothes are up there along with everything they've ever owned. I need to sort through it. And Eli's going to help. We've put this off long enough."

She rubbed his arm. "After work, I'll help, too."

"I'd like that."

That night he went to sleep with Grace in his arms. He didn't feel guilty or disloyal. He felt an incredible peace that he was getting on with his life.

All it took was one woman to open his eyes.

All it took was Grace.

CHAPTER FIFTEEN

THE NEXT MORNING Grace slipped from the bed, careful not to wake Tuck. But he was a light sleeper. The moment she moved, he woke up. He scooted up against the headboard.

"Are you leaving?"

"Yes." She slipped into jeans. "I want to be in the office by eight. The day care opens today and I want to make sure everything goes smoothly. I also need to have a meeting with the partners to explain my absence."

She fastened her bra, pulled a wrinkled T-shirt over her head and leaned over, whispering, "See you tonight."

"Grace."

She stopped in the doorway and looked back. Morning light was creeping into the room, bathing him in a golden light, a fairy-tale kind of light. At that moment she knew Jeremiah Tucker was her Prince Charming.

"Aren't you going to kiss me goodbye?"

She shook her head. "If I kiss you, I won't leave and I have to go to work. I'll make up for it tonight."

He winked. "You have a deal. Good luck."

Grace found her purse in the kitchen, took a moment to pet Sam and hurried to her car.

Within the hour she was in her apartment, showered

and dressed in a beige power suit with a brown silk blouse. She chose a pair of Manolo Blahnik shoes, slipped her feet inside and waited for the feeling.

Nothing happened.

A smile split her face. She'd finally found something better than shoes—Tuck's love. She twirled around and said the words aloud, "I love you, Tuck." Then she wrapped her arms around her waist and enjoyed that all-encompassing feeling.

Now she had to make her job fit back into her life. Her time would be split, but she could make it work.

She had to.

GRACE WAS IN THE DAY CARE at eight. Doris Hayden was already checking in some kids. She looked up, saw Grace and immediately came to her side.

"Ms. Whitten, I'm so glad to see you." There was obvious relief on her face and in her voice. Of medium height with graying dark hair, Doris had been a nurse for twenty years and had a spotless record. On the first interview, Grace knew she was going to hire her. Doris had worked on the pediatric ward of a large hospital and loved children, but she wanted her nights and weekends free.

"How are things going?"

"Wonderful. We have fourteen children registered. If this keeps up, we'll need more help."

"I was thinking we might need some extra people anyway. I want every child to receive the best care."

"Yes, ma'am. I must say the decorators did a wonderful job."

The main room was open and appealing, the walls a soft yellow and a pastel green. Balloons, a train and cartoon characters were hand painted on them. Furniture of red, green, blue and yellow made the room even brighter. A babies' room was to the left and through the double doors at the back was a room with a large TV screen for watching movies or cartoons. There was, of course, a kitchen.

"Yes, they did," Grace responded.

"Ms. Whitten." Grace turned to see Nina standing behind her with her two-year-old daughter. "Am I glad to see you."

"We'll talk upstairs," she said, not wanting to get into a conversation about her absence in front of everyone. Grace shook hands with several employees and made her way to her office.

Nina was a few seconds behind her. Grace took a deep breath and resumed her role as managing partner. "I'd like to see Byron in thirty minutes. Set up a meeting at ten for the partners—all partners, no excuses. I expect everyone to be there."

"Yes, ma'am." Nina scribbled on her pad, and then looked up. "I'm glad you're back."

"Thank you."

After Nina left, Grace wanted to call Tuck, just to hear his voice, but she would see him later. She would be content with that.

Opening a drawer, she pulled out a phone book and looked up the hospital where Brady was. She made an appointment to see the CEO and the hospital administrator.

Then she walked to Byron's office. His secretary

jumped to her feet. "Oh, Ms. Whitten, Mr. Coffey was coming to your office in a few minutes. I'll let him know you're here."

"Since I'm early, I'll let him know I'm here." She opened the door and stepped inside. She wanted the upper hand with Byron and surprise was a good tactic.

Byron was on the phone and he immediately hung up. Standing, he said, "Grace, did my secretary get the time wrong?"

"No, Byron, I finished with my other appointments early." She looked directly at him. "I'm sure you've already talked to my father."

He frowned. "The last conversation we had he said we weren't hiring Mann and that he'd be in touch, but I haven't heard from him."

Grace thought it was time to bring everything out into the open. "I want to get a few things straight." She stepped farther into the room, her eyes holding his. "I'm not the ditzy blonde you think I am."

"Grace…"

She held up a hand. "Let me talk, please.

"I'm well aware that when my father ran for judge and won, he retained fifty-one percent of this law firm in a blind trust for his daughters—until the time one of us was willing to take over as managing partner. You drew up the blind trust and my father paid you very nicely to keep his secret. The secret being that he still had control of every major decision made by this law firm."

"It wasn't…"

"It was just like that. And neither you nor my father

thought I had—" she narrowed her eyes in thought "—what do you guys say? You didn't think I had the balls to run this company."

"That's crude."

"Yes, it is, and it's even cruder that you and my father thought I would never notice the manipulation and under-the-table tactics."

He stiffened visibly. "Stephen and I have known each other since law school, I've always been very loyal to him, even when he ran for Congress."

"But you resented his wish to have one of his daughters running the firm."

He stiffened even more. "I've been loyal to you, too, Grace."

"Yes, you have, and I appreciate that and I also appreciate your help in adjusting to the role as managing partner."

"You're a natural."

"Thank you. And I wanted to let you know that I won't be spending as much time in the office. I will have a personal life, too."

"I see."

"I make all major decisions concerning this law firm and you will not report anything that goes on in this firm to my father. Are we clear on that?"

"Yes. We're very clear."

She felt she didn't need to say any more. She'd made her point.

The board meeting went off without a hitch, and then she dealt with two lawyers who had complaints. Grace couldn't wait to get away. She could almost feel that strict, stern exterior lifting from her as she made her way to the hospital.

The administrator was more than glad to accept her money for comfortable chairs for the pediatric ward. He warned her there wasn't a lot of room and they'd do the best they could. Grace could see that just donating the money was no guarantee it would be spent how she wanted it.

After some more negotiating, he agreed to let her buy the chairs and have them delivered. Then she made a quick stop at a furniture store and bought three leather recliners. She talked the manager into delivering them that day. Tonight Barbara Wilcott would be able to rest comfortably.

On impulse, she went back to the hospital to see how Lisa, Keith and Brady were doing. On the way she picked up food for Barbara. Everything was quiet on the ward. Barbara was flipping through a magazine and Grace was surprised to see Brady in his bed. Keith and Lisa weren't there.

"Where are the Templetons?" she asked Barbara.

"Lisa was really sick and Keith took her home." Barbara laid down her magazine. "She's probably coming down with something."

"How's Brady doing?"

"Better, but he keeps watching the door. I think he's looking for Ranger Tucker. That's my personal opinion."

Grace thought she was probably right. Even at Brady's age, he knew Tuck cared about him.

"How's your little girl?"

"No change."

"I'm sorry."

"My husband and I are still praying and hoping."

"Have you eaten today?"

Barbara nodded. "Yes. I've had a snack this morning. I don't need much."

Grace held up a bag. "How would you like a hamburger, fries and chocolate malt?"

"You're one of a kind." Barbara smiled and took the bag without any protest.

"The good part is you can eat it in here before anyone sees you."

"Thank you, Grace."

As Barbara ate, Grace walked over to Brady. He was walking around his bed, eyeing her warily.

"Hi, Brady." She smiled at him.

He touched one eye.

She clapped her hands. "Yes. I see those long eyelashes."

Loud noises came from the corridor and Grace knew the chairs were being delivered. She had wanted to be gone before that happened.

"Goodbye, Brady." She waved and walked out into the hall.

Jennifer was arguing with the deliveryman.

"No one told me about any chairs," Jennifer was saying. "We don't have luxuries like that here. You must have the wrong hospital."

"Lady, I'm not stupid," the man snarled. "I can read a delivery order."

"I'll have to call the administrator."

"Go ahead."

Grace poked the elevator button, hoping to be gone before Jennifer spotted her. Her luck didn't hold.

"Ms. Whitten," Jennifer called.

Grace waved and stepped onto the elevator. She wasn't waiting around for Jennifer to ask her if she knew anything about the chairs.

She didn't want to lie.

TUCK SPENT MOST of the morning at the district attorney's office going over details of the embezzlement case, then he stopped in to see a friend from college, an architect. Tuck told Joel what he wanted and Joel made plans to come look at the house. After that, he'd draw up plans for Tuck's approval.

From there Tuck went by Caleb's office to let him know that he'd only be taking a week off instead of the month they'd planned. Caleb said that was okay and wanted to make sure Tuck could handle Caleb's office when the baby came.

Tuck razzed him about being nervous, but he assured Caleb he would be there for him. The McCains were big on togetherness and Tuck found he was, too.

He returned home to an empty house. Sam barked at him and Dee curled around his leg, as usual. Although nothing really had changed in the household, something seemed different. The scent of lilac lingered in the room and reminded him Grace wasn't here. Suddenly she was becoming the center of his world. Glancing at his watch, he wondered how much longer she would be.

To keep from thinking, he would start cleaning out the attic. The stairs to the second floor went up from the den. The banister was made of cedar and he probably wouldn't change that. Two bedrooms, both small, occupied the floor. He and Eli shared one for a lot of years. Tuck would like to make the rooms bigger and put in a bathroom.

When he pulled the cord in the ceiling of the small hallway, the attic ladder slid down and he began to climb. The sight took his breath away. Junk, clutter, dust and cobwebs covered the place. He coughed a couple of times to clear his lungs.

The place was a mess. He hadn't been up here since Ma had died and he stored away some of her things. He picked up a lava lamp Ma had bought in Vegas when they had gone on one of their rare trips. Pa hated the lamp and Tuck couldn't say he was all that crazy about it. So why was he keeping it? For the memories? He was living in the past and it was time to savor those memories and then let them go.

He could do that now.

"Tuck, where are you? I'm back." When he heard Grace's voice, he shimmied down the ladder in half the time it took to go up it.

"I'm coming," he shouted. Taking the stairs two at a time he saw her in the kitchen, holding Sam with Dee curled around her leg.

"Look," she said, staring down at Dee. "She's finally made friends with me."

He cupped her face. "You're just too hard to resist." He kissed her soft lips and Sam yelped. They laughed and Grace set Sam on the floor. Tuck sat down, pulling her into his lap. "How was your day?"

"Pretty good. Byron knows where I stand." She played with the hair curling at his neck and lazy, languid feelings filled him. "I stopped by the hospital."

"Why?" He was immediately alert. "Is something wrong?"

"Yes. Barbara Wilcott has no place to sleep."

He blinked. "What?"

"I had a meeting with the CEO and the administrator of the hospital and they were very excited I wanted to donate some money. They had all sorts of causes that needed it, but I said I wanted to buy recliners for the pediatric ward. They tried to appease me with other, more urgent needs and I quickly told them what my bottom line was. Since I'm rather pushy, they eventually saw it my way. Tonight Barbara will be able to stretch out with a hand on her child and go to sleep in some measure of comfort." She paused. "This is just between you and me. I don't want Barbara or anyone else to know I purchased the chairs."

Tuck stared at her and thought, *She's the one. Grace is the woman for me.* So many times he'd wished he could help Barbara, but he didn't know what to do for her. Grace, on the other hand, went out of her way to see that something was done and at her own expense.

"You're wonderful," he murmured, and tucked her hair behind her ear. He noticed that worried look in her eyes. "What's wrong?"

"I stopped in to check on Brady and the Templetons, but Barbara said that Lisa had become ill and Keith had taken her home. Brady was all alone. I just hope everything's okay."

This news sobered him and he reached for the phone on the wall to call Opal.

"Hey, Opal, how are you doing?"

"Ranger Tucker, I'm doing just fine."

"How's Brady?"

"So that's the reason for the call."

"I heard Lisa Templeton is ill."

"Twenty-four-hour bug, nothing else. She'll be back at the hospital in the morning."

"Good. I was just checking."

"You have a hard time letting go, don't you, Ranger Tucker?"

"Yes, ma'am, but I'm getting better."

"Good for you. Take care now."

"You bet."

Tuck relayed the conversation to Grace.

"Good." She seemed relieved. "What have you been doing all day?"

He told her about his day. "I just had a look at the attic and it's a nightmare."

"I'm here to help." She kissed the tip of his nose.

"There are cobwebs up there." He knew her fear of spiders and it didn't take long to see that fear in her eyes.

"Oh."

"Don't worry. I'll slay your spiders."

"Ah, my hero."

He took her lips in a long, deep kiss.

Soon they'd have to make decisions about the future—their future. Now, he knew they had one.

EACH DAY TUCK CONTINUED his work, cleaning out the attic. Grace helped when she arrived after a full day at the office. Each day, her workday was getting longer and longer. This was minor, he told himself. Soon he'd be back at work, too.

He had a pile of things for Eli to go through and he was after him to get it done. He carried all the clothes and old furniture to a homeless shelter. Old papers and bank records he burned behind the house in a barrel. The attic was beginning to look bare.

The highlight of Tuck's day was waiting for the sound of Grace's car in his driveway. He couldn't help but wonder if this was a pattern for their relationship. He knew she was having problems at work and he was trying very hard to be understanding. The plumbing had burst in the day care and it had been a big mess, and then two lawyers were at odds over a trial and Grace sat in on the proceeding to ensure harmony and a fair trial for their client. She carried an enormous load, and Tuck knew her loyalty and dedication to the firm.

But he missed her.

That night they were keeping Jesse. Caroline had called saying they had plans to go out with Caleb and Josie but didn't have anywhere to leave Jesse. Her sitters were engaged in other activities. Grace laughed and said to bring him over. Her sitters were open for business.

Grace barely had time to kiss Tuck before Caroline and Eli arrived. "I'm sorry," she whispered. "We never have enough time."

"I know. We'll have to talk about that."

Before she could respond, Eli carted in Jesse's Pack

'n Play. Caroline was holding Jesse and Grace grabbed him immediately, soaking up the sweet smell of the baby. She'd missed him.

"About time you two came up for air," Eli said. "And no hanky-panky stuff in front of my son."

Caroline slapped Eli's shoulder. "Will you stop it?"

"What?" Eli acted innocent.

"We should be home around ten," Caroline said, and kissed Jesse. "Bye, sweetie."

"Take your time," Tuck said. "We'll be here. And, Eli, you're not getting your son back until you agree to go through some of this stuff." Tuck glanced at the boxes stacked on the floor in a corner.

"Okay, okay. I'll come by first thing in the morning."

"I have your word."

"God, you're relentless." Eli sighed. "You have my word."

After they left, Tuck and Grace spent the evening playing with Jesse. Soon the baby grew drowsy and Grace gave him a bottle and put him in the Pack 'n Play for the night. Jesse went to sleep almost instantly.

She curled up in Tuck's arms in his recliner as they watched an old movie. She sensed the tension in him. "Are you upset with me?"

"Of course not. I just miss you."

She relaxed. "I'm thinking of hiring a personal assistant."

"Would that help?"

"I don't know, but I have to do something. I'm not happy being away from you, either."

"I go back to work on Monday and our time together will be shorter."

She raised up. "We have a problem, Jeremiah Tucker."

He smiled and her pulse raced. "Kiss me and let's see if we can't make it better."

She obliged, and it made everything better.

For now.

CHAPTER SIXTEEN

THE NEXT MORNING Grace hurried off to work while Tuck and Eli went through the remaining things.

"I don't know why you're insisting I go through this stuff," Eli complained.

"Because it belongs to both of us, so stop whining," Tuck told him.

"Okay." Eli sat on the edge of the den sofa, looking around at the boxes and strewn items. "It's a big mess in here. Where do we start?"

"Let's start with the lava lamp."

"You're kidding, right? I do not want that gaudy thing."

"Ma loved it."

"She saw beauty in everything."

Eli was right. Ma never saw the bad in anything or anyone. "Okay. I'll keep it." He pointed to a gun propped against the wall. "There's an L.C. Smith shotgun and this knife." He fished it out of a box. "Both were made in the twenties and have Pa's initials on them. Which do you want?"

"You choose."

"I'll take the gun."

"Good. I'll take the knife." Eli reached for it,

opening up the blades. "Look at the pearl inlay. This is a cool knife."

Tuck knew Eli would rather have the knife. That's why he chose the gun.

Tuck pointed to a box. "There are all your high school and college photos and trophies."

Eli frowned. "I don't want them."

"Caroline might. And Jesse might want to see them one day."

"Sometimes you're worse than an old woman, Tuck."

Tuck let that pass and squatted by a box. "Here are Ma's and Pa's old country albums." He sorted through them. "Some are signed by the artist—Ernest Tubbs, Porter Wagoner, Loretta Lynn, The Wilburn Brothers, The Louvin Brothers, The Carter Family and some I don't have a clue who they are. I think I'll keep them and the record player."

"Fine. I don't have any use for them."

Tuck reached for a small box. "This is Ma's and Pa's wedding rings."

"Those are yours. I already have a wedding ring."

Tuck sat in his chair, staring at the gold bands. "I might use these."

Eli stopped digging through a box and gaped at him. "What?"

"I might use these," he repeated.

"The man who said he was never getting married is thinking about marriage?"

"Yes," Tuck replied without hesitation.

"Wow. I thought I'd never see this day."

"Me, neither, but how many times have you told me that my day was coming?"

"Too many to remember." Eli scooted back on the sofa. "So you're giving up your plans to take in foster kids?"

Tuck closed the velvet box. "I'm not sure. Grace understands me more than any woman ever has. All I know is that my need to be with her is stronger than anything I've ever felt."

"How does Grace feel?"

"We haven't made a commitment to each other. We're taking it slow, finding each other, enjoying our time together."

"But soon you have to face reality."

"Yeah." Tuck nodded. "Soon we have to talk."

"And you're scared to death."

Tuck raised his head. "You could be right. I've never allowed a woman to change my way of thinking."

"Are you afraid she doesn't feel the same way?"

"No. I'm afraid of the obstacles standing in our way."

"Like what?" Eli asked.

"Like her job and her father."

"Grace has always been dominated by Stephen but lately she seems to be breaking free."

"She's changing, too."

"You two need to have a good, honest talk."

Tuck fingered the box. "Tonight I plan to do that. As long as we're honest with each other, we can make it work. I know we can."

"Do you realize this will make us brothers-in-law? And let me tell you something. You're getting the

Whittens fifty-fifty. There's no need for them to be camped out at my house all the time."

"But you have the grandson." Tuck laughed.

"You can change that, too."

Tuck held up a hand. "Don't rush things. I can only take so many changes at one time."

"It's good to see you happy," Eli said.

"It's been cathartic going through Ma's and Pa's belongings. I can't keep my life as a shrine to them. I finally can see that and I have peace about it. I'll probably never let go of the kid thing, though. Helping kids is just a part of me. Grace and I will work through it."

He returned the velvet box to the larger cardboard one and pulled out a humidor. "Remember this?"

"Damn, I'd forgotten about that thing. Is it locked? Pa always kept it locked." Eli scooted closer to Tuck.

"Yes, but Ma taped the key to the bottom when Pa died." Tuck flipped the dark walnut case over and found the key. Flipping it back, he unlocked it.

The pungent smell filled his nostrils and memories swirled around him. He and Eli were never allowed to open the box. Ma forbade Pa to smoke in the house or around the children. He would take the box to the porch and sometimes Tuck and Eli would slip out to watch Pa ready a cigar to smoke, unless Ma spotted them and made them come inside.

"There are cigars still inside," Eli said, and reached for one and sniffed it. "Man, that reminds me of Pa."

Tuck opened a drawer near the bottom. "The cigar cutter and lighter are here, too."

Eli stuck the cigar in his mouth and leaned back.

"This smells great. If I lit this thing, it would probably blow off my head. I'm not too sure about aged tobacco, but it doesn't smell tainted or anything."

"Pa loved his cigars, and wait—" he lifted the half-empty tray "—there's a full tray below this one."

Eli handed him the cigar. "Put this one back."

Tuck looked at it. "You've slobbered all over it."

"So? No one's ever going to smoke it."

"I guess you're right." Tuck slid the cigar in with the others and tried to put the tray back, but the humidor wouldn't close. "Something's wrong. I must have the trays in backward. Hold this one." Eli took the tray and Tuck lifted out the other. There was a piece of yellowing paper beneath the bottom tray.

"What's this?" Tuck asked, pulling it out.

"Who knows? Maybe something Pa didn't want Ma to see."

"Pa never kept secrets from Ma."

"Tuck, he was human. Sometimes you forget that. Open the letter and let's see what kind of secret Pa was keeping."

"Maybe we shouldn't," Tuck said. "It's been hidden all these years. Maybe we should just let it be." Tuck didn't know why he was hesitant, but he was.

"Give me that," Eli snapped. "It's probably an old receipt or a bond worth millions. Now wouldn't that be a kick in the pants."

Tuck held on to the paper, not letting Eli have it. Slowly he opened the old, yellowing, thin paper. There was a printed heading of an orphanage, Sisters of the Guadalupe. Tuck knew the place. He passed it many times on the outside of Austin. The letter was handwritten and still legible.

Goose bumps popped up on his skin in chilling intensity as he read. Anger slammed into his stomach. Eli gasped over his shoulder.

The letter read:

Dear Mr. Tucker,
The baby has been born and he will be left at 6:00 a.m. as we discussed. Please pick him up immediately as we would not like him in the elements any longer than necessary. The mother's only request is that he be called Jeremiah.
We, the sisters, know you will give this child a good home.
And, Mr. Tucker, remember you have promised before God to keep this secret forever.
May God bless you and your family.
Yours in Christ,
Sister Frances O'Rourke

The letter was dated the day Tuck was born.

Tuck and Eli were frozen in place. They couldn't move or speak. The only sound was the grandfather clock ticking as loud as a gunshot. Tuck tried to absorb what he'd read, but anger kept blocking his thinking.

He knew. He knew. Pa knew, kept ripping through his mind like bullets at a target.

Tuck jumped to his feet, the humidor tumbling to the floor. He waved the letter at Eli. "Pa knew who my mother was. He lied to me. Pa lied to me. He said he did a thorough investigation and there were no clues. He lied! He knew exactly where I came from and he never told me even after I was grown. How could he?"

Eli walked around the chair and faced him. "Calm down and let's think about this rationally."

"I'm not in a rational mood." He pushed past Eli. "I'm in a mood for some honest answers and I'm going to get them."

"Tuck." Eli grabbed his arm.

"Let me go," Tuck shouted.

"Not until you calm down."

Eli might be bigger and stronger, but Tuck was functioning on pure adrenaline. He jerked his arm away and Eli grabbed him again. Tuck shoved him and Eli went flying backward. Tuck made a dash for the back door.

As he swung open the door, Grace stood on the other side. He ran, unable to talk to her. Unable to talk to anyone.

"Tuck," Grace called, running after him.

He jerked open his car door and got in. Grace jumped into the passenger seat before he could back out.

"What's wrong?" She saw Eli standing at the back door and she was sure he was cursing. "Did you and Eli have a fight?"

He handed her a piece of paper he clutched in his hand. It took about five seconds before she fully understood the situation and she felt an incredible sadness for him. But she had other concerns first.

Tuck was driving fast and erratic.

"Pull over and let me drive."

Tuck didn't respond, just stared straight ahead at the country blacktop road. Luckily it was a farm-to-market road and there wasn't any traffic. Trees and ranches whizzed by.

"Tuck."

They turned a corner, swerved to miss a car and plowed through a bar ditch and came to a stop.

Grace let out a long breath, her hands gripping the dash. Glancing at Tuck, she saw him lean his forehead on the steering wheel. He was crying. Her heart twisted at the sight.

She leaned over and wrapped her arms around him. "Tuck, don't, please."

"Pa lied to me," he mumbled brokenly.

"I'm so sorry. Let's go back to the house and talk."

"No." He wiped at his eyes. "I have to go to the orphanage. I have to have some answers."

"Okay." She brushed away a tear. "I'll go with you, but slow down, please."

He backed out of the ditch and they headed for the main highway. She wished she could ease his pain, but all she could do was be there for him and offer him comfort when he needed it.

She was so glad she'd left work early to spend more time with Tuck. If she hadn't, he would have been gone with this terrible pain in his heart. Being with Tuck was suddenly the most important thing to her. Not her work. Not her family.

But Tuck.

She would always be here for him.

CHAPTER SEVENTEEN

THEY DIDN'T SPEAK as Tuck drove steadily toward the orphanage. He seemed to know where he was going and Grace didn't bother him with questions. He was lost somewhere in the past, somewhere within himself.

He turned off the highway and pulled up to an ancient gray stone building with a traditional bell tower. Huge live oaks shaded the courtyard and a religious statue surrounded by blooming flowers adorned the center. The orphanage was in the shape of a horseshoe, with a main building and a wing on each side. The yard was neatly maintained, but there was an austere feeling about the place.

Tuck killed the engine and stared straight ahead. "I was born here."

"So it seems." She couldn't stand the torment on his face. "Tuck, it was so long ago. Maybe it's best to just…"

"No." He cut her off. "I have to know."

He got out and she quickly followed. They took the walk to the main building. A nun came out a door and walked briskly toward a wing.

"Sister," Tuck called.

The nun stopped and glanced at them. She wore a habit so it was difficult to determine her age. Grace didn't think nuns wore the traditional robes anymore, but evidently some orders still did.

"Yes, my son," she asked, in a soft almost whisper.

"Could you tell me where the main office is, please?"

She pointed. "It's right through that arch, first door on the left."

"Thank you."

"Bless you," she replied and moved on.

They walked through the arch and approached the door.

Tuck paused for a second, and then he opened it. A musty, old smell mixed with the fragrance of incense greeted them. He removed his hat and spoke to a nun sitting at a desk. The room was very stark, equipped with just the bare essentials and a few candles and religious statues.

"May I please see the nun in charge?"

"That would be Sister Theresa." The nun rose to her feet. "I'll let her know someone wishes to speak with her."

"Thank you."

In a minute, she was back. "This way, please."

They walked into a small room with a desk, typewriter, filing cabinets and more candles and statues. Large windows looked out onto the playground where children of all ages ran and played. A nun sat at the desk and rose to her feet. She was tall and thin, and Grace guessed she was somewhere in her sixties.

"May I help you?"

"Yes. I'm looking for Sister Frances O'Rourke," Tuck said.

"I'm sorry. Sister Frances is in declining health and is no longer in charge of the orphanage."

"I still would like to speak with her."

"May I ask why?"

Tuck held out his hand. "I'm Jeremiah Tucker, Texas Ranger, and this is Grace Whitten."

"It's very nice to meet both of you."

The nuns took politeness to a new level.

"I was born here," Tuck said bluntly. "And I'd like to know who my mother is. Sister Frances knows."

"Oh, my son, Sister Frances is very elderly and feeble. She can't help you. Her memory is faulty."

Tuck's eyes didn't waver from the nun's. "I'm trying to be nice, Sister, but I can have a court order within an hour to search every file in this place. So what's it going to be?"

Sister Theresa waved a hand. "Sit down. Maybe I can help you."

They took seats in straight-back chairs across from the desk.

"Why are you so sure you were born here?"

Grace still had the letter in her hand and Tuck reached for it. He laid it in front of Sister Theresa. "I found this in my father's things."

The nun glanced over the letter. "Jess Tucker was your adoptive father?"

"Yes and…" Tuck paused as the door opened and Eli stepped in. "This is my foster brother, Elijah Coltrane." He introduced Eli as if it was quite normal for him to show up. But Grace knew Eli was worried about Tuck. She was, too.

"I see. Both of you were raised by the Tuckers."

"Yes. Did you know my father?"

"I knew Mr. Tucker well. He helped us out on many occasions. He and your mother are sorely missed."

"He told me he didn't know who my mother was, but he knew. He kept a secret for Sister Frances, but now I want to know."

"Sister Frances is eighty-nine and very crippled with arthritis. We try to keep her comfortable and I'm afraid I can't disturb her."

"I don't plan on disturbing her. I just want to talk to her."

"She's in her room in her bedclothes and it's just not allowed."

Tuck studied the nun. "Sister, I'm forty-two years old and I've waited a long time to find out about my mother. I don't plan to do anything with the information. I just have a need to know. I'm sure you can understand that. All I'm asking for is a few minutes with Sister Frances. And I know God wouldn't mind if I spoke with her in her room. You might have heard, He's very forgiving."

Sister Theresa's lips twitched. "Yes. I've heard that." She tapped her fingers on the desk in thought. "Please give me a few minutes."

"Sure." Tuck rose, his hat in his hand as the nun left the room. He stared at the children in the yard, the unwanted ones, and Grace's heart broke at the anguish in his eyes.

"Tuck…"

He didn't respond to her and fear edged its way into her chest.

Eli placed a hand on Tuck's shoulder. "Tuck, it doesn't matter anymore."

Tuck clenched his jaw. "It does to me."

"I'm sorry. I really am."

"I know."

The nun returned. "Sister Frances will receive visitors."

"Thank you, Sister."

They followed the nun down a long corridor. The hall seemed to be made of stone and their footsteps echoed eerily, sadly and with a morbid reckoning. It was a morose feeling and Grace couldn't shake it.

As the nun unlocked a door, Grace realized they were going into the nuns' quarters, a place where secular people weren't allowed.

They were ushered into a sitting room with dark walls, threadbare sofas and shelves of religious books. Grace stared at the huge cross that hung on one wall, a table of candles around its base. She rubbed her arms, feeling something she couldn't describe.

"Have a seat." Sister Theresa motioned toward a sofa. "Sister Frances will be here shortly. Please don't expect too much. Some days Frances is forgetful and uncooperative. I hope you get the answers you desire."

"Thank you, Sister."

Another nun wheeled a woman in a wheelchair into the room. She was dressed in a white robe; her long gray hair hung over one shoulder. Thin and feeble, Sister Frances's gnarled hands shook slightly in her lap.

"Frances, this young man is here to see you," Sister Theresa said.

"But I'm not dressed." Her voice was raspy, weak.

Tuck pulled a wooden chair close to her and sat down, facing her. "That's okay. I just want to ask some questions about the baby you left at the Tuckers' mailbox many years ago."

Sister Frances blinked at him and her gray eyes looked enormous behind the wire-rimmed glasses. Tuck wasn't sure she'd understood what he'd said.

A gnarled hand suddenly reached for his face, shaking against his cheekbone. *"Bernadette."*

"Excuse me?"

"I'd know those eyes anywhere. You're Bernadette's son."

Tuck swallowed. "Bernadette who?"

Sister Frances glanced at Sister Theresa. "What was Bernie's last name?"

"Martel, I believe," Sister Theresa replied.

"Yes, yes, that's it."

"Tell me about Bernadette," Tuck asked, his stomach feeling queasy. "Tell me why she gave me away."

"Oh, my son, is it wise to stir the ashes of the past?"

"I've waited forty-two years to find out the truth. I'm old enough to take it."

Sister Frances nodded several times. "Then you shall know."

"Thank you."

"Theresa, it's cold in here." Sister Frances wrapped her arms around her waist. The other nun placed a gray blanket over Sister Frances's knees. "That's better," she mumbled, and looked at Tuck. "Who are you?"

Tuck took a hard breath. "Jeremiah. Bernadette's...son." The words felt strange, unreal.

"Oh." The nun blinked as if she didn't know where she was.

"Sister Frances, please stay focused. I want to talk about Bernadette. Tell me about Bernadette."

"Okay." Her head bobbed up and down, but she didn't say anything.

"Sister Frances…"

"Yes, my son?"

"Please tell me about Bernadette."

"I'll do my best. Let's see—" her dull eyes grew distant "—Bernadette lived with an aunt and uncle and their children. Her parents were killed when she was very small, I believe. The uncle was a mean drunk and beat them often." She made a clucking sound with her tongue. "One day he was beating one of his daughters. Bernadette intervened and tried to protect her. The man broke her jaw, her arm and her leg, and then began the round of despicable foster homes for her. She was about fourteen, I think, when she was finally placed with the Tuckers. God was watching out for her. He always does." She bobbed her head again. "Yes, He was. At the Tuckers' Bernadette found out about family, love and faith."

She stopped talking and Tuck drew a breath as painful as any he'd ever taken. It burned his throat, his insides, and all the way to his soul.

His mother had been one of the Tucker kids. Grace was right.

Sister Theresa handed Sister Frances a glass of water with a straw in it. She took a sip.

"What happened to her after that?" He pushed the words past his scorched throat.

"She was very happy with the Tuckers, but at sixteen she made a life-affirming decision. Jess and Amalie tried to talk her out of it, but she was adamant."

"What was it?

"She joined the convent."

"What!" Shock ran through his system.

"She was Sister Bernadette, but we called her Bernie."

"My mother was a nun?" He had a hard time processing that.

"Yes. She enjoyed teaching the children. The outside world had been so cruel to her, but she found peace in our structured, secure environment."

"But something changed?"

"Yes."

Tuck waited, but she didn't say anything else.

"Sister," he prompted.

Sister Frances looked around. "Where are we?"

"We're in the sitting room," Sister Theresa replied. "Are you getting tired?"

"Yes."

Sister Theresa glanced at Tuck. "We'd better take her back to her room."

"Sister, please, just a few more minutes," Tuck pleaded. This was his only chance to hear about his mother.

Sister Theresa nodded. Tuck scooted close to Sister Frances. "Sister, please tell me how Bernadette became pregnant."

"My son, some things are best unknown." She leaned forward and whispered, "We shouldn't be talking about this."

"Please, Sister, whatever you tell me stays here in this room. I just have to know."

"Well." She kept her voice low. "We had a man who helped out with the maintenance of the orphanage. He was a nice fellow and did things for free. Sometimes

Bernie would help him when he needed someone to hold a ladder or hand him something. She was very friendly and he mistook her friendship for something more."

"He fell in love with her?"

"Yes."

"But she didn't love him?"

"No. She had given her heart to God."

That queasy feeling became intense and he shoved it down, taking several deep breaths. He'd wanted the truth so now he had to face it. "What happened?" he asked in a voice that came from deep within him.

Sister Frances took another sip of water. "My son, I can't tell you these things."

Tuck swallowed hard and forced out the words. "He raped her?"

"Don't use that word," she ordered in a loud voice, her body shaking.

"Please don't get upset." Tuck tried to calm her, but inside he was shaking like a leaf in a windstorm. He couldn't allow himself to think. Not now. He rubbed his hands together, preparing himself for the next question. "Was this man arrested?"

"No. The next day he came and asked for her forgiveness and Bernadette forgave him."

"Why?"

"In some way she felt she had tempted him and it wasn't in her nature to be vindictive or to judge him. The man was truly sorry for his sin and we are taught to forgive, my son."

"But…" Tuck stopped, swallowing the bile in his throat. "What happened to him?"

"He was very distraught afterward and at work he

wasn't paying attention and slipped and fell from a scaffold on a construction job. They say he died instantly."

Tuck linked his fingers together, feeling his sweaty palms. But he had to keep going. "Where is my mother now?"

"Don't you know?"

"No, Sister. I don't."

"She died a month or so after you were born. I can't remember exactly. The guilt, the shame and the dishonor got to her spirit. She died quietly in her sleep."

His mother was dead. Tuck was trying to assimilate everything, but he just had a huge burning knot in his gut. He had to keep going, though.

"Why did she want me named Jeremiah?"

"It was her father's name."

He'd had a grandfather. The word sounded surreal in the extreme in connection to him. He'd never had grandparents. He was just Jess Tucker's son and in that instant he knew that's the way he wanted it to stay. *Forever.* Exposed secrets were tearing him apart and accepting them would take time.

"What is that?" Sister Frances spoke sharply to Grace, who held the yellowing letter.

"It's the letter you wrote to Jess Tucker," Tuck explained.

"Jess was supposed to destroy that. He promised before God—no evidence." She grew agitated.

"It's all right, Sister. No one ever knew. Jess Tucker kept his word."

"Good." Sister Frances seemed to relax. "Jess Tucker was an honorable man."

"Yes, he was," Tuck agreed. His father had kept the secret he'd sworn to keep. Even though he'd probably wanted to tell Tuck, he would never break his word. So he hid the letter away in a place Tuck would only look after his death. That's why he was adamant that Tuck and Eli never touch the box. Tuck could only know after his death. Suddenly things were beginning to become clearer, but something still bothered him.

"Did Amalie know who my mother was?"

"That was the one thing Jess was insistent about. He had to tell Amalie. Bernadette agreed."

They both knew. That's why they'd told him repeatedly that he was a gift from God.

"Thank you, Sister. I appreciate your talking to me."

Sister Frances frowned. "Who are you?"

"Jeremiah Tucker—Bernadette's son." This time he said it without pausing.

"Yes, yes." She nodded. "Go in peace, my son."

Sister Theresa motioned to the other nun and she wheeled Frances away. Sister Theresa slipped her hands into the pockets of her habit. "She fades in and out, but I believe it's close to the truth."

"I do, too," Tuck replied, feeling numb.

Sister Theresa looked him straight in the eye. "Remember your promise to never use this information."

"I would never do anything to tarnish my mother's memory. Her secret will always be safe."

"Bless you, Mr. Tucker, and may you find some peace."

"Thank you, Sister."

A nun guided Tuck, Grace and Eli down the long corridor, their footsteps echoing on the cold, hard stone.

The gates of hell. The wages of sin drummed through his mind, mimicking the echoes. They stepped out into the warm April sunshine, but Tuck didn't feel it. All he could feel was the pain. He blinked, his eyes adjusting after the dimness of the orphanage.

"Are you okay?" Eli asked.

Tuck placed his hat on his head. "I'll be fine. I just need some time alone."

"Tuck."

"Eli, please. Just give me some time."

"Okay." Eli nodded. "If you want to talk, you know where to find me."

"Thanks."

Eli strolled away and Tuck walked briskly to his car. Grace broke into a run to catch up. Tuck didn't speak on the drive home. He couldn't and he could feel himself shutting down and shutting everyone out—even Grace. He needed time. Time to understand what he'd just heard. Time to learn to live with one of life's hard truths.

He was the son of a rapist.

LIKE ELI, GRACE WANTED Tuck to talk, but she knew Tuck wasn't ready. He'd heard so many truths today and she wondered how long it would be before he fully accepted them—both the circumstances of his birth and his adoption.

When they reached the house, Tuck hurried inside and studied the names on the table.

She picked up Sam. "What are you doing?"

"Her name should be here."

"You mean your mother's name?"

"Yes." He jabbed at the table. "There it is. Bernadette."

Grace glanced down. To the right of Bernadette was Tuck.

Tuck noticed it, too. "We're together. I wonder if Ma and Pa planned it that way."

"They…" But Tuck wasn't listening to her. He tore toward the hall. She placed Sam on the floor and quickly followed.

She found him in the spare bedroom, going through the photos they'd stored in the plastic container. Kneeling, he hurriedly removed the frames, exposing the back of the photos.

"Tuck…"

"Ma wrote names on the back of all the photos. Her photo is here. I know it."

Grace didn't try to stop him. He somehow had to do this—to keep searching until he had all the pieces to the puzzle of the past. Of his life. Suddenly he sank to the floor, leaning against the wall, holding a photo.

Easing down by him, she read the names on the back: Carol, Bernadette and Nancy. "All dressed up for Easter services" the caption read.

Tuck turned the photo over, staring at the girls. "The middle girl is my mother." The words came out in a hoarse whisper.

Grace looked at the smiling young girl. "She has dark hair and eyes."

"Like me."

Grace touched his face. "Yes, like you."

He pulled away and her heart sank. "Tuck."

"Go home, Grace. I need time—alone."

"I'm not leaving you like this."

"Will you for once not argue with me and respect my wishes?"

He sounded like the old Tuck who was always snapping at her. She waited for an apology, but she didn't get one. Instead, he said, "We made a mistake. We should never have gotten involved."

She bit down on her tongue to keep from crying out. "You don't mean that," was all she could manage.

"I do. I'm sorry if that hurts you."

"Yes. It hurts me, but it hurts me more to see you like this." She took a deep breath. "None of what we found out today matters to me. You're still the man I've fallen in love with. I don't care who your parents are. They're not who you are."

"Save your love for a man who deserves it and who can give you all you need. I'm not that man."

"Why not?"

"Leave it alone."

The tone of his voice should have deterred her, but it didn't. "Why not?" she persisted, fighting for their relationship. Fighting for their love.

He scrambled to his feet in an angry movement. "Because I've always had control of that empty place inside me, a place that belonged to the unknown—my mother. It was protected, secure, but now it's wide-open and the pain and the heartache is pouring in. I can't stop it. I can't do anything but feel that pain. The pain of knowing that I'm the son of a rapist. I'm no good to you or myself or to anyone. I'm completely spent, completely empty." He turned toward his bedroom.

"You don't need control. All you need is love."

He didn't respond. His back was rigid, straight and unyielding, telling her more than she wanted to accept.

"You're an incredibly good man. I know that. Everyone knows that. What happened between your biological parents doesn't change that. It doesn't change you. You've spent your life giving to others. It's all right to take some of that back. It's all right to have a life. It's all right to fall in love."

"I don't love you, Grace," he said clearly and effectively. It crushed whatever hope she had and the fight left her. She knew when to give up.

But she would never give up on their love.

She ran from the room, tears streaming down her face. She made it to her car and called Eli. Tuck was hurting and alone and she couldn't stand that. Eli said that Tuck needed time and they should respect his wishes, but he would check on him first thing in the morning.

She drove home feeling as if her world had suddenly come to end.

WHEN TUCK HEARD the door close, he made his way into the den. He laid his mother's photo on the table and picked up the humidor from the floor. Pulling the letter from his pocket, he placed it on the bottom as it had lain for so many years. After putting the box back together, he sat in his recliner letting his mind take him places he didn't want to go.

He'd had horrible feelings when he'd learned Pa had lied to him, but now he knew he had his reasons. Pa would never break his word. He was that type of man.

Thoughts followed about his biological father. What type of man forces himself on a nun? The lowest kind. But this man had also given Tuck life. That was harder to accept. He honestly didn't know if he ever would.

Unable to stop them, tears rolled from his eyes. He hadn't cried since Ma had died, but now he cried for a mother and the pain she must have endured. He cried for his adoptive parents and the torment they must have suffered at keeping their secret from him. And he cried for himself and the agony he couldn't get through.

Lastly, he cried for Grace and all that could have been. He prayed one day she would forgive him.

CHAPTER EIGHTEEN

THE RINGING OF THE PHONE woke Tuck. It took a moment for him to realize what it was. The sound stopped and he instinctively reached for Grace, then everything came flooding back with painful clarity.

Grace wasn't here. She wasn't ever going to be here again.

He sat up, realizing he was still in the recliner. He ran his hands over his face, feeling as if he'd been slam-dunked through a net of barbed wire. Each scar ran deep and wide inside him and he couldn't get past the truth.

His father...

He swallowed hard, unable to complete the thought. Did the truth somehow change him?

Tuck didn't have any answers. All he knew was that he had started to believe that he could have a life, a family—with Grace. But now...

Feeling the weight of despair, he slowly stood and a deep, tortured sigh escaped him. He had hurt her in a way no man should hurt a woman, but he was powerless to change that. She deserved someone better than him. She deserved love, happiness and everything that entailed.

He couldn't give her that.

Not now.

TUCK'S CELL RANG and he reached for the phone on his waist.

"Tuck, this is Sheriff Wheeler."

"Morning, Sheriff."

"Remember that hit-and-run case you investigated about a year ago?"

Tuck headed for his bedroom as he talked, Sam trailing behind him. "Sure. Luis Rodriquez is well hidden in Mexico."

"The Mexican authorities just called. Luis is tired of running and he's ready to turn himself in and face charges here in Texas. They'll bring him to the bridge in Laredo. Since the Rangers have jurisdiction, I thought you might like to be the one to walk across the bridge and arrest him."

"You bet." Tuck had spent a lot of hours on the case, trying to find Rodriquez after he'd run from a car crash. The young girl he'd hit died instantly. Rodriquez was drunk and fled the scene before police had arrived. His family quickly got him to Mexico. The girl's family had been waiting a long time for this day.

"How soon can you be in my office?"

"In about forty-five minutes." This was what he needed—to throw himself into work. It would keep him busy and his mind on other things.

He hung up, took a shower and dressed. Carrying his boots and gun into the den, he sat down to put them on.

His back door opened and Eli walked in. "Morning," he said, sinking into a chair.

"I'm not in a mood to talk, so go home."

"I'm just checking to see if you're okay."

"I'm fine." He slipped a foot into a boot. "I'm going to Mexico to pick up Luis Rodriquez. He's turning himself in. I won't be gone long, but would you check on Sam and Dee?"

"Sure. No problem." Eli picked up the photo of Tuck's biological mother from the coffee table. He flipped it over and read the back side. "You found a picture of your mother."

"Yeah."

"You have her coloring."

"I know." He slipped his other foot into a boot. "I wonder what I inherited from my father."

Eli looked straight at him. "All his good qualities."

He clenched his jaw. "I don't feel like going over this."

Eli fingered the photo. "You've been through a lot lately. Just take some time and think this through. You're the most caring, giving man I know. There isn't a part of you that's bad."

Tuck attached his gun to his belt, trying to block out Eli's words, trying not to think, but somewhere in the corner of his soul he could feel that soiled part of him, like a scarlet letter. He would never be able to change that. He gulped in a breath.

He looked at his brother. "Then why do I feel so tainted?"

"Tuck, give this time. Whoever your biological father is doesn't mean a thing. It's the man you've become that matters. The man we all love. Ask any kid you've mentored. Ask Grace."

"Leave Grace out of this."

"Tuck, for heaven's sake, don't throw away what you have."

Tuck sucked in a painful breath. "It's over. I know that."

"Tuck—" Eli stopped for a second. "Okay, think about your biological father. He helped out at the orphanage for free. A bad person doesn't do that. He's human and fell in love with a nun. I'm not saying that what he did was right by any means, but your mother forgave him. And you have to, too."

Without a word Tuck attached his badge to his shirt.

"You're not the spawn of the devil," Eli said firmly. "Even if you were I'll still love you. Caroline and Jesse will, too, so will the McCains. Even Grace will. Do you know why?"

"No, but I'm sure you're going to tell me."

"Because we know you. And soon you'll realize that, too. Just don't throw away everything that's good in your life."

Tuck didn't reply. He had nothing to say.

Eli stood with an aggravated sigh, glancing at the boxes. "What are you going to do with those?"

"Put them back in the attic for now."

Eli settled his hat on his head. "Tuck."

"Go home, Eli. And tell the McCains I don't want to talk to anyone."

Eli shrugged. "Sure. But you know Beau. He's going to want to help, as all of us do."

"Eli…" Tuck couldn't take much more. He had to get away from everyone.

"I'll get the point across," Eli added quickly.

"Thanks."

"Are you okay?"

Tuck saw the worry in his brother's eyes. "No." He didn't lie. "But I will be."

GRACE CURLED UP on her sofa, clutching the peignoir she planned to wear for Tuck, her tears soaking it. Everything had been so wonderful and now it just seemed lost. What hurt the most was that she couldn't reach him. Her love wasn't enough.

Her doorbell rang and she ignored it, then she heard the key in the lock. *Caroline.* Why did she ever give her sister a key?

"Grace, where are you?" Caroline called.

"Go home, Caroline."

Caroline flopped down beside her and Grace rose to a sitting position. Caroline brushed away Grace's tears. "Oh, Gracie, I'm so sorry."

"I love him, Caro, but…" She hiccuped. "But he doesn't love me."

"Tuck's hurting. Just give him some time."

"I'm so afraid that I'll never be able to reach him."

"Then fight for what you want. You do that better than anyone I know. Make a decision, fight for it with all your heart and the fear will go away."

"I'd like to be alone," Grace mumbled.

Caroline hugged her. "Sisters first—sisters always."

"That's not true anymore. You have a husband and a baby. Our lives are changing."

"But we will always be sisters. Nothing will ever change that."

"No." Grace wiped at her eyes. "I never dreamed love could hurt this bad."

"Gracie…"

"But I'll survive. I was taught to be strong."

"You have to be strong to survive in a man's world." Caroline dropped her voice to sound like their father.

Grace wanted to smile, but she couldn't.

"How about I get us some chocolate?"

"No." Grace shook her head. "I really want to be alone to wallow in my heartache. Then I'll pick myself up and decide what I'm going to do."

"Okay." Caroline pulled the peignoir out of her hands. "You're ruining this beautiful garment."

Grace snatched it back. "I was going to wear it for Tuck, but now…"

"This isn't like you to indulge in self-pity."

"Sometimes a woman has to cry."

"I'll give you that, but not for long. Tuck needs you."

"Goodbye, Caroline."

"I'll call you in a couple of hours."

"No. Don't."

"I'm not leaving you alone like this. Eli has Jesse and I have to go, but I'll check on you later."

"Whatever." Grace curled into a ball. When the door closed, she burst into tears. She let the tears flow freely, cleansing, washing away, holding on to the peignoir and her dreams.

After that, she got up, dressed and went in to work. She sat in her big office unable to concentrate. The law firm used to be her life, but it wasn't anymore. She wasn't happy here. She'd once told Caroline that she wanted to be happy with herself and her life. For a short period of time she had been, and then she'd come back to the firm and gotten bogged down with the daily problems of being head of The Whitten Law Firm.

She walked to the window and stared out at the city of Austin, but she didn't really see it. Her gaze focused on the oaks in the distance. Several miles behind them was the hospital. She wondered how Brady was, if he'd gone home. She wondered about Barbara, Molly and the other baby.

They'd touched her in a way she hadn't expected. They'd touched her heart and awakened a part of her she hadn't even known was there.

Just the way Tuck had awakened her heart.

Caroline had told her to make a decision and fight for it. She wanted a life with Tuck and she was going to fight for it with all her heart. First, she had to make changes.

She turned toward her desk and froze. A spider inched his way across the hardwood floor. Fear jumped into her throat and her natural response was to shout for Nina. But not today. She drew a deep breath, walked over and stepped on the spider with her Manolo high heel. She flinched, but she crushed that sucker.

Raising her arms in the air, she did a victory dance. "Yes. Yes. Yes."

This was a big step. The last step.

Dancing on the dead spider, she now knew who the real Grace was—a woman who wanted it all with a man named Tuck. And she wasn't afraid to fight for that.

She opened a drawer for a Kleenex to remove the spider from the sole of her shoe and then threw it into the trash can. After straightening her suit, she reached for a button on her phone. "Nina, please tell Byron I'd like to see him as soon as possible."

"Yes, ma'am."

She took her seat and readied herself for this meeting and the changes that would follow.

Within minutes Byron walked into her office.

"Please have a seat," she said.

Byron sat down and crossed his legs, his eyes watching her. "Is there a problem?" he asked.

She leaned back. "I'm offering you your heart's desire."

"What are you talking about?"

"I spend too much of my time at this firm and I don't plan to do that anymore."

His eyes narrowed. "I'm not sure what you're talking about. I thought you cut back on your hours."

"I tried, but this is a very time-consuming job." She took a moment. "I've found something that's more important to me, so I'm offering you a comanaging partner deal. I will maintain my fifty-one percent and control, but I will leave the daily operations to you, except I will have approval of everyone who is hired."

Byron wiped a speck from his immaculate slacks. "Have you spoken to your father?"

"No. My father has nothing to do with this firm anymore. The decision is mine and it's final. As a courtesy, I will inform him after we come to an agreement."

It took thirty minutes to iron out the details. Byron was in agreement on almost every issue. He'd been waiting a long time for this.

"So, Grace, what are you going to do?"

"I plan to take on a lot of charitable causes, helping

people who can't afford an attorney. And I'm getting involved with child advocacy, offering my services to help protect children."

"That doesn't sound like you."

"It is, Byron. Trust me."

Byron stood and shook her hand. "Thank you, Grace. I won't let you down."

The decision made, she picked up the phone and called her father. After the initial shock, the conversation went well. He spent five minutes trying to talk her out of it, but she stuck to her decision. In the end he told her he just wanted her to be happy. She told him she planned to be.

And she meant it.

Tuck wanted time and she would give it to him. But not for long. Happiness to her was being with Tuck, sharing his life.

Now she had to convince him of that.

CHAPTER NINETEEN

TUCK AND A DEPUTY made the long, tiring drive to Laredo. They met with the sheriff in that county who was talking to the Mexican authorities. After everything was in order, they drove to the bridge. At the signal Tuck walked across the bridge to meet Luis Rodriquez. He snapped handcuffs on him and escorted him to their waiting vehicle.

Within minutes, they were on the road back to Austin. Tuck drove and there was very little conversation. He preferred it that way. He wasn't in a mood to talk.

It was late when they checked Rodriquez into the jail. Tuck told the deputy to go home to his family and he'd fill out the necessary paperwork. There was no one waiting for Tuck. And that's the way it had to be.

He was dead tired when he crawled into his car to go home. When he reached his house, he fell across his bed. The scent of lilac filled his senses. It was everywhere—on the pillow, the sheets, his skin and in his heart. Grace's face swam before him and a ragged moan escaped him as he was claimed by sleep.

THE DAYS MOVED SLOWLY. Tuck was never far from Grace's thoughts but she restrained herself from calling him. She was giving him the time he wanted and it wasn't easy. She stayed busy, though, waiting for his call, or some response from him.

April turned into May and Grace was working on a plan to have meals provided to all the parents who stayed by their children in the pediatric ward. She had another meeting with the CEO and he told her Brady was still a patient, so afterward she took a moment to check on Brady, Lisa and Keith.

She walked into the room and stopped dead. Barbara was gone and Molly's crib was empty. Her heart fell to the pit of her stomach. *Oh, no.* Tears gathered in her eyes and she pushed them away. They'd probably gone home, that's all.

As she tried to convince herself of that, the door opened and a bed was pushed inside with Molly in it— sitting up and looking around. *Molly was awake!* Barbara followed with a smile on her face.

Unable to stop herself, Grace grabbed Barbara and hugged her. "Molly's awake. I'm so happy."

Barbara's arms tightened around Grace. "Thank you, Grace. It's so good to see you. My baby's going to be okay."

Grace drew back and brushed away a tear. "I was so worried when I saw the empty bed."

"We went for some tests."

The nurse lifted Molly from the bed and the baby held out her arms for Barbara. "Mama," she cried.

Barbara quickly took her child, holding her close. Molly's head was still bandaged, but she looked fine and healthy.

"So everything is going to be okay?"

"The doctors think so. They're running a battery of tests, but she's talking and she knows her family. All good signs, the doctor said."

"I'm so happy for you and Molly and your family."

"Thank you." Barbara sat in the recliner. "I've been getting a lot more rest since we got these wonderful chairs." She gently rocked Molly, sparing Grace a glance. "You wouldn't know anything about that, would you?"

Another nurse entered the room preventing Grace from answering. She was grateful for that.

She turned to the nurse. "I came to see Brady and he's not in his bed. Have the Templetons taken him home?"

The nurse looked up from the paper in her hand. "No. He's in the playroom with Cathy, a nurse's aide." Her eyes narrowed. "And you are?"

Grace held out her hand. "Grace Whitten. My law firm represented the Templetons."

"Natalie Dunbar, head nurse."

"I'm surprised that Brady is still here."

"He had a staph infection and the doctor ordered another round of antibiotics. He thought it was best to keep him in the hospital until he was completely well. Actually, the Templetons preferred it that way." Something in Natalie's eyes changed and Grace got the impression she did not like Lisa and Keith.

Nurse Dunbar turned to Barbara. "How did the test go?"

"Molly did great," Barbara replied, kissing her baby's cheek.

"Good. Marcie will take her vitals and if everything stays the same, it looks like you'll be able to go home in a couple of days."

Barbara smiled. "I know. It's wonderful."

Natalie looked at the paper in her hand. "I just got a call from the hospital administrator. Your meals will now be sent up from the cafeteria. Every mother on the ward will get their meals free. Not sure what's going on, but it seems we have a benevolent benefactor."

"It seems that way." Barbara glanced at Grace. "It's very generous and compassionate."

Grace winked at her, not hiding it, but not admitting it, either. That would happen soon enough. She'd set up the Stephen Whitten Meal Fund to supply meals to parents who sat with their children around the clock. The news would be revealed to the media next week, but first she had to inform her father. She had a feeling he wasn't going to have a problem with it.

The door opened and a nurse walked in, holding Brady. He was rubbing his eyes and Grace could see that he wasn't feeling well. Her heart contracted. Where were Lisa and Keith?

The nurse placed him in his crib and Grace walked over to her. "Is he okay?" Grace asked.

"He's just tired and ready for a nap," the nurse replied. "I'll go get him some juice."

Nurse Dunbar followed the girl out and Grace turned her attention to Brady. "Hi, Brady." He stared at her with dark, gorgeous eyes, clutching his stuffed dog. His hair was growing out and curling against his scalp. "Are you tired? Would you like for me to rock you?" Grace held out her hands, but Brady made no move toward her. He just kept watching her. She patted the mattress. "Lie down, Brady, and I'll sing to you."

Brady touched his eye.

Grace felt a catch in her throat. "Yes. You remember. I love those long eyelashes."

Suddenly Brady ran toward her, his arms outstretched. Grace lifted him out and held him against her, her heart melting from the contact. She sank into the recliner, cuddling him close. "I'll rub your back and sing you a lullaby. Okay?"

Brady touched her face and her throat muscles locked for a second.

"Hush, little Brady, don't you cry. Grace is gonna sing you a lullaby." As she started to sing, Brady rested his head against her chest. She sang on, rubbing his back until Brady's eyes closed. She stood, gently placed him in his bed and covered him.

She turned to Barbara, her heart heavy and troubled. "What's going on?"

"Like Natalie said, he's had a staph infection, he's been running a low-grade fever and he's been sluggish, not his usual fighting self."

"When was the last time Lisa and Keith were here?"

"Yesterday morning, but Lisa became ill again and they went home."

"But what about Brady?"

"The nurses are taking very good care of him. When he's awake, they keep him at the nurses' station so they can watch him closely."

This was unacceptable. She had to do something.

The aide came back with the juice. "Oh, he's asleep."

"Yes," Grace replied.

"I'll save it for later. He's always thirsty when he wakes up."

As she walked out, Barbara said, "I think the stress is getting to Lisa. I don't mean to be critical, but she's having a hard time."

"Something has to be done. This isn't right." She glanced toward the empty crib in the corner where the other baby had been.

"They removed his tube at the beginning of the week," Barbara said.

"Oh." A deep pain pierced her for all the abused children in the world. As she stood there she realized something about herself—she cared deeply for the unwanted children. She cared about kids and people. And she was going to make sure Brady had the very best care.

Lisa and Keith had a lot of explaining to do.

TUCK ROLLED OUT OF BED with a start. He'd overslept and he never did that. He hurriedly took a shower, shaved and dressed. He had to get to his office, then he'd promised to drive Dillon and Sheila to the bus station. They were leaving today. Damn. This late start was going to put him behind.

Dillon was quiet on the way to the station and he held on tight to Tuck for an extra second before he joined his mother boarding the bus. Tuck waved until the bus was out of sight. Saying goodbye was never easy, but he knew this goodbye had a happy ending. There weren't enough of those.

As he crawled back into his car, his cell rang. It was Gladys Upchurch.

"Ranger Tucker, I'm so worried."

"What is it?"

"Micah left for school, but the principal just called and he's not there. I don't know where he could be."

"Did anything happen?"

"Some kids in school are picking on him, calling him a killer's son, and he has a hard time dealing with that. I'm worried, Ranger Tucker. He's never run off before."

"Don't worry, Mrs. Upchurch. I'll find him and bring him home."

"Thank you. I knew I could depend on you."

He clicked off. That's who he was—someone who was there for these kids who had no one else. Someone they could depend on. Sitting there staring at the sunbeams reflecting off the hood of his car he knew there was nothing in his genes that would ever change that trait in him. Eli had told him that, and Grace had, too. But he couldn't allow himself to believe them. He was still struggling.

He was still feeling the pain.

IN HER CAR GRACE CALLED her office for messages before going to Lisa and Keith's home.

"Oh, Ms. Whitten," Nina said. "I'm glad you checked in. Mr. Templeton has called three times. He wants to see you. He said it's urgent."

She wanted to see him, too. "Call him back and tell him I'll be at his house in about twenty minutes."

"Yes, ma'am."

With the heavy traffic, it took Grace exactly twenty minutes to reach Lisa and Keith's home, an English Tudor in an exclusive neighborhood. Grace hurried up the walk and rang the doorbell.

Keith opened it immediately. "Grace. I'm so glad you came. Lisa's in the bedroom."

Grace glanced around the tastefully decorated house and didn't see any toys or anything to indicate a child was going to live here. She followed Keith through the foyer, formal living room, a hall and into a spacious bedroom. Lisa lay in bed propped up against pillows in a silk peignoir similar to the one Grace had bought.

"Oh, my, are you ill?"

"No, Grace," Lisa replied. "I'm really fine. Have a seat."

Keith brought a Queen Anne chair and Grace eased into it, not having a clue what was going on especially since they both were smiling.

"You look wonderful, as always," Lisa said, perusing Grace's suit and shoes.

"Thank you," she replied. "What's going on, Lisa? I just left the hospital and Brady really needs you."

Lisa chewed on her lip. "I haven't been feeling well and…and I wanted to explain to you first."

"What?"

Lisa let out a bubbly laugh. "We're pregnant."

"Oh, how wonderful! Brady will have a little brother or sister."

The joy on Lisa's face vanished. "That's what we

wanted to talk about. To carry this baby to full term the doctor has ordered complete bed rest. I can only go to the bathroom. I'm stuck here for the duration." She hesitated. "We won't be able to take Brady now."

"What!" Grace was immediately on her feet. "Why not?"

"We have to think of our own child," Keith said.

"Brady is supposed to *be* your child," Grace pointed out. "You've been visiting him, forming a bond, a connection. Now you're just going to walk out on him?"

"We have no choice, Grace." Keith's voice rose. "Brady's very aggressive and he could hit Lisa in the stomach and cause her to lose the baby. We have to be very careful. I'm sorry."

"Ranger Tucker can have him now," Lisa said.

Grace was shocked at Lisa's sheer audacity and she wanted to slap her. She found she had to restrain herself to keep from doing so. "So just hand Brady off to the next available parent? I'm sure that will be very good for his self-esteem."

"I'm sorry we let you down." Lisa tied the tiny pink bow on her bed jacket.

"I am, too, Lisa. And I'm really sorry you let Brady down." She started for the door and Keith followed.

"Should we call Ann Demott or what?"

"I'll take care of it," she flung over her shoulder.

"Grace."

But Grace wasn't listening. She walked stoically to the front door and let herself out.

Back in her car she called Tuck. He had to be the first one to know this. No answer. She left a message for him to call her as soon as possible. She drove directly to the Whitten Firm, spoke to Ann, and then called Judge Farnsworth. No way in hell was she letting anyone take Brady from Tuck now.

After that she called Beau, making sure she had all her bases covered. Everything was in place, except Tuck. Why wasn't he calling her back?

Where was he?

ON A HUNCH TUCK DROVE over to Patterson Park. It wasn't far from Micah's house and the boy went there a lot to fool around. As Tuck drove up, he saw him sitting under a large oak tree, his backpack beside him.

He parked his car and walked over to him.

"My grandmother call you?" Micah asked without looking up.

"Yep." Tuck eased down beside him. "She's worried. I am, too. Why didn't you go to school?"

"I'm never going back there. The kids call me names, bad names, and I can't handle it anymore. I'm running away, but I haven't made up my mind where to go yet."

"I see." Tuck drew up his knees and rested his forearms on them. "My Pa used to say that running never solved anything. Now, he was a big John Wayne fan and Mr. Wayne's motto was to stand and fight."

"I don't want to fight. I hate fighting." He buried his head on his knees.

"Fighting doesn't have to be physical. It's an inner strength of facing these bullies every day and letting them see that their taunts are not affecting you. Never react to them and soon they'll tire of their little games."

"It makes me angry when they call me a killer's son."

A wound opened inside Tuck. *It made him angry to be a rapist's son.*

He clenched his hands, concentrating on Micah instead of himself. "It's okay to be angry. We all are at some point in our lives, but in your case you can channel all that emotion into your fastball. For someone your age, you throw a fastball better than anyone I've ever seen."

Micah raised his head. "You think so?"

"Sure. Stay in school, get good grades, keep playing sports and a college scholarship is just waiting for you. After that, the sky is the limit."

"But everyone thinks I'm a bad person because of what my father did to…"

"I don't."

Micah didn't answer, just picked at the grass.

To help Micah, Tuck knew he had to bare a part of his soul, a part that was as alien to him as anything he'd ever felt. He had to do it, though.

But could he? He suddenly saw Grace's face and it gave him strength. Courage.

He clenched his hands tighter. "Do you think I'm a bad person?"

Micah looked at him. "No, you're the best person I know."

"I'm going to tell you something I've never told another human being."

"What?" Micah's eyes grew big.

Tuck's fingers turned numb. "My biological father was a rapist."

Micah's eyes grew bigger, if that was possible.

"So do you think I'm a bad person because of what my father did?"

"No. No." Micah threw himself at Tuck. "You're the best."

Tuck held him for a moment, then drew back looking into Micah's tear-filled eyes. "You see, we have certain genes from our parents, but that doesn't make us our parents. We're each a unique individual and we know right from wrong. Our behavior, attitudes and actions determine our destiny."

As he said the words he knew they were true. Never in his life had he committed a violent act and learning the truth about his father wasn't going to change that.

"Yeah," Micah echoed in barely a whisper.

"You keep practicing that fastball and one day I'll be watching you play in the major leagues." Tuck ruffled his hair. "Let's go get a burger and fries and then I'll take you to school."

Micah jumped to his feet. "I'm going to be strong, Tuck, just like you."

Just don't be blind like me.

When Tuck left the school, he checked his messages. Grace had called four times. He wondered what she wanted. Without hesitation, he called her back, but didn't get an answer. Now they'd play phone tag.

He had to testify at a murder trial in the afternoon. Afterward he had a meeting with the assistant D.A. to go over some details, and then he went home to change. He was going to see Grace. He'd been in limbo too long. A part of him was helping kids; the other part was loving Grace. He suddenly had a need to tell her that.

For the first time in days he felt alive again.

WHEN TUCK PULLED INTO his driveway, Grace's car was parked behind his truck. He drove into the carport, placed his hat on the seat and got out, wondering why she was here. But he didn't care. He was just happy to see her.

She opened her car door and slipped out, Sam in her arms. The con artist was glad to see her, too. In a power suit and heels, dog hairs on her blouse and jacket, she looked great. The wind tossed her hair across her face and she flipped it back as she made her way to within a couple of feet of him. A sudden warmth flooded his body.

They stared at each other for a full ten seconds. His eyes feasted on her. God, he'd missed her. He'd been going through his daily routine, but it wasn't the same. His life wasn't the same without her. She'd said it was okay to have a life, to fall in love.

Had he ruined all hope of that?

"How are you?" she finally asked, and that concerned voice broke through the barriers he'd erected around his heart.

"I'm fine. I'm coming to grips with everything."

"I'm glad."

Somehow they'd reverted back to the tense conversations they used to have and that hurt—because he was the cause of it.

"I've been trying to reach you for most of the day," she added.

"I returned your call and left a message."

"I got it a little while ago and thought I'd come out here in person to tell you."

His first thought was of Eli, Caroline and Jesse. Had something happened? Fear tugged at his insides.

"What happened?"

"The Templetons are pregnant and have withdrawn their petition for custody of Brady."

"What!" Had he heard her correctly?

"The Templetons no longer want Brady."

"My God." He swiped a hand through his hair. "I have to call Beau and go…" He frowned. "Where is Brady?"

"He's still at the hospital."

"Why?"

"He's had a staph infection and is running a low-grade fever. They just finished another round of antibiotics. At the time, the doctor thought it best to keep him there."

"Didn't the Templetons want to take him home?"

"Lisa been sick a lot lately from the pregnancy, and I don't think she was up to caring for him."

"Damn it. So Brady's all alone?"

"No. The nurses are taking very good care of him and I've been there most of the day. I've also spoken with the doctor and he feels the staph infection is now under control and Brady is ready to go home."

He reached for his cell phone. "I have to call Beau."

"I've already called Beau and I'm taking over the case. It's okay with him if it's okay with you. I just need your approval. I've already spoken with Judge Farnsworth and after applying a little pressure she's put the hearing on the docket for Monday at one o'clock. She also agreed not to accept any more petitions for Brady."

He watched her closely. "Thanks."

"I'm so sorry for what the Templetons have done and I have to make this right—for Brady and for you."

"You certainly have things rolling."

"I just need your approval to go forward."

As he stared into her green eyes he knew without any doubts that she still loved him. She was doing everything in her power to make sure he and Brady were together. But that wasn't enough now. He and Brady needed her. So many times he thought he could do this alone, but Brady needed a mother. His friends' wives were right. Brady needed something that Tuck couldn't give him, but then again, he could.

"You have it," he replied, realizing she was waiting for his answer. Dealing with the lowest part of his life, he thought he was unworthy of love. Today proved him wrong. Spending time with his little brothers made him see that. Everyone was worthy of love, even him. As he'd told Micah, each person can control their own destiny. And he intended to do that.

She turned to go back to her car and he wanted to say so many things. But "I'm sorry" and "Please forgive me" seemed stuck in his throat.

"Grace."

She glanced at him.

Sam was still clutched in her arms. "You have my dog."

"Oh, I'm sorry." She placed Sam on the ground. "Bye, Sam."

"Grace."

She looked up.

"I'm sorry I hurt you." They stared at each other and

he hoped she saw all the regrets in his eyes. He hoped she saw the love.

"Me, too," she replied, and continued to her car.

Most of his adult life he'd been searching for a woman to love and accept him for who he was. He'd finally found her. Grace had told him that all he needed was their love. She'd been right. He had to tell her. And he had to do it now or he was going to lose her. "Grace."

She stopped, but didn't turn around and his heart stilled in his chest.

Grace took a deep breath, fighting for strength. *Please, let me go.* He'd asked for time and she was trying very hard to give him that, but if she looked into his eyes one more time she was going to throw herself at him.

"I love you." The words came low and husky and sounded better than any Brahms she'd ever heard.

She whirled around, stared into his love-filled eyes and took off running, in high heels, which was something she didn't do well. She tripped and fell into his arms and he swung her round and round until she was dizzy—dizzy with happiness. Dizzy in love.

"I'm sorry. I'm sorry," he whispered a moment before his lips claimed hers. The pain and the sadness faded away.

When they came up for air, she stroked his face, his hair. "Are you okay?"

"I'm fine." He kissed her gently. "Thank you for not giving up on me."

"I'll never give up on you, Jeremiah Tucker." Her tongue stroked his lower lip. "I love you."

He groaned and kissed her deeply. After a moment, he took her hand. "Let's go inside and talk."

She followed. She'd follow him anywhere.

Inside Grace felt that comfort and peace she'd found here. She didn't intend to ever let it go again.

Tuck walked to one of the boxes, knelt down and rummaged through it. Grace knelt beside him. Pulling out a small box, he looked at her.

"Grace Whitten, will you marry me? Will you be Brady's mother? Will you be the mother of any children we decide to have?"

She bit her lip. "Are you saying…"

"I'm saying I want a life, a complete life with you. You did say I had a right to take some back and a right to fall in love."

"Yes. Yes." Tears filled her eyes from sheer joy.

"I'm ready to do that, so will you marry me for better or worse?" He held up the box. "These are my parents' wedding bands. I'd like for us to use them if it's okay with you."

"Yes. Yes. If you don't kiss me soon, I'm going to start blubbering like an idiot." She threw herself at him and they tumbled onto the area rug, locked in each other's arms.

He kissed her until there was no more sadness, no more pain. Grace lost herself in the joy of being back in his arms, in his life. Finally Tuck scooted up against his recliner and pulled Grace onto his lap.

She stroked his hair. "You said you've come to grips with everything."

He turned his head and kissed her hand. "I'm sorry I hurt you, but I've never felt that desolate before."

"And now?"

He told her about Micah. "He was just feeling so much pain and I knew I had to share my pain for him to understand he wasn't a bad person because of what his father had done."

"And it helped you to understand that you weren't a bad person?"

"Yes. I could see it so clearly."

"All the love you've given these boys saved you."

He kissed her cheek. "In a way. To help Micah I knew I had to accept the circumstances of my birth, to accept that I was still the same man these boys depended on and was always there for them. I had to open up and share to completely accept it, to believe I was worthy of a life and all that it entailed." He caressed her arm. "But it wasn't Micah's, Dillon's or Pablo's faces I saw at the end of that long, dark tunnel of pain. It was yours. Seeing your face in my mind gave me the strength to do it."

She buried her face in his neck, her arms wrapped around him, and Tuck felt an indescribable peace. "Beau told me once he hoped I found an incredibly selfless woman to share my dream. I just found an incredible woman."

"Ah. Thank you. I'm so sorry you were hurt like that," she whispered against his skin. "But I had to give you time like you'd asked for and for a bossy, pushy woman that wasn't easy."

"Hey. You're talking about the woman I love. She's concerned and enthusiastic."

"Mmm. I like that." She raised her head. "Is Micah okay?"

"Yes. I'll be keeping a close eye on him."

"Oh." Her eyes grew bright. "Molly woke up."

"Is she going to be okay?"

"They think so." She glanced at her watch. "We'd better go. I don't want to leave Brady too long."

They rose to their feet and Tuck slipped his arms around her, twirling her around the room. He stopped, buried his face in her hair, just holding her. "I wish we had time to…dance."

"Me, too," she groaned as he kissed her ear. "But later…we'll…have plenty of time…later."

He grinned and took her hand, walking toward the back door.

Suddenly he thought of something that had to be done. He went to the mantel for a small knife Pa used to carve the names on the table.

"Come here," he said as he moved toward the kitchen table. "We're going to carve your name in a place of honor."

He wrapped his arms around her from behind and guided her hand as they etched Grace next to Tuck. "That's forever," he murmured, kissing her cheek.

She trembled and turned into the circle of his arms. "Forever."

WHEN THEY REACHED the hospital, Jennifer told them Brady was in the playroom and they quickly made their way there. Brady, in a gown and socks, squatted on the floor, pushing a toy truck around.

"Hey, buddy," Tuck said.

Brady glanced up and his eyes grew big, his mouth

forming an *O*. Today there was no anger in those eyes, they were bright and clear. Quickly Brady stood and turned away. Tuck didn't know what he was doing until Brady reached for a ball and rolled it his way.

Tuck swallowed the lump in his throat. Brady remembered. He picked up the ball and walked to Brady. Squatting in front of him, Tuck said, "How are you, buddy?"

Brady just stared at him.

"I've been gone for a while, but I promise from now on I will always come back. You can count on that. Do you understand that?"

Brady continued to stare at him.

"If you understand, nod your head," Tuck prompted, nodding his head.

Brady moved his head up and down.

"Good, Brady." He was responding and Tuck felt joy spiral through him. "Is it okay if I hug you?"

Brady kept nodding and Tuck lifted him into his arms, holding him tight. Brady laid his head on Tuck's shoulder and he knew he and Brady were meant to be together.

Just as he and Grace were.

She'd filled an empty place in his life and in his soul.

Grace wrapped her arms around them.

Now they would be a family.

THE NEXT COUPLE OF DAYS were hectic as they took turns staying with Brady, never leaving him alone. Eli, Caroline and the McCains chipped in and helped to get the house ready for Brady. It became a family effort.

He and Grace had decided to get married before the

custody hearing. They wanted to be a complete family before they brought Brady home.

On Monday, Tuck dressed in his best suit and dancing boots. He was getting married today. He was becoming a father today.

He took a moment to savor that, embrace it and to remember the wonderful gifts he'd been given in his life. Those gifts made him the man he was today. Not the least of those was Grace. He now knew why he felt a need to keep her at arm's length when they'd first met. Because subconsciously he'd recognized she had the power to change him. And he resisted change. Now he was ready to accept the future and to live life to the fullest. With Grace. And with Brady.

He slipped his parents' rings into his pocket and stopped for a moment in Brady's room. Grace had made a quick trip with Caroline, picking out what she'd wanted for the room. Elise, Josie, Macy, Eli, Jake, Caleb and Beau had taken it from there.

A new three-quarter bed of maple wood, with a side rail, dresser and chest were there. One wall was brick red, the others khaki. The bed linens were red and green with horses and cowboys on them. The trim on the sheets was like a red bandana, as it was on the comforter. Horses and cowboys were also on the wide red bandana border on the ceiling. A rocking horse sat in one corner and a large toy box filled to the brim with every toy imaginable in another. Stuffed animals littered the bed. The room was perfect for Brady.

Not for the first time he realized that he had an incredible extended family. Brady was going to love them.

Just as he did.

DNA did not make a family—love did. And he was going to make sure Brady felt that from now on.

He straightened his tie, getting ready for the best day of his life.

TUCK PACED in the judge's chambers. It was almost one. Where was Grace? He couldn't believe how nervous he was.

The door opened and she walked in dressed in a white suit with a flower in her hair. She looked more beautiful than he'd ever seen her.

"Wow! You look great. May I kiss the bride?"

"Not yet." Her eyes twinkled. "Later we're going home and getting reacquainted."

"I can hardly wait."

"Me, neither." She smiled, but that was all the time they had as the bailiff announced Judge Farnsworth's arrival.

He took her hand and they walked forward.

The judge took her seat. "Ms. Whitten, this is quite an unusual twist."

"Yes, Your Honor, it is. But a very happy one."

"Thank you for agreeing to marry us on such short notice," Tuck said.

"Ranger Tucker, after all that's happened I'm inclined to grant you anything within reason. And I'm a big fan of romance."

Grace's heart was about to soar out of her chest, then the door opened at the back of the room and Jennifer stepped in with Brady in her arms. Opal, the caseworker, was behind them.

She glanced at Tuck with a lifted eyebrow.

"Thank you, Your Honor, for allowing Brady to come here today," he said.

Oh, she loved this man.

"Normally I wouldn't," Judge Farnsworth replied. "But this is a happy occasion and I'm anxious to meet this young man."

Grace saw Eli and Caroline ease into the room followed by her parents, Jake and Elise, Caleb and Josie, Beau and Macy. All their family and friends were here to share their happiness.

Tuck looked at her. "We couldn't get married without our family."

She touched his loving face. "Do you know how much I love you?"

"You can show me later." He grinned.

Brady had had enough. He wiggled in Jennifer's arms, shouting, "No, no, no," trying to get down. Tuck nodded at Jennifer and she set him on his feet. Brady toddled quickly to Tuck, wrapping his arms around Tuck's legs. Tuck lifted him into his arms and they faced the judge.

Eli and Caroline strolled forward. "We're maid of honor and best man," Eli said.

Joanna ran forward with a white bouquet. "She has to have a bouquet," Joanna said.

"By all means," the judge replied.

"Do you mind if I take pictures?" Caroline asked, holding up her camera.

The judge nodded and glanced toward the back. "Congressman Whitten, are you taking part in this ceremony?"

"You bet." Stephen walked to stand by his wife. "Normally I would give the bride away, but my daughter is a strong, independent woman and she doesn't need me to give her away. So I'll just give her and Tuck my blessing."

"Thank you, Daddy." A bubble of laughter escaped Grace's throat and she thought she was going to burst with pure happiness. She got it right this time and she was going to love Jeremiah Tucker for the rest of her life.

Tuck reached for Grace's hand while holding Brady in his other arm. Brady made a dive for Grace and she caught him and clutched him tightly, tears filling her eyes.

Looking into Grace's brimming eyes he repeated vows he would keep for the rest of his life as he slipped his mother's gold band onto her finger. He had a family and he would cherish that every moment of every day.

He'd once told Eli that he and Grace could work out their problems. He now knew with certainty they could. Whatever the future held, they would work at it together.

Like a family should.

EPILOGUE

Eight months later...

DECEMBER WAS WARM and festive in Waco. The home of Althea and Andrew Wellman reflected the cheer of the season, but the McCain family wasn't gathered to celebrate the holidays. They'd gathered at the home of Jake's, Beau's and Caleb's mom and stepfather to celebrate new life.

Brett Andrew had been born to Caleb and Josie. Faith Jane had been born to Beau and Macy. Both babies were healthy and basking in the glow of their loved ones. Today the babies had been christened and their grandparents honored them with a catered barbecue.

The whole family and the in-laws gathered. Boone Beckett, Cousin Ashley, Lencha and Gertie were there for Josie. Macy's mother, Irene, and her father, Ted, were there with their respective spouses. The Stephen Whittens, Aunt Vin and Elise's mom were also there. No one had been left out.

Since the weather was so nice the Wellmans had the dinner outside under the live oak trees. Later in the week, the temperature was forecasted to drop into the thirties. But today they'd been blessed with a beautiful day.

Tables with white linens dotted the backyard. White roses with baby's breath adorned each table. More flowers decorated the covered patio where two white lacy bassinets sat. The women were "oohing" and "aahing" over the infants. The men clustered together, talking sports, mostly about upcoming Bowl games.

The kids played in the yard. Jesse, Zoë and Brady sat in a wagon and Ben pulled while Katie pushed the smaller kids around. Bandy, the Wellman's dog, barked and played with them.

Tuck watched his son. Brady had adjusted so well over the past few months. He didn't bite or hit anymore and he was now saying words. Once he started talking, they couldn't seem to stop him. Nor did they want to. Daddy and Mommy were favorite words around their house. Even though Brady was a little older, he and Jesse were becoming very good friends. They would grow up as best friends, just as Tuck and Eli had.

All of Brady's progress was due to Grace. He couldn't have done it alone. He could admit that now. Never again would he want to do anything alone. It was so much better with Grace—a woman he loved with all his heart.

The remodel on their house was now completed and they had a larger master bedroom and an extra bedroom and bath downstairs. Upstairs they'd added a bath and a large playroom. It was now their house, made that much more special because they'd done it together.

Grace only worked half days and some days not even that. Brady stayed in the day care while she was at the office. Brady was learning that his parents would always come back.

Stephen had won the election, but after this term he planned to retire. At that time, Stephen and Grace would sit down and make a decision about the firm. Tuck and Grace had talked at length about this. He wanted her to do whatever would make her happy and he knew she would probably never completely leave the firm. That was fine with him. He didn't want her to give up something she'd worked so hard to achieve.

He'd always thought of Grace as perfect and she was as close to perfect, in his mind, as one could get. She was now on the board at the hospital and she also volunteered her attorney services for an advocacy program for abused and battered children. She wore many hats and did every job wholeheartedly, most of the time with Brady on her hip.

Every day he loved her more, if that were possible. She kept in touch with Barbara and they had visited Molly several times at home. He now saw that Grace had a need to help others. He had never seen that in her before. Opal had called about a little girl who had been beaten by her stepfather. She had multiple injuries plus a broken leg. Opal wanted to know if they could keep her until the grandmother arrived from Tennessee.

Tuck hesitated, but Grace said to bring her. The child was nervous and frightened, but Grace made her feel at ease. She held her, hugged her, kissed her and made her feel loved. Grace had to bathe her, help her dress and take her to the bathroom. Not once did she complain. He'd watched Grace with love in his heart so big that it completed him in ways he'd never imagined. He'd found the perfect woman—for him.

At first, Brady didn't take this new child in their lives too well, but Grace had a way of making him understand that Kayla needed them. She had him carrying Kayla's food or getting things for her. She made him part of helping the little girl.

When Kayla's grandmother arrived, Kayla didn't want to leave. They all had tears in their eyes as they said goodbye.

After that, they agreed to take children who needed a place to stay for a few days. Emergency cases like Kayla. When Brady was older, they would look further into helping more children. They made decisions as a team and it was working well. At night when he held her, he knew he had everything he'd ever wanted. More than he'd ever planned.

Grace stood on the patio, peering into a bassinet with Caroline, but her eyes never strayed too far from Brady. Stephen was now pulling the wagon while Ben pushed. Katie ran to look at the babies.

Stephen stopped and squatted in the grass, talking to the kids. All three kids giggled and toppled out into Stephen's arms. Joanna hurried to help. She picked up Brady, hugging and kissing him. Stephen and Joanna treated Jesse and Brady equally and Tuck and Grace were very grateful for that. Brady now had grandparents.

Caroline glanced at Macy. "May I hold Faith?"

"Of course," Macy replied. "She loves to be held. Beau is spoiling her rotten."

Caroline carefully lifted Faith out of the bassinet. "Eli, come look at this angel."

"Oh, no, I'm not falling for that. There's yours." He

pointed to Jesse, who was now rolling around on the grass with Brady.

"He's getting so big. Hold Faith. Just for a minute," Caroline pleaded.

"Hey, what's wrong with Brett?" Caleb asked, lifting his son into his arms.

"He's adorable," Caroline replied. "But I have one of those."

"You're damn right he's adorable," Boone, Josie's grandfather said. "He has Beckett blood." He reached for a cigar in his pocket.

Gertie, a cousin of Andrew Wellman, snatched the cigar out of his mouth. "Like that's something to be proud of."

"Give me my damn cigar, woman," Boone snapped.

"Act your age, Boone," Lencha, Josie's mother's friend and Boone's worst enemy, piped in. "And stop using bad language."

"Don't start with me, Lencha."

"Enough." Josie held up a hand. "This is our son's christening and I expect good manners from everyone. And I mean everyone." She looked directly at Boone.

"Ah, all right." Boone slumped in his chair.

"Thank you," Josie said.

"We all appreciate it," Ashley piped in, kissing her grandfather's cheek.

Caroline placed Faith in Eli's arms. "Oh, my," Eli said. "She's light as a feather. I don't think Jesse was ever this light."

"Daddy, Daddy," Zoë called. "Get me." She held out her arms, waiting for Beau.

"Ah, three women always wanting my attention,"

Beau joked on his way to Zoë. He swung her up in his arms and kissed her. "How's my baby?" She wore pink ribbons in her pigtails to go with her new dress.

Jesse and Brady ran toward the house, their shirttails hanging out of their pants and grass and dirt stains on their clothes. Jesse looked up at Eli with the baby and said, "Daddy, me, me, me."

"See, Caroline. I've got a problem here."

"Let me have Faith," Irene said, and Eli gladly handed off the baby and picked up Jesse.

Brady ran straight to Grace and held up his arms. "Mommy, Mommy." She lifted him, kissing his flushed cheek.

"Is my baby tired?"

Brady buried his face in Grace's neck. "I tired, Mommy."

Tuck immediately went to her side. "Let me have him."

She smiled at him and his heart wobbled. "I'm fine."

Tuck held out his hands. "Come to Daddy."

"Daddy." Brady leaped into his arms.

Stephen and Joanna strolled leisurely to the patio. Tuck looked at his wife. "Do you want to do it now?"

She stroked his face. "You're just dying to tell everyone, aren't you?"

"Yes." He kissed her fingers. "Everyone, I'd like to make a toast."

"We need beer, then," Jake said, and handed Tuck a glass. Elise gave Grace a glass of tea and between the two of them they made sure everyone had something.

"Can I...toast, too, Mommy?" Ben asked.

"Yes, baby," Elise replied. "I'll get fruit juice for you and Katie."

When Elise had handed the kids drinks, Jake took her hand. Ben and Katie stood in front of them.

Everyone waited.

"I know what this is about," Eli said. "You and Grace have decided to adopt another child."

"No, that's not it." Tuck shook his head.

Caroline slipped an arm around her husband's waist. "Let him talk."

Tuck raised his glass. "Here's to family, love and happiness. I've experienced all three firsthand as a husband and as a father. It's better than I'd ever imagined."

Everyone made to touch their drinks together. "I'm not finished," he said in a rush.

"Tuck, I've never known you to be long-winded," Beau said, holding Zoë with an arm around Macy, who now held baby Faith.

"That's Beau's department." Caleb laughed, laying his son gently into his bassinet and wrapping both arms around Josie.

"Be nice," Althea said to her sons. "Let Tuck finish."

"Here's to new babies, new beginnings and new lives." He took a deep breath. "And here's to the new baby we're expecting in June."

"Hot damn, now isn't that something?" Eli said. "I told you. I told you it would happen."

Stephen and Joanna rushed forward to hug Grace and Tuck.

"Andrew, we need champagne," Althea said to her husband.

"Yes, dear." Andrew disappeared into the house.

They were bombarded with well wishes, hugs and love. This was family and they had endured the good and the bad times. Their bond would sustain each of them through the future and make them stronger. Tuck was now a part of it.

Glancing toward the sky, he knew three angels were watching over him. The fourth angel was there, too. He'd come to terms with his biological father. He had an inner peace about his past. These days there were no doubts or insecurities about who he was. He was a husband, a father, a friend and a Texas Ranger.

He wrapped an arm around Grace, his fingers resting on her slightly swelling stomach. In the other arm, he held Brady.

He had it all.

HARLEQUIN®
Super Romance®

Welcome to our newest miniseries, about five
poker players and the women who love them!

Texas Hold'em

When it comes to love, the stakes are high

Beginning October 2007 with

THE BABY GAMBLE

by USA TODAY *bestselling author*

Tara Taylor Quinn

#1446

Desperate to have a baby, Annie Kincaid
turns to the only man she trusts, her ex-husband,
Blake Smith, and asks him to father her child.

Also watch for:

BETTING ON SANTA *by Debra Salonen* November 2007
GOING FOR BROKE *by Linda Style* December 2007
DEAL ME IN *by Cynthia Thomason* January 2008
TEXAS BLUFF *by Linda Warren* February 2008

Look for THE BABY GAMBLE *by* USA TODAY
bestselling author Tara Taylor Quinn.

Available October 2007 wherever you buy books.

REQUEST YOUR FREE BOOKS!

2 FREE NOVELS PLUS 2 FREE GIFTS!

HARLEQUIN®

Super Romance®

Exciting, emotional, unexpected!

HARLEQUIN®

Mediterranean NIGHTS™

Sail aboard the luxurious Alexandra's Dream and experience glamour, romance, mystery and revenge!

Coming in October 2007...

AN AFFAIR TO REMEMBER

by
Karen Kendall

When Captain Nikolas Pappas first fell in love with Helena Stamos, he was a penniless deckhand and she was the daughter of a shipping magnate. But he's never forgiven himself for the way he left her—and fifteen years later, he's determined to win her back.

Though the attraction is still there, Helena is hesitant to get involved. Nick left her once...what's to stop him from doing it again?

ATHENA FORCE

Heart-pounding romance and thrilling adventure.

A deadly masquerade

As an undercover asset for the FBI, mafia princess
Sasha Bracciali can deceive and improvise at a
moment's notice. But when she's cut off from
everything she knows, including her FBI-agent
lover, Sasha realizes her deceptions have masked
a painful truth: she doesn't know whom to trust.
If she doesn't figure it out quickly, her most
ambitious charade will also be her last.

Look for

CHARADE

by *Kate Donovan*

**Available in October
wherever you buy books.**

#1446 THE BABY GAMBLE • Tara Taylor Quinn
Texas Hold 'Em

Desperate to have a baby, Annie Kincaid turns to the only man she trusts—her ex-husband, Blake Smith—and asks him to father her child. Because when it comes to love, the stakes are high....

#1447 TEMPORARY NANNY • Carrie Weaver

Who would guess that the perfect nanny for a ten-year-old boy is Royce McIntyre? Not Katy Garner, that's for sure. But she has no other choice than to ask her handsome neighbor for help. Never expecting that Royce might be the perfect answer for someone else…

#1448 COUNT ON LOVE • Melinda Curtis
Going Back

Annie Raye's a single mom who's trying to rebuild her life after her ex-husband, a convict, tarnished her reputation. But returning home to Las Vegas makes "going straight" difficult because she's still remembered as a child gambling prodigy. And it doesn't help when Sam Knight costs her a good job. So she sets out to prove the private investigator wrong.

#1449 BECAUSE OF A BOY • Anna DeStefano
Atlanta Heroes

Nurse Kate Rhodes mistakenly believes one of her young charges is being abused by his dad and sets in motion a series of events that jeopardize the lives of the young boy and his father, who are forced to go into hiding. To right her wrong, she must work with Stephen Creighton, the legal advocate who's defending the accused father, and find the pair before it's too late.

#1450 THE BABY DOCTORS • Janice Macdonald

When widowed pediatrician Sarah Benedict returns home after fifteen years in Central America, she wants to set up a practice where traditional and alternative medicine work together. And she hopes to team up with Matthew Cameron, the friend she's loved since she was eight. Loved *and* lost, when he married someone else. Except now he's divorced...and she doesn't like the person he's become.

#1451 WHERE LOVE GROWS • Cynthia Reese

Becca Reynolds has a job to do—investigate the suspicious insurance claims of several farmers. Little does she realize that she "knows" one of the men in question. Could Ryan MacIntosh really be involved? And will she be able to find out before he figures out who she is?